"WHAT DO YOU MEAN YOU'VE LOST CONTACT?" RIKER ASKED.

"Precisely that, Commander," answered Data. "We have lost contact with the captain and the away team."

"What about sensors?" Riker snapped.

"Useless," replied the android. "The area where they beamed down is undergoing intense volcanic activity. The volcanic ash is highly magnetic and is disrupting our sensors. Even if the away team survived and stayed in the beam-down position, it's doubtful we could beam them back up until the volcanic activity subsides.

Riker was seething. "Damn," he cursed to himself. "I don't like the sound of this."

Look for STAR TREK Fiction from Pocket Books

Star Trek: The Original Series

Star Trek: The Next Generation

#7

STAR TREK ®
THE NEXT GENERATION

MASKS

JOHN VORNHOLT

POCKET BOOKS

New York   London   Toronto   Sydney   Tokyo   Singapore

An *Original* Publication of POCKET BOOKS

POCKET BOOKS, a division of Simon & Schuster Inc.
1230 Avenue of the Americas, New York, NY 10020

ISBN: 0-671-70878-3

First Pocket Books printing July 1989

10 9 8 7 6 5 4

POCKET and colophon are registered trademarks of
Simon & Schuster Inc.

Printed in the U.S.A.

For my wonderful parents, who never cease to be
supportive and enthusiastic

Thanks to Nancy and Sarah, my wife and daughter, for making themselves scarce. I missed them.

To Ashley Grayson, for telling me how to get the planet right.

To The Group: Susan, Janie, Marilyn, and Linda. What day are we meeting?

And to my ST:TNG experts: Kevin J. Ryan, Barbara Beck, and Andrea and Kevin Quitt.

Chapter One

THE MASK LAY ON THE TABLE, glistening even in the subdued light of the *Enterprise*'s Ten-Forward lounge. Lights from ten thousand stars played upon its burnished metal surface, which was intercut with opaque ribbons of black and navy blue flowing from the nose hole of the mask like the strands of a spiderweb. Its two eye sockets were outlined with green and yellow jewels that might have been emeralds and topazes. Sweeping eyebrows made of rubylike stones gave the mask a faintly quizzical expression. This was offset by an oval of stern black jewels, which encircled the mouth opening, offering no hint of expression or emotion. The chin of the mask was exaggerated, jutting out boldly then curling protectively under what would be the wearer's own chin. The mask's outer edges swirled back into short but perfectly formed wings tipped with lavender feathers. The handmade mask was improbably beautiful.

"It's gorgeous," murmured Katherine Pulaski, reaching tentatively for the artifact. "May I hold it?"

A tall athletic man, clad in leather frontierstyle clothing and wearing his sandy hair to his shoulders, reached out to stay her hand. His creased face smiled, kindly but determinedly. "No, Doctor, you may not. I don't want anything to happen to this mask before we reach Lorca. You see, it's my calling card."

Wesley Crusher noticed Kate's disappointed expression. The young man liked the ship's new doctor and her frankness. "It looks heavy," Wesley observed, trying to change the subject.

"It's not really heavy, lad," said Lewis. "It's made out of an alloy that's mostly aluminum. There's lots of aluminum on Lorca."

Wesley saw Guinan among the handful of onlookers admiring the mask. But unlike the others, the dark-skinned humanoid seemed more interested in Fenton Lewis than in the rare artwork.

"Are those real animal skins you have on?" she asked innocently.

Fenton Lewis narrowed his gaze at Guinan, who seemed completely oblivious of his scrutiny. "Trading in animal skins is illegal in the Federation," he observed.

"There are a great many places that aren't *in* the Federation," she answered.

"That's true," agreed the ambassador, "and I've been to many of them. Wild places. You know, many of the old Earth explorers wore animal skins in the wilderness. Skins wear better than fabric and cut down on the human scent." He smiled as he fingered a cuff that was worn smooth and dark. "This outfit has seen me through many scrapes. I get the information I need to do my job—without asking too many questions."

"Speaking of questions," Guinan responded cheerfully, "did I ask you what you wanted to drink?"

"I'll take some of that damned Ferengi juice," growled Lewis.

"One synthehol coming up."

Guinan hurried back behind her counter just as the doors breezed open to admit Jean-Luc Picard and William T. Riker. Though Riker was taller than Picard and built much more powerfully, there was no doubt who commanded. The wiry, balding Picard had an aura of strength and authority born of character and of the respect accorded him. The crowd in the room parted to allow the captain and his first officer to approach Fenton Lewis.

"Ambassador Lewis?" asked Picard, gazing at the colorfully garbed stranger. He maintained his dignified demeanor only a few seconds before spotting the gleaming mask. He leaned over it excitedly. "Is this mask genuine? Is it Lorcan?"

"Absolutely, Captain," said Lewis, motioning to the artifact. "A genuine Ambassador's Mask. It didn't come cheap, I can tell you that. Feel free to examine it."

Riker smiled slightly at his captain's unexpected show of excitement. "This is Captain Jean-Luc Picard," he said, "and I am Commander William T. Riker, first officer of the *Enterprise*. We would have preferred to meet you in the observation lounge. Normally, this facility is reserved for crew members and ship's residents."

"Noted," said Picard, never taking his eyes off the striking mask. "But I think we can make an exception in the ambassador's case. He's come a long way and has a very important mission."

"And he's very thirsty," Lewis added, as he gratefully took a small glass from Guinan. He downed the drink in one gulp and handed the glass back to her. "Hit me again, and this time make it a double."

Guinan winked at Wesley. "He's lucky Data's not here."

"Data?" asked the ambassador.

3

"Our android," explained Wesley. "He takes language very literally."

Captain Picard carefully lifted the Lorcan mask with both hands and stared into the hypnotic visage. "Stunning, absolutely stunning."

Katherine Pulaski murmured in Wesley's ear, "He wouldn't let *me* touch it."

As if he overheard her, Picard replied, "You have no idea how rare these masks are. A Lorcan has to be killed to be separated from his mask. Isn't that true, Ambassador?"

"Not entirely," said the long-haired civilian. "In some instances, Lorcans have to be defeated in hand-to-hand combat before they will relinquish their masks, but even in those cases, the combat isn't always to the death. The Ambassador's Mask is one of the few masks that's allowed to leave the planet and to be worn by off-worlders."

Guinan handed Lewis a fresh drink, and he took a long sip. "I'm surprised and relieved, Captain, that you know so much about Lorca," the ambassador said.

"I know very little about it," Picard admitted, turning the mask over to inspect its leather bindings. "But I'm an incurable romantic about a place where chivalry is still in force and where the most dangerous weapon is a sword. Perhaps I have an idealized view of Lorca, but that's the view I've absorbed in the computer library."

"We'll know the truth soon." Fenton Lewis smiled. "Perhaps you'll accompany me on my mission."

Commander Riker cleared his throat respectfully but firmly. "Normally the first officer leads the away teams. The captain is too valuable to risk."

"It's the chance of a lifetime," remarked Lewis, slyly cocking one eyebrow. "As the captain said, the Lorcans have nothing more dangerous than swords."

"Swords can kill," Riker said with finality.

Still mesmerized, Captain Picard continued to stare at the mask of flowing silver metal festooned with gemstones and feathers. "How dangerous can a people be who would make something so beautiful?"

Picard handed the mask back to Fenton Lewis with great reluctance. "We reach planetary orbit in eighteen hours, and we'll have a complete briefing in the observation lounge at zero-four-hundred. We'll decide then who, if anyone, is to accompany Ambassador Lewis."

Will Riker was troubled some hours later when he repaired to his quarters for his sleep period. He thought Fenton Lewis had overstepped his position by encouraging the captain to join him on the away team. Of course, Riker had to admit, Captain Picard hadn't seemed to need much encouraging, as enamored as he was with barbarous cultures. The first officer could only hope that Worf, as security chief, would second his opposition to the captain leaving the ship with a buffoon like Fenton Lewis. The ambassador might be a colorful character, but that didn't entitle him to the run of the *Enterprise* after ten minutes on board. And it certainly didn't entitle him to turn the time-tested procedures of a starship upside down. Most of all, Riker's instinct told him to watch Lewis, closely.

Riker stripped off his tunic, revealing a broad, well-muscled chest. Then he manipulated the console on his desk.

"Computer," he said.

"Yes, Commander Riker."

"Tell me about Ambassador Fenton Lewis."

"One moment please." After a brief pause, the soothing feminine voice of the ship's computer continued: "Ambassador Fenton Lewis. Age: forty-six. Place of birth: Alpha Centauri IV, Lewis Colony."

"Lewis Colony," Riker snorted. That figured.

"Shall I go on?" the computer queried.

"Yes, please."

"Educated on Earth. Graduated with honors from Oxford University with degrees in anthropology and sociology. After completing his graduate studies, Fenton Lewis was offered admittance to Starfleet Academy but declined in order to join a civilian trading mission to the Klingon Empire. Sole survivor of the crash landing of the freighter *Nystrom Egbert,* he lived in the wilderness of Orestes VII for three years, during which time he mapped eight thousand square kilometers of the planet's surface. After his rescue, he joined the Diplomatic Service as an intermediary first class. Twice received the Federation Medal of Honor for sacrificing personal safety in order to mediate armed conflicts. Promoted six years ago to the post he currently holds: ambassador-at-large with special duties. Author of three books on wilderness survival."

"Hmmm," said Riker grudgingly. He might have been born with a silver spoon in his mouth, but Lewis had earned the right to a somewhat cocky attitude.

"That is the brief biography of Ambassador Lewis," the computer added. "More data is available. Do you wish a more detailed report?"

"No," answered Riker. "Just tell me, does he have any black spots on his record? Any unfortunate episodes?"

"Certain portions of Ambassador Lewis's record are classified," replied the computer. "But the Ferengi Alliance has tried and convicted him in absentia for murder."

"Murder?" said Riker, raising his eyebrows. "That doesn't sound very diplomatic."

"I don't understand," the computer replied.

"Never mind. What exactly happened between Lewis and the Ferengi?"

"Data removed," answered the computer, "by request of Ambassador Lewis."

The man did pull some weight within the Federation, Riker decided. He turned off his console and lowered the lights in his cabin to a warm golden glow.

Will Riker washed up and lay in his bed for some time before falling asleep.

From the aft turbolift, three relief crew members filed onto the bridge and stood silently at attention. Jean-Luc Picard noted their arrival and rose from his control seat. Riker was already standing and shifting uneasily on his feet. He looked like a teakettle that was about to boil over. And why shouldn't he? Picard smiled to himself. Riker's job was to protect his captain from all hazards, including himself. A good first officer—and Riker was certainly that—considered the captain no more expendable than any other integral part of the ship, like the matter-antimatter reactor or the computer. Unlike the computer, however, the captain had a mind of his own.

"Ensign Crusher," Picard said, "maintain course at warp speed."

"Yes, Captain," Wesley answered briskly.

"Number One, Worf, Data, La Forge, to the observation lounge," Picard ordered. He turned back to Wesley. "Please ask Ambassador Lewis, Counselor Troi, and Dr. Pulaski to join us."

"They're already there," answered the teenager.

"Good."

Silently the two humans, the android, and the Klingon followed the captain off the bridge as the relief personnel manned the vacated consoles.

Jean-Luc Picard sensed that his first officer wanted to tell him something, but the big man held his tongue. Not that Picard couldn't guess what he would say if given an opportunity to speak. Well, he would have that opportunity, but not until everyone had been fully briefed on Ambassador Lewis's mission.

When they reached the observation lounge, they found Deanna Troi and Katherine Pulaski studying the Lorcan mask. Apparently, thought Picard, Lewis was not letting it out of his sight. The ambassador himself stood at the huge port windows, watching the spectacular view of stars stretching and popping through the sky at warp speed. His plainsman outfit and long unruly hair made him look more like a refugee from a history book than one of the Federation's most honored diplomats.

"A phenomenal sight," he said to no one in particular. "With so much out there, it makes you want just a small piece of it for yourself." He turned to the others and smiled charmingly. "Of course, home is a nonexistent concept to a career diplomat. We're always on somebody else's turf."

"Turf?" asked Data quizzically. "Do you refer to the term for an athletic playing field?"

"Ah, you must be Data," the ambassador nodded. "The lad told me about you."

"Ambassador," said Picard with a sweep of his hand, "may I also introduce you to Lieutenant La Forge, chief engineer, and Lieutenant Worf, security chief."

Fenton Lewis nodded to Geordi, who looked deceptively stern behind the visor that covered his sightless eyes. Then the ambassador turned to Worf and uttered something indecipherable in a language full of guttural growls and clicks. After his initial surprise, Worf responded in kind.

With some annoyance, Riker tapped his insignia badge. "My translator doesn't seem to be activated."

"Excuse me, Commander," said the Klingon, his massive brow still wrinkled with surprise. "The ambassador was merely saying that he was honored to meet me."

8

"I'm honored to meet all of you," Lewis replied expansively. "I wish I had more time to get to know each of you. But we shall arrive at Lorca in a matter of hours, isn't that right, Captain?"

"Yes, it is."

"Then we'd better get started." Lewis motioned to the conference table, and the *Enterprise* crew members took their seats. "Much of what I'm about to tell you you could find out from your computer, but I've made a special study of Lorca and have talked to some recent Federation visitors to the planet. I believe nobody else in the Federation is as well versed in Lorcan customs as I am.

"Lorca was settled about two hundred years ago by two separate groups from Earth. One of them was a wandering theater company—in fact, the planet's name is taken from a famous Earth playwright. They used Lorca as a rest and recreational stop, a place to rehearse new productions, put on play festivals, and house their nontraveling family members. The other group was a cult of antitechnologists who went there seeking a paradise where they could live a simple communal life. The fruit-and-berry folk hired the acting company to take them to Lorca in their ship, and that was the last Earth ever heard of either group.

"Communications being what they were two hundred years ago," he continued, "Earth thought the ship had been destroyed en route with all aboard. But it turned out that the ship did make it to Lorca, and later on, perhaps a thousand of the settlers survived a cataclysm that can only be compared to all-out nuclear war. As a result of a number of sudden and savage volcanic eruptions, Lorca was transformed from a paradise into a fire storm as volcanoes spewed enough ash into the air to lower the surface temperatures by at least half. But somehow, though all of their technology was destroyed, a thousand or so hardy souls survived. Over the course of time, they have developed a warrior-run feudal society that is completely devoid of technology."

He held up the startling Ambassador's Mask and rotated it dramatically. "One thing they never forgot from their theatrical heritage was the use of masks. The entire society is structured around masks such as this one. Everyone's standing in this rural community is based upon the type of mask he or she wears. A person of lesser rank shows obedience to a person of higher rank. Therefore a serf wears a simple clay mask, and a nobleman wears a mask made from the rarest feathers, gems, and metals. And I don't mean they wear these masks on special occasions—they wear them all the time. Appearing in public without a mask would be akin to us walking buck naked in public. It simply isn't done."

Deanna Troi held up a hand to ask a question, and Lewis nodded to the exotically beautiful Betazoid.

"Can these people rise from one social rank to another," she asked, "merely by wearing a different mask?"

"Ah," the ambassador said, "that is where the warrior mentality comes in. At any time, one citizen of Lorca may challenge another's right to wear the mask of a certain rank. If mere words or a show of wealth and entourage are not enough to substantiate the right, a duel ensues. Most of these swordfights are ritualistic, with the winner sparing the loser's life and taking his mask as a prize. If the mask is of greater value than his own, the victor may begin wearing it, thus increasing his stature in the community."

"Fascinating," remarked Kate Pulaski, leaning forward with her usual intensity. "Theoretically, then, a person could wear any mask he chooses?"

Lewis nodded. "As long as he can obtain it and defend his right to wear it."

Will Riker narrowed his gaze. "Are the duels always simply ritualistic?"

"Almost invariably," the ambassador answered.

"Almost?" Riker countered.

Fenton Lewis smiled. "Lorca is a violent planet. None of our information has been verified." He stepped closer to the conference table. "That's why I'm going there, to get all of our questions answered. Recent reports have shown that the planet may be due for another series of cataclysmic eruptions, which could cause another devastating volcanic winter. We'll send a team of geologists to make a final evaluation later on, but first we need to open diplomatic relations. After all, we owe something to these people, who are of Earth stock, even if they hardly remember it."

Fenton Lewis stalked back and forth. "The Federation is also concerned because a number of Lorcan masks have been showing up at Ferengi art auctions. Given the history of the Ferengi, we're worried that they might turn Lorca into one of their infamous mining colonies, or worse. If Lorcans ask for protection, we'll be able to provide it.

"On the other hand," he added, "maybe the Lorcans are too warlike to allow us to establish diplomatic relations with them. One of the problems is that they don't seem to have a centralized government. Their nominal head of state is a semi-mythological figure called Almighty Slayer."

"Almighty Slayer?" asked Geordi incredulously, breaking into a wide grin.

"I hope he exists," said Fenton Lewis, "because he's the one I'm going there to find."

Everyone sat still for several moments, letting the scope and danger of Fenton Lewis's assignment sink in.

Worf finally spoke: "You'll need a full security detachment."

"No, no," Lewis said determinedly, "I don't want to show up there with an army. The Lorcans are eager

11

enough to fight as it is. The good thing about this custom of wearing masks is that a small party of off-worlders can blend in with the natives without attracting attention."

The group gradually shifted their eyes to Captain Picard, who, so far, hadn't said a word and was massaging the cleft in his chin as he compiled his thoughts. "Ambassador Lewis," he finally said, "your mission presents the *Enterprise* with several problems. First of all, we know so little about Lorca that it may take weeks or even months to find the appropriate parties with whom to negotiate. We don't have any other business pending, but if I know Starfleet, they're not going to allow us to orbit this planet indefinitely."

"I realize that," Lewis replied, "and I'm prepared to beam down alone. It wouldn't be the first time. The *Enterprise,* or another ship, could check on my progress after a prescribed period of time."

"Unacceptable," said Picard. "Our orders are to deliver you and *protect* you. I don't relish the idea of reporting back to the Diplomatic Service that we dumped one of their key people on a warlike planet and then deserted him. We can't leave until we're certain of your safety."

"I shall welcome your company," the ambassador replied, waving his hand magnanimously.

"You may not," continued the captain, "after you hear my conditions. A time limit must be set for this mission—say, thirty Lorcan days. Also, it must be *my* responsibility to determine when the danger is too great and the mission should be aborted."

A deep frown creased Fenton Lewis's face, and he started to protest. Finally, he settled back in his seat and drummed his fingers on the table. "As long as you don't interfere in matters of diplomacy, I bow to your expertise in matters of security. Of course, Captain, you must come with me if you are to make this determination."

Will Riker leaned forward and leveled a stern gaze at the long-haired civilian. "As I stated before, Ambassador Lewis, standard procedure dictates that the first officer lead all away teams."

"I insist that Captain Picard come along," challenged Lewis, returning Riker's stare. "He can't determine the danger on the planet unless he is there!"

"I will be there," said Picard slowly. Now it was his turn to receive Riker's bristling stare. "I know what you're thinking, Number One, and I'll entertain your objections in private when this meeting is over. We will beam down a minimal complement—myself, Ambassador Lewis, Security Chief Worf, and Counselor Troi. With her empathic and telepathic abilities, Counselor Troi is best suited to determine the peaceable or belligerent intentions of the Lorcans."

The captain then turned to Worf. "Lieutenant, consult with Ambassador Lewis and determine what equipment and clothing we will need."

"At least Worf won't need a mask," added Geordi.

The joke broke the tense atmosphere in the room, and even Riker managed a faint smile.

"I had thought I would go alone," Fenton Lewis admitted. "All of you *will* need masks."

"We are not going to pass ourselves off as Lorcans," answered Picard.

"That's not the reason you need the masks," said Lewis. "The Lorcans might take offense at your naked faces. Wearing masks isn't a ceremonial custom; it's a fact of everyday life."

Jean-Luc Picard frowned thoughtfully. "I doubt if the replicator has any masks in memory, except for some Halloween masks. Would those do?"

"Very well," said the ambassador. "They would be ideal, in fact; they would never be challenged."

Picard turned to Deanna Troi. "Counselor, will you check with the entertainment director and see what he has in the way of masks? Try to select some that are appropriate."

Briskly Picard stood. "This briefing is adjourned to make preparations for the away team."

"Captain?" interjected Riker, as the others filed out of the room.

"I haven't forgotten you, Number One."

The commander waited until he and the captain were alone in the observation lounge. The stars streaking by outside the gigantic port windows usually filled Riker with excitement and wonder, but now he felt only dread. He didn't mind taking command of the *Enterprise* while Picard was away; ordinarily he relished the opportunity. But not when it placed his captain in harm's way.

Gone were the days when starship captains were swashbuckling heroes, thumbing their noses at death. Too often in the early days death had thumbed its nose back, and Starfleet had lost captains of great experience and ability. Now the death or incapacitation of a captain was considered as serious as the loss of a starship. Sometimes Riker felt that his concern for Picard's safety bordered on the irrational, but this protective instinct had been drummed into him and every other cadet at the academy.

Despite his strong feelings, the first officer decided to be tactful. "I can well understand your wanting to see Lorca," he remarked offhandedly. "It sounds like a fascinating planet."

"But you can't agree with my decision," Picard replied, "and you're going to do everything possible to talk me out of it."

"I believe, with Worf and Deanna along, I can determine if the danger becomes too great to continue," Riker said evenly.

"I'm sure you can." Picard nodded. "But can you persuade Fenton Lewis to leave even if it means his mission will be a failure? Thus far, the two of you haven't gotten along very well."

"I don't know why," muttered Riker, "but I don't trust him. Did you know that he was tried and convicted for murder?"

"By the Ferengi," added Picard, "who consider the Federation a threat to their commerce. For all we know, you and I may be wanted for some crime or another by the Ferengi."

"All the same, Captain, I don't trust Lewis."

"He strikes me as unorthodox, too," the captain agreed. "But Starfleet assigned him this task. You obviously reviewed his record, and so did I. If anyone stands a chance of ferreting out the leadership on this planet, Fenton Lewis is the one. He has reached a station in his career where he is allowed a bit of eccentricity." Picard met the younger man's intense stare and softened his own stare with a smile. "And so have I."

"Then you insist on leading the away team?" Riker asked, his tone now bordering on resignation.

Picard nodded. "Can't let you have all the fun. I'll quite understand, Will, if you wish to state your objections in the log."

"That won't be necessary," Riker replied. He was beginning to feel like a selfish curmudgeon for trying to deny the captain a chance to satisfy a strong personal desire. "Just be careful."

"You can rest assured of that."

Three Halloween masks lay on a shelf in the transporter room, along with the rest of the supplies destined for Lorca: heavy boots and dark blue parkas for the cold weather; the Ambassador's Mask; canteens and freeze-dried food; a collection of scanners, clothing, and toilet articles; backpacks to hold it all; and pistol phasers in heavy-duty shoulder holsters.

Captain Picard inspected the freight closely, and, like a sergeant inspecting raw recruits, he didn't look happy. Then his eyes struck the Halloween masks, and he smiled in spite of himself.

One mask sported the grinning white-faced visage of Harlequin, the clown of Earth's sixteenth-century commedia dell'arte theatrical troupes. Another had the bulging pink cheeks, flared snout, and cocked ears of a pig; a tiny green top hat was attached to it. The third mask was the typical red devil's face, with a leering grin, a goatee and mustache, and short yellow horns. Despite the flimsy elastic bands that secured them to the wearer's head, all three masks looked reasonably well constructed.

Picard turned to Deanna Troi, who had chosen the masks and was now trying to hide her embarrassment. His eyes twinkled. "Counselor, do you really suppose we will be inconspicuous in these masks?"

"I am sorry, Captain," she said a bit shamefacedly, "but these were the only halfway appropriate full-face masks I could find. There were a few others, but they were even more hideous. Halloween is a rather bizarre holiday."

"Yes, it is," Picard agreed. He turned to Fenton Lewis. "Will these suffice?"

The ambassador studied the masks closely and then nodded. "As I said, ideal."

Picard's lips thinned as he shifted his attention to Worf. "Lieutenant, I have some disagreement with your choice of equipment. These pistol phasers," Picard continued, hefting one of the sleek instruments, "are too threatening. Let's go with hand phasers, set to stun."

Worf nodded and started to say something, but Fenton Lewis cut him off. "I disagree with you there, Picard. We may need the firepower. We don't know what to expect down there."

"Even firing a phaser on another planet is a violation of the Prime Directive," the captain reminded him firmly. "The people of Lorca have developed into a feudal society out of choice or necessity, and we can't interfere in that development. I don't want them to see phasers or any other technology they might get curious about. Is that clear?"

"Perfectly, Captain," said Worf in his basso profundo voice.

Lewis smiled wistfully. "I have no desire to change Lorca. I think I'll like it the way it is."

"Let's hope so." The captain nodded. He turned to Lieutenant Data, who stood at the transporter console. "Have you chosen the coordinates yet?"

"Population on the planet is extremely scattered," Data replied, never taking his eyes off his readouts, "and the energy sources are very faint."

"They don't even have electricity," Lewis added.

"The best I can do, Captain, is to set you down next to what appears to be a gathering of life-forms."

"Data, don't set us down next to any life-forms," ordered Picard. "Put us a few kilometers away, so that we can approach them normally."

"Wise strategy," the ambassador concurred.

"We are ready, Captain," said Worf, after loading the backpacks.

Picard lifted one of the hooded parkas. "Is the cold-weather gear really necessary?"

"I'm afraid it is," Worf answered. "Lorca is expecting a temperature of four degrees today."

"Very well." Picard nodded. He pulled his communicator badge from his tunic and pinned it on one of the parkas, then checked to be sure that his phaser was set to stun. "We are going to look fairly nondescript."

"That may not be entirely bad," Fenton Lewis remarked.

The four members of the team pulled on the boots and heavy parkas, eschewing the hoods for the moment. Worf slipped his backpack on and helped the others with theirs. The entire party looked unobtrusive, with their uniforms totally hidden beneath the heavy parkas.

"To the grand adventure!" Lewis exclaimed, raising a clenched fist. "To the Lewis and Picard Expedition!"

"Pardon me?" The captain blinked.

"One of my ancestors was Meriwether Lewis, of Lewis and Clark fame," said the ambassador proudly. "They were the first to chart the American West. And the Lewis Colony was the first civilian settlement in the Alpha Centauri system. I guess you could say exploration runs in my blood."

"Let's hope our mission is half as successful as those of your ancestors were," Picard replied, striding to the transporter platform. Ambassador Lewis, Lieutenant Worf, and Deanna Troi quickly followed. The captain glanced around to see that every member of the team was in position, then he nodded to Data.

"Energize."

Chapter Two

THE TRANSPORTER DEPOSITED the away team on a vast veldt. A mountain range of dark amber towered in the distance, dominating the horizon and clashing with the red salmon sky. The Lorcan sun was visible only as the fiery center of a red cloud that seemed to encompass the entire rose-hued planet. Even the ground was orange, with beige plants sprouting in gnarled heaps and puddles of blue-black water spotting the semiarid plain. From hidden geysers, pillars of steam streaked into the air, only to be blown to pieces by the brisk wind. The *Enterprise* crew pulled their parkas tighter around them and zipped them up to their chins, but the wind sneaked into every crevice and stole the breath clouds from their mouths.

Fenton Lewis looked exhilarated as he strode several steps deeper into the vast wilderness and tightened the straps of his pack around his wiry frame.

"'Our actions are our own; their consequences belong to heaven,'" quoted the ambassador somberly. "Saint Francis of Assisi," he added.

"We may need a saint to get through to the

Lorcans," Jean-Luc remarked. "Worf, have you spotted any life-forms?"

"Over there, Captain," answered the Klingon, motioning to the forest directly behind them. To the south, a wave of dense brown vegetation had encroached upon the forbidding flatlands, and a pack of red-furred creatures squatted on the ground at the forest's edge. Occasionally, one of the lithe beings would reach up into the trees with impossibly long arms and lift itself effortlessly out of sight. Their laconic manner didn't disguise the animals' intense scrutiny of the new arrivals, nor did it hide the fear that kept them at a safe distance.

"So much for arriving unannounced," grumbled Picard.

"I do not sense a high intelligence," Deanna Troi observed, after studying the long-armed creatures for a moment.

Worf adjusted the brightness of his scanner readout to compensate for the red glare of the sky. "No correlation with species found elsewhere in the Federation."

"There'll be time enough to study the flora and fauna later," muttered Lewis. "Let's find some people to talk to." He lifted the Lorcan Ambassador's Mask and put it on with movements that seemed obscenely pretentious and, at the same time, admirably elegant and regal.

Captain Picard stepped forward, gently testing the soil with his feet. The odd circular puddles strewn before them made the planet's surface appear to be of the consistency of swiss cheese. The ground felt and sounded crunchy, like permafrost, and seemed none too substantial as Picard prodded it with his insulated boot.

"Soil readings?" he ordered, shifting his weight from one foot to the other and listening to the curious crackling underneath.

"High iron, clay, and water content," Worf responded, checking his scanner. "The topsoil is clay-based, and the bedrock is slate. Most of the surface consists of thin strata of hardened clay with pockets of water between them."

"Underground streams," Lewis replied. "If you listen carefully, you can hear the water flowing."

Picard listened, but he heard nothing save the call of a scavenger bird circling above them on gigantic glider wings and, from every direction, the spewing of geysers. This was a wild place, he concluded.

"We've met our first inhabitants," said Fenton Lewis, digging a gloved hand into the soil and coming up with a handful of clay, some of which was moving. "Worms," he remarked, "or grubs, I'm not sure which."

Picard nodded at the crawling mess and tried to ignore Lewis's mask, which now seemed garish. "We'll send a biology team later. Ambassador Lewis, do you feel confident enough to take point?"

"Sure, I'll lead the way," the masked figure declared, striding across the alien soil and sweeping an arm in a wide arc to indicate the boundless expanse of mountains, forests, and plains. "Let's head south, toward those red-furred creatures," he said finally. "Perhaps they will lead us to an inhabited region."

Then Fenton Lewis kicked a stone, which skimmed across the clay and tufts of sickly grass before plopping into one of the dark blue puddles. It sank without a trace, except for a few thick bubbles that gurgled to the surface. "These are sinkholes. They may be very *deep* sinkholes, so I advise everyone to give them a wide berth."

Picard glanced at Worf and Deanna, both of whom were standing tautly at the ready. "Understood?" he asked.

"Understood, Captain," said Worf. Deanna Troi nodded, managing a brave smile. Picard fought the temptation to tell the delicate Betazoid that he shouldn't have brought her here, that the dangers and unpredictability of Lorca were too great. But she was a member of his crew, no different from any other, and no one aboard the *Enterprise* was more qualified to judge the intentions of the Lorcans than Counselor Troi, Picard thought ruefully. The vast land stretching before them belied the idea that Lorca had been settled. The planet seemed primeval and unfinished, not ready for human habitation.

As if to confirm the captain's private musings, one of the far-off mountains suddenly exploded, belching a fiery red cloud into the flame-streaked sky. The ground beneath the away team trembled, and the nearest sinkholes became steaming cauldrons of hissing bubbles.

"Volcano!" Worf shouted. "Cover your faces!"

"The masks!" shouted Deanna.

At once, the queer Halloween masks became indispensable apparatus, as Picard, Worf, and Deanna pulled them out of their packs and strapped them over their faces. Within seconds, a thick cloud of red ash and black sand swept over them, carried by the icy wind. Deanna fell to one knee, and Worf leaned protectively over her. As if daring the sudden sandstorm to knock them off their feet, Captain Picard and Ambassador Lewis stood shoulder to shoulder, facing into the gritty tempest. They shielded their eyes with their hands.

"These masks!" Lewis shouted over the din. "They're not just decorative."

"Neither is this planet!" the captain shouted back. "I would say it's highly unstable."

"Unfettered power usually is unstable."

Already the cloud of sparks and steam was receding, and Picard could look toward the volcano with unprotected eyes. The sky over the mountains was now an even deeper red, as if the mountains were bleeding

22

into the sky. The sun was buried in the scarlet clouds, and Jean-Luc Picard was thankful that it was morning on Lorca; the sun would rise higher, perhaps affording warmth as well as untamed splendor.

If they headed away from the mountains, they would have the volcano at their backs in case of another eruption. "Let's make those trees!" Picard ordered. "Double time!"

At once, the party was galvanized into action and began a steady jog toward the oasis of brown vegetation to the south. Worf shoved his pig mask up onto his forehead, letting it rest upon the crevices of his Klingon brow like a pink beret. Deanna kept her mask in place, and Picard thought that the white Harlequin face was entirely unlike the serious olive-skinned Betazoid underneath. Self-consciously, he pulled his goateed devil's mask off and stuck it back in his pack. The captain had never been one for disguises. Only Fenton Lewis wore his Lorcan mask proudly, though it weighed considerably more than the Halloween masks.

"March time," the captain ordered, slowing to a brisk walk and making sure the others did the same. He wanted to enjoy strolling under the angry red sky in the Lorcan morning.

They carefully avoided the dark sinkholes, which became less numerous and less prone to spouting steam the closer they got to the forest. The graceful furry creatures were gone, presumably frightened away by the volcanic eruption. Though he had asked Ambassador Lewis to take the point, Captain Picard decided to lead the way himself, with Worf close at hand. Deanna Troi wasn't surprised. She removed her mask and found herself walking beside Fenton Lewis, who kept the gleaming Ambassador's Mask over his face. It cut off his peripheral vision, allowing her to stare openly at him without being noticed. The mask suited him, she thought, with its sweeping curves and jarring colors.

In all her experience, she had never known any other human whose mind control was so strong or whose mind was so secretive. Undoubtedly his natural charm did much to disarm his audience. Still, she could see that Fenton Lewis was an extremely determined individual. One might even call him selfish, but it wasn't selfishness that made him a diplomat, a man whose persuasive powers were impressive enough to stop wars. Deanna could sense compassion and empathy in him. But he obviously didn't let emotion get in the way of reason, and he tried never to show his feelings. Now, with his astonishing mask, he was well protected against revealing his true self.

"I know you're taking me apart," he said matter-of-factly, startling Deanna. "That's why I'm keeping the mask on."

"The mask," she replied, gracing him with a smile, "it suits you." He wasn't the only one who could be charming.

"Now that I know you approve of it, I'll take it off," he said, gripping the mask by the chin and pulling it back over his head. His sandy hair cascaded onto the animal skins that covered his rangy shoulders, and Deanna noted with interest that his coloring matched the coloring of the planet, from the deep beige of his tanned face to the azure of his eyes to the sun-bleached streaks in his hair.

He cocked one eyebrow merrily. "I suppose, Counselor, exploring planets is old-hat to you."

"I've been on my share of away teams," she said, trying to sound as matter-of-fact as he had.

"Usually you go with that strapping first officer . . . Riker? Is that his name?"

"That's his name," she replied coolly. She didn't like the leer in Lewis's voice.

"That must be convenient," Lewis said bluntly, "because you two are lovers, aren't you?"

Her astonishment lasted only seconds, but Deanna felt the color, and the anger, darken her cheeks.

"That was in the past," Deanna said simply and truthfully. "I had no idea the Diplomatic Service was so well informed."

Lewis shrugged. He warmed her with his most gallant smile. "I meant no disrespect, Counselor Troi, believe that. I merely wanted to satisfy my perverse curiosity."

"I understand. And I was satisfying *my* curiosity earlier."

"Then we're even," the ambassador replied.

Worf stopped ahead of them to adjust his backpack. The wind seemed warmer and less fierce, with the forest directly ahead of them acting as a windbreak. Gnarled plants and hardy vines stood at the edge of the woods, fighting off the gusts of sand, ash, and steam from the bleak prairie. The forest plants were obviously dying away, from the look of the wizened stumps of their ancestors, which poked through the reddish soil.

"Erosion is killing the vegetation," said Deanna to no one in particular. "The wind and the volcanic ash are winning."

"Just here," answered Fenton Lewis, striding toward the outer edge of what appeared to be an endless woods. "There's a lot of planet out there."

"Lieutenant Worf, you may contact the ship," Picard said to the Klingon. "See if they can warn us the next time a volcano's about to erupt."

"Yes, Captain." Worf tapped his communicator insignia, but there was no answering tone and no signal. He tapped it again, and this time he studied his fingertips as he pulled them away from the distinctive Starfleet badge. Fine black granules clung to them; the granules looked like iron shavings—fine enough to work themselves into delicate instruments and ruin them.

Picard stiffened and slapped his own communicator. He, too, was greeted by silence. "Troi," he ordered, "try your communicator."

Deanna touched hers and then massaged it, but it remained as mute as the others. Her fingertips also came away covered with metallic shavings. The shavings were highly magnetized, she noticed, sticking together in barely discernible clumps and clinging to her clothing, hair, and equipment. She looked dumbfounded at Picard and Worf.

Fenton Lewis howled with laughter at their solemn faces. "Y'know, I never agreed with the policy of pinning communicators onto people's clothes. I liked the old kind, the ones you stuck in your pocket." He laughed again.

"I fail to see the humor in this situation," Captain Picard responded sternly.

"But there's a lesson to be learned here, Captain," said Lewis, draping a rawhide-clad arm over the smaller man's shoulders. "All the technology in the world won't save you from poor planning."

"The *Enterprise* crew will be worried," Worf observed.

"Why?" Lewis shrugged. "They know the original coordinates. All we have to do is go back to the original spot for beam-up. Isn't that right, Captain?"

"Theoretically, yes," Picard agreed. "That doesn't change the fact that Commander Riker will be worried. We should have checked in by now."

Suddenly the ground trembled, and the small landing party whirled to face the mountain range, which again spewed flaming clouds into the choked atmosphere. No one needed to give the order to put on masks or seek safety in the thick vegetation. Within seconds, Deanna Troi, Jean-Luc Picard, J. G. Worf, and Fenton Lewis had vanished into the Lorcan forest, and the red plain was barren except for the plumes of geysers.

"What do you mean, you've lost contact?" Riker asked Data.

"Precisely that, Commander," answered Data, his lilting cadence giving his turn of events no more importance than would be given to the report of a shortage of whipped cream in the Ten-Forward lounge. "We have lost contact with the away team."

"What about sensors?"

"Useless," replied the android. "The area where they beamed down is undergoing intense volcanic activity. The volcanic ash is highly magnetic and is disrupting our sensors. Even if the away team stayed in the beam-down position, it's doubtful we could lock on to them to beam them back up until the volcanic activity subsides."

"Damn," Riker cursed to himself. "I don't like the sound of this."

Geordi La Forge turned away from his engineering station on the bridge to look glumly at the acting captain. "This is the worst example of Murphy's Law I've ever heard of."

"Murphy's Law?" queried Data. "Is that a new law of physics? Does it explain the malfunctioning of the communicators?"

"It explains everything," sighed Geordi.

Riker was seething. "It doesn't explain why we risked our captain on a dangerous mission. And it doesn't explain why the away team was beamed down next to an active volcano."

"Finding a spot on Lorca that is not near an active volcano would be very difficult," Data explained. "The captain and Ambassador Lewis requested to be beamed down in the vicinity of planetary life-forms. I obliged. Perhaps I should have done more than a routine sensor sweep. I failed to consider a worst-case scenario."

Not even the calm yellow eyes could hide Data's concern. Commander Riker was moved to put his hand on the android's shoulder.

"It's not your fault," Will said kindly. "This mission has been ill conceived from the beginning. But now we have a new mission—to get our captain, Deanna, and Worf off that planet. Fenton Lewis can stay there forever, if he likes."

Riker lifted his chin determinedly and spoke in a booming voice: "Riker to sickbay."

"Dr. Pulaski here," came the reply a moment later.

"Doctor, can you be ready to beam down to the planet in twenty minutes?"

"Absolutely. Has something gone wrong?"

Riker swallowed hard as he reported, "We've lost contact with them."

"Where are we meeting?"

"Transporter Room One."

"I'm on my way."

Riker cleared his throat and spoke even louder: "Riker to Security!"

"Yes, sir," came an eager and youthful voice. "Ensign Salinger on duty." He corrected himself, "Acting Security Chief Ensign Salinger."

"Well, Acting Security Chief, this is the acting captain. I want two armed security officers waiting in Transporter Room One in twenty minutes. This is a dangerous away mission with possible combat, so send me two people who can handle themselves."

"Yes, sir," snapped the ensign crisply.

"Request permission to join you, sir," said Geordi, stiffening to attention.

"I'd love to have you along, Geordi," answered Will, "but I need you to stay home and mind the ship."

"Excuse me, Commander," said Geordi hesitantly, "what am I to do, in case—"

"Don't send anyone else down to the planet's surface," insisted Riker. "That is an order. If you don't hear from us in forty-eight hours, report to Starfleet and ask for further orders."

"Yes, sir," Geordi replied. He turned to look at the big chair in the center of the bridge. It was really the same construction as the other chairs on the bridge, but the aura of command made it loom as large as a king's throne he had once seen on Earth, at Windsor Castle. He was going to sit in that chair for a matter of hours, or days, but he wasn't going to sit easily. He knew that.

"Is Ensign Crusher remaining on board?" he asked.

"Of course," Riker replied. "I'm not risking a single life that I don't have to risk."

"Commander?" asked Data. "May I accompany you in search of the captain and his party? I feel somehow responsible."

"You may join us," agreed Will Riker.

Travel through the Lorcan woods was surprisingly easy for the away team. In such a cool climate, buffeted by shifting winds, only the hardiest plants survived. No thick underbrush clogged their footsteps, and they didn't need to use phasers to cut a path. Fenton Lewis had found what appeared to be a trail, and he was leading the single column, followed by Picard, Deanna, and Worf. The big Klingon was content to be the rear guard, keeping his eye on the other members of the team.

Sinkholes were rare now; apparently the trees and vegetation absorbed all the available water, despite their sickly appearance. The trees towered high, but they all seemed strangely denuded, except for brittle needles and a brown fur that covered every centimeter of bark and leaf. Perhaps, thought Worf idly, the trees and stubby bushes were actually green underneath the drab moss, but he didn't have time to even take a scraping to find out.

They were on a forced march, hoping to meet some Lorcans before nightfall. The tentative plan was to find the Lorcan leader, Almighty Slayer, then return to the ash-strewn plain and beam back to the ship. With precise coordinates, they could return to Lorca later and conduct their business with a measure of efficiency. Captain Picard was determined not to leave Commander Riker in doubt as to the party's status one minute longer than necessary. Worf recalled the first officer's objections to the captain leading the away team and he knew Picard was feeling guilty and somewhat chastened by the turn of events.

Actually, no one was in very good humor except Ambassador Lewis. He appeared to thrive on the uncertainty of the situation, and Worf was beginning to grant the human ambassador a modicum of respect. Here was a man who was single-minded and fearless—like a warrior, not like the vast majority of human beings. Even an extremely brave human could be paralyzed by countless fears and concerns. But Ambassador Lewis, marching straight into the unknown with a smile on his face, was the kind of human a Klingon could understand.

Suddenly Picard stopped and raised his hand. "Stop."

Deanna and Worf responded instantly to the familiar voice, but Fenton Lewis plowed ahead several more strides before stopping. "What is it?" he asked impatiently, not turning around.

"We've been marching half the day," said the captain, slightly winded. He pointed upward. "The sun is directly overhead. If we don't meet any Lorcans soon, we won't get back to our arrival point before nightfall."

"Who wants to go back there?" asked Lewis with mock revulsion. "We won't find any humans living near those volcanoes."

"He may have a point, Captain," Deanna Troi admitted. "I sensed no intelligence in the area."

"We have to think of the *Enterprise* crew," Picard answered. "They'll be looking for us there."

Fenton Lewis rolled his eyes, as if to beg release from such backward thinking. "Captain," he explained, "the communicators were only our umbilical cord to the ship. They aren't important. The ship is of no help to us down here, and we can't be of any help to the ship. You gave me a month to accomplish my mission, so why don't you relax and enjoy this grand adventure? I'm not interested in hogging all the glory. This is the Lewis and Picard Expedition as far as I'm concerned."

"Ambassador," replied the captain, barely controlling his irritation, "I'm not interested in glory, yours or mine. You have only a mission to worry about. I am responsible for the safety and well-being of a starship. You wouldn't have gotten to this planet without the *Enterprise,* and you won't get off it without her. Whether you like it or not, the *Enterprise* and her crew are part of your mission."

"All right," answered Lewis in a conciliatory tone. "So we're stuck with each other. And you're stuck on this planet without your communicators. What good will it do us to turn back? Believe it or not, this is an actual footpath we're following, and I would be willing to bet that we'll meet up with some Lorcans by tonight, or tomorrow at the latest. Take that gamble, Captain."

Fenton Lewis smiled disarmingly. "Think of the European adventurers exploring the New World, or my own relatives establishing the first colony in the Alpha Centauri system. They trekked for years to get where they were going, and they were completely cut off from help of any kind. No gigantic ship was hovering overhead, waiting to beam them up at the slightest sign of trouble. This is life, Captain, enjoy."

Jean-Luc sighed. The adventure that started so smoothly had gone sour with the loss of the communicators. The excitement of those early morning hours had been replaced by a quiet concern and resolve. Already, Picard could hear his first officer saying, "The captain is supposed to stay with the ship." And what was the problem, really? A simple loss of communications. If the roles had been reversed, as they so often were, and Picard was on the *Enterprise* tracking Commander Riker on the away team, he wouldn't panic. Nor should Riker. After half a day, panic was hardly justified.

"All right," said Picard determinedly, "we shall continue until we make contact with the Lorcans. After that, if there is no danger, Counselor Troi and I will return to our arrival point."

"That's the spirit!" Lewis bellowed, slapping the captain on the back. "Now let's make history!"

Impatiently, Will Riker paced the narrow confines of Transporter Room One. He had originally wanted to leave in twenty minutes, and already it had been thirty-three minutes since he had given the order. Kate Pulaski sat calmly on a box behind the transporter console, checking her medical supplies. The two security officers, Whiff and Greenblatt, stood at attention by the door, looking uncomfortable in their overweight parkas. Except for the pistol phaser shoulder holsters on Whiff and Greenblatt, the second away team was dressed identically to the first.

Whiff was a giant humanoid with a hairless pink face, an Antarean ranger only recently commissioned by Starfleet. Greenblatt was a blond woman of deceptively slight stature. Riker remembered her from the weekly T'ai Chi classes and he knew she could toss any one of them, including the gigantic Whiff, clear across the room. The transporter technician fiddled with his controls and checked his settings. But where was Data?

"Commander," said Pulaski, in a tone that bespoke a healthy skepticism, "did we ever receive any communication from the away team?"

"No direct communication," Riker answered. "But Data was monitoring their position, so we know their communicators were working until the eruption."

"Are you afraid they were trapped in the volcanic debris?" asked Kate softly.

Riker answered with more certainty than he felt. "No. For one thing, they were some distance from the volcano; they weren't right at the foot of it. And Data picked up life-form readings in the area before and after the eruption. It's just that the readings are inconsistent because of these magnetic clouds, and we can't be sure what's going on down there."

"Then there's every possibility," Kate concluded, "that the away team is all right."

"Every possibility," Riker agreed.

"Then why are we going down?" the doctor asked simply.

He kept thinking about Fenton Lewis's tales of masked barbarians bashing each other's heads in with swords over the right to wear one mask or another. Lorca frightened him, and Fenton Lewis frightened him even more.

"We're going down," he said solemnly, "to ascertain the status of the away team."

"No," answered Kate Pulaski, shaking her head. "We're going down there because you're a man of action and you can't stand sitting around waiting."

"I didn't know you were also the ship's psychologist," Riker said sarcastically.

"Not officially." The doctor smiled. "That's just my hobby."

The turbolift door blew open, and Data rushed into the room. He brushed past the two security officers and joined the technician behind the transporter console. "May I enter the transporter coordinates?" he asked politely.

"Be my guest," said the man.

"Data!" snapped Riker. "Where have you been?"

"Triple-checking these coordinates," the android answered, never removing his eyes from the flashing monitors embedded in the console. "This time I have arrived at the optimum location to beam down to the planet: far enough away from volcanic activity to ensure proper scanner and communicator operation, yet close to scattered pockets of life-form readings."

"But will we be close to the captain and *his* party?" asked Riker.

"Unknown," Data replied. "We do not know where the captain is."

Riker shook his head. "Will we be close to where we think they might be?"

"We will know the direction to go to find them," answered Data. He turned to the technician and nodded. "Be *my* guest."

Data strode to the platform, as Riker, Pulaski, and the security personnel picked up their equipment and struggled after him. Pulaski suddenly looked stunned, as if she had forgotten something important.

"Masks!" she gasped. "We don't have any masks to wear!"

"There's no time," snapped Riker, glancing at his pistol phaser. He checked to see that everyone was in position, then he gestured to the transporter technician.

"Energize!"

Chapter Three

RIKER'S PARTY MATERIALIZED in a great forest, with huge brown trees towering on all sides of them. So imposing were the trees that the two security officers drew their pistol phasers and fanned out to protect the away team.

"Phasers set to stun," Riker reminded them.

Whiff and Greenblatt double-checked their weapons, as the others stared in awe at the monstrous trees. Kate Pulaski's gaze finally reached the pinnacle of the nearest one, and she marveled at the pink clouds that hovered over its tip like cotton candy on a long stick. She was suddenly startled by a hairy creature staring down at her from the top branches of the giant tree.

"Commander," she whispered, backing up closer to Riker and pointing, "there's something alive in that tree." The long-limbed creature chattered shrilly and threw a seed pod at them.

Now everyone's attention was directed toward the tree, and Whiff and Greenblatt were nervously aiming their weapons in the direction of the lanky creature. Gracefully, it shifted from one scrawny bough to another, arms, legs, and tail moving with such speed that it was impossible to tell which appendage was which. It rested for a moment, dangling upside down by its prehensile tail while it stripped the seed pods from a lower branch. It examined each pod in turn and either rejected it, sending it clattering to the ground, or pried it open and ate the seeds.

Now that the creature was still for a moment, Kate decided that it was less like a monkey and more like a sloth, with arms and legs of equal length and a similar body. It probably never walked upright like a primate. Why should it walk at all, when its long, thin limbs were perfect for swinging through trees? The animal's matted fur was a golden-red and would probably have been beautiful were it not so filthy.

"At ease," said Riker with a smile. "Data, do you think that's one of the life-forms you've been picking up?"

"Possibly," the android replied.

"May I suggest," said Kate Pulaski, "that it has seen humans before? It's obviously not afraid of us."

"A reasonable assumption," Data agreed. "I wonder how intelligent it is?"

Riker sighed. "Which way should we go, Data?"

Data checked his tricorder. "Our position is southeast of where the captain's team landed. However, I am picking up more life-forms directly to the west."

"More of these?" Riker asked, pointing to their arboreal friend.

"No," Data answered with slight surprise in his voice. "One of the creatures is quite large."

"Let's go," said the commander, motioning toward a path between the trees. "Greenblatt, you lead the way. And try to keep your phaser holstered."

"Yes, sir," she said.

Twigs snapped above their heads, and the entire party whirled to look up. The same hairy sloth they had seen earlier, or its identical twin, now perched directly above them. It chattered what seemed to be words of encouragement to the travelers.

"It appears to be following us," Data said quizzically.

"That's all we need," grumbled Riker, "an escort."

"Or a mascot." Pulaski smiled.

The Antarean, Whiff, apparently having no interest in cute furry creatures, had wandered ahead. "Commander Riker!" he called in a lilting accent. "I see a road ahead."

Seconds later the party emerged onto a dirt road, complete with wheel ruts and stumps where trees had been felled to make the road wider. Between the ruts in the red clay were the half-moon shapes of hoofprints. Data bent down to study the markings more closely.

"These tracks were made by a very primitive conveyance," he said.

"A wagon of some sort," Riker answered. "At least they have roads."

Ensign Greenblatt stiffened to attention. "Listen," she hissed.

Kate Pulaski half expected to be serenaded by their treetop mascot again. Instead, she heard a sound that was disarmingly like real singing. As the seconds dragged past, the voice in the woods became very clearly that of man singing, accompanied by the rhythmic clattering of a vehicle of some sort. Riker crouched down and motioned to the others to take cover.

The doctor found herself kneeling next to Ensign Greenblatt behind a fallen log. To the young officer's credit, she kept her phaser in its holster, exactly as ordered. She also kept her attention riveted upon a portion of the road that curved out of sight behind a dark stand of canelike plants. Kate marveled at the ensign's acute hearing; to her own ears, the off-key warbling seemed to come from everywhere at once, including the treetops. But it soon became clear that Greenblatt was right. A bedraggled slump-backed pony emerged from the cane, pulling a small but garishly painted wagon.

Sitting in the driver's seat was what looked like a large sunflower, and Pulaski realized with a start that she was looking at a real live Lorcan, complete with mask. The mask riveted her attention, almost making her forget the grating but spirited voice coming from behind it. The mask was perfectly round and predominantly yellow, with strange signs painted in blue on the forehead and cheeks. The signs were duplicated, Kate realized, on the wagon, which was painted gold with blue lettering. Red filigree curled across the roof of the wagon. It reminded Pulaski of an artifact from Earth's past she had seen at the Smithsonian Institution: a circus wagon. Even the pony was wearing a mask of blue, which added to the festive effect.

Kate started to look for Commander Riker to see what he planned to do, when something streaked out of the trees and landed on the roof of the wagon with a jarring thud. It was the furry sloth, which looked gangly and awkward away from its arboreal habitat. The sloth reared up on its hind legs and gave a shriek that would have curdled synthehol.

"Whoa!" shouted the driver, reining in his pony. "What is it, Reba? What is it, girl?"

The thing bounded up and down, flapping her impossibly long arms and pointing to the hidden off-worlders. Kate thought the jig was up.

Commander Riker apparently thought so, too, as he emerged from his hiding place. "We mean you no harm!" he shouted.

"Aaagh!" wailed the man in the sunflower mask, throwing his arms over his eyes. "Infidels! Heathens! Pagans!" He turned his back on Riker and cowered in his seat. "Spare my life, demons! Spare me—I am but a poor peddler!"

"We aren't demons," Riker replied, exchanging alarmed glances with the other team members who now joined him in the center of the road. "We are visitors."

"Demons!" the man squealed. "Make my death quick, I beg you! And don't steal my soul." The sloth, Reba, climbed down from the roof of the wagon and threw herself protectively over her master's back. The two of them wailed in unison, certain of their impending death.

These were the ferocious Lorcans? thought Riker. He motioned to the others to stay back, as he took a few tentative steps toward the wagon. "Honestly," he said in a calm voice, "we mean you no harm. We are not demons, just visitors from a far-off place."

"Then where are your masks?" the peddler demanded.

"We don't wear masks," Will answered honestly.

The man whirled around, anger seething in his voice even if his features were hidden. *"No masks?"* he asked incredulously. "You should be put to death for such immodesty!"

Will smiled slightly. "Have you seen or heard of any others like us? Visitors from a far-off place?"

"If I had, they would be in their graves!" The Lorcan suddenly reached back into his wagon and drew out a huge double-edged sword, its handle glittering with gemstones. "Pray to your gods to welcome your heathen souls!"

Whiff and Greenblatt stepped forward, their hands tensing around their pistol phasers. "Put that down," Whiff ordered.

"Wait!" barked Kate Pulaski with authority in her voice. She stepped between Whiff and Greenblatt as she addressed the man in the sunflower mask. "If we agree to wear masks, will you help us search for our comrades?"

The sunflower cocked slightly, and the sword was

lowered a few centimeters. "Will you be my vassals and show me obedience?"

"Vassals?" growled Riker, tasting the word and spitting it out.

"Only until after the fair," the peddler assured them. "With an entourage so large, I will be able to wear the Proprietor's Mask and demand a larger space to sell my wares. Higher prices, too!"

"What type of mask are you wearing now?" asked Data.

"This?" answered the man with obvious contempt. "A poor Peddler's Mask. I can justify no other."

Data was obviously fascinated. "What type of masks would we wear?"

"All right," sighed the peddler, as if conceding a huge bargaining point, "all of you may wear the Apprentice's Mask instead of the Vassal's Mask. But you must show me obedience . . . at least in public."

The doctor edged closer to Riker. "I don't think we can go anywhere on this planet without masks," she whispered.

Riker nodded and looked up at the wagon. He saw a decrepit pony, a gangly hairy pet, and a man wearing a dinner plate on his face. He fought the temptation to call Geordi and have them beamed back to the ship immediately.

"We'll wear the masks," said the commander. "But how long does this fair last? Our primary concern is to find our comrades."

The peddler shrugged. "I can't imagine they will be anywhere but the fair. Unfortunately, it's a long journey—yet a fortnight."

"That is two weeks," Data added.

"If we don't hit any boggles," the peddler remarked, tossing his sword back into the wagon.

"Boggles?" asked Pulaski.

"Fire storms," the Lorcan explained. "They can kill

people and animals. If we hit a bad one, I'll have to repaint my wagon."

"What happens during these storms?" Riker asked, narrowing his gaze.

The man shook his head. "You are from far away, aren't you? You've never seen the ground open up and the fire fly in the air? You have never felt the hot breath of the dragon who lives at the center of the world?"

"Volcanoes," said Data somberly.

"Why would you have to repaint your wagon?" the doctor asked.

"The paint burns, and the wagon gets black. Who will buy from a peddler with a black wagon?"

Riker reached for his Starfleet communicator-insignia and plucked it off his tunic. "We'd better keep all sensitive instruments under cover. That includes the scanners and the phasers."

"Put your belongings in the wagon," said the Lorcan, leaping to the ground. Riker was surprised to see how tall and fit he was, considering how old his voice sounded. The masks could be very deceptive.

"I am Day Timer," he said, grasping Will's forearm.

The commander returned his grasp. "Will Riker."

"Now, Will Riker, tell your vassals to help me dig for clay."

"These aren't my vassals," Will replied. "They're my companions. And why should we dig for clay?"

"Because," said Day Timer somberly, "you must have masks to wear as soon as possible." His own mask swiveled in the direction of Ensign Greenblatt, and the young woman shifted warily under the disconcerting scrutiny of the yellow disc.

Day Timer's voice took on a strange hoarseness. "I haven't seen the naked face of a woman in six years. If you were her kinsman, you could put me to death for looking at her now."

Kate Pulaski stepped closer to Will. "Let's help him dig for clay."

As the salmon-colored clouds dropped lower over the treetops, a light rain began to fall. Fenton Lewis stopped in his tracks and pulled the Ambassador's Mask over his face. The mist beaded against its polished surface. "I suggest that all of you put your masks on," he said. "The rain comes from those same volcanic clouds and must be full of ash and debris."

Deanna and Worf glanced at the captain to see what he would do. He nodded, and they pulled on their masks, trying to ignore how ridiculous they looked. After all, there was no one in the Lorcan woods to see the pig, the clown, and the devil in the company of a silver sunburst.

Picard peered nervously at the darkening sky. "We're going to have to make camp soon. Any idea how far we've come?"

"Counting the time in the desert," answered Lewis, "I'd say about ten kilometers. But the path is widening—we should hit a road soon, or a village."

Worf was fooling around with one of his scanners. He gritted his teeth and growled, shaking the thing like a baby's rattle. "This one's useless, too!" he muttered. "I don't think we have a single device that still works!"

"What about our phasers?" asked Deanna Troi. "They haven't been exposed to the volcanic dust."

"That's right," agreed Lewis, "and the captain now appears to have been very judicious in making us bring hand phasers instead of pistol phasers. See, Picard? Not everything has turned out badly."

The captain nodded, his face feeling clammy inside the plastic devil's mask. He wanted to take it off and feel the rain on his face. "With everything that's happened today," he said slowly, "I think I understand what happened to the Lorcans."

"So do I," Deanna replied.

Picard removed the useless communicator-insignia from his parka and studied it. "Two hundred years ago, the people who settled this planet were just as dependent upon technology as we are. They were space travelers and colonists. Then increased volcanic activity blanketed the planet in dense clouds and lowered the temperature. And the same thing that happened to our equipment must've happened to theirs.

"We've only been here one day, and already I feel like a primitive, totally dependent upon my wiles and my instincts for survival. The Lorcans have spent two hundred years here. And whatever customs have built up around the use of masks, we know they have a practical application as well."

Jean-Luc paused in thought. "Odd, we haven't even met a single Lorcan yet, but I feel like one of them."

"I couldn't agree with you more," Deanna conceded. "Perhaps we were meant to be welcomed this way."

The tiny party stood in the center of the vast forest, dwarfed by the dark trees, which rose out of sight into the encroaching mist of clouds. The wood and its scarlet canopy were as hushed and awesome as the grandest cathedral. Even the rain was a polite whisper.

Riker crawled on his stomach under the peddler's wagon to escape the drizzling rain. Dr. Pulaski and Ensign Greenblatt were sitting inside the wagon watching Day Timer and Data, who were building a fire under a gigantic evergreen, meticulously scraping the brown moss off each twig and branch destined for the flame.

The clay gathering had been a trivial task, since most of the topsoil was clay. After extracting the worms, they had mixed the fresh clay with rainwater to create mud, from which Day Timer had hurriedly molded five circular masks. They were similar to his but slightly smaller. Eye, nose, and mouth holes would be carved out later to fit, he said, just before the clay set.

For the moment, the masks remained inside the wagon with Dr. Pulaski and Ensign Greenblatt, who had to remain out of sight lest their unmasked faces offend the Lorcans. As soon as the fire was ready, they would be placed near the flames to dry. Day Timer had said that sunlight was preferable for drying clay masks, but a large enough fire might dry them by morning.

Riker glanced up at the darkening amber sky. Surrounded by the immense forest, it was impossible to see the sun or how close it was to setting, but twilight on Lorca lasted a long time, he noted. Will pulled his communicator-insignia from the inner pocket of his jacket and squeezed it gently. The answering tones were reassuring.

"Riker to Enterprise."

"Hello, Commander Riker," said an eager voice. "This is Geordi. Any luck yet?"

"As a matter of fact, no," grumbled Riker, not bothering to conceal his frustration. "Any sign of the first away team?"

"Nothing," Geordi replied. "We continue to scan their last coordinates, but even when the sensors are working, we can't find any life-forms in the area."

"Commander, Wesley has been studying the geology of the planet, and it doesn't look good. Lorca has no surface oceans and only a few lakes, but there are vast underground oceans with opposing hot and cold currents. What isn't water is molten lava, all of it straining to burst through the thin upper crust. The entire planet is like a honeycomb loaded with explosives."

"We know volcanoes are common here," Will acknowledged. "They're called 'boggles.'"

"Whatever they're called, stay away from them. The colder parts of the planet are probably the safest."

"Make sure you stand prepared to beam us all aboard at a moment's notice," Riker warned. "That may be all the time we'll have."

Geordi sounded confident. "All the transporter rooms are on round-the-clock alert, and we have auxiliary personnel at full standby. We're all with you. Let's get our captain and our crew back."

"That's the plan," answered Will. "Anything else?"

"No, sir."

"Thank you, Mr. La Forge. Riker out."

Commander Riker put his badge back into his inner pocket and zipped it shut. Despite his greater concerns, one smaller and more immediate concern was gnawing at his stomach at the moment: he was hungry. And he wasn't looking forward to the food in his pack. The mysterious peddler seemed to be well fed and spry enough, thought Riker. Maybe he knew where they could find some real food.

The first officer rolled out from under the wagon and stood up, noticing that the rain had waned to a fine mist. He brushed the red clay from his clothes as he strolled to where Day Timer, Data, and Whiff were working in impressive unity to carve a shelter from the thick lower limbs of a giant evergreen. "Everbrown" would be a better term, thought Will, although he did notice some green twigs among those in the firewood pile.

"Are you really going to build a fire inside that tree?" he asked doubtfully.

"It is quite amazing," said Data, holding up a leafy branch that was caked with brown moss. "Day Timer says this moss is naturally flame-retardant, even when the moss and the tree are both dead. Of course, the moss is a parasite and eventually kills the tree, but it allows the tree to survive fire. A curious trade-off."

"But a necessary one," Riker observed. "How long would this forest last, surrounded by volcanoes, if it weren't impervious to fire? Judging by the height of some of these trees, I'd say they've been here for centuries."

"Watch," said the masked peddler as he drew a strange contraption from the oversize pocket of his pants. It consisted of a thick rope, tied in a coil, one end of which poked through a bronze flint-holder attached to a crude striker wheel. He struck the wheel several times with the palm of his wrinkled hand until finally the sparks from the wheel against the flint set the rope on fire. Carefully, he blew on the smoldering rope until it was burning well enough to light his pile of kindling.

"I sell these," he said proudly. "Very popular."

"Are you planning to cook something on that fire?" Riker asked hopefully.

Day Timer was lying on his chest, nursing his fire with a few well-directed puffs. "Do maskless people eat fish?" he asked.

"Certainly." Will smiled, pleasantly surprised. His mouth watered at the thought of fresh food. "Is there a place to go fishing?"

"Fishing?" scoffed Day Timer. "You people are truly backward. First, you don't know about masks, and now you say you don't know about werjuns either?"

"Werjuns?" asked the commander.

"The animal," Data replied, nodding up at Reba. The gangly sloth dangled by her tail from a branch far overhead. Now that she knew they were talking about her, she stopped her leisurely swinging and listened intently to the conversation.

Day Timer kept his mask angled toward the rising flames. "Go get them fish, Reba," he said. "Find them a bog." He motioned toward Riker. "That one there looks like he could eat a bushel."

"I could," the commander admitted. "What can we do to help?"

"Just follow Reba," the Lorcan answered. "And take the women, too, so they will stop going through my wares. Be careful you don't fall into a bog, or that will be the end of you."

"We'll be careful," Riker assured him. He waved up at the red-furred quadruped. "Lead on, Reba."

The animal swung gracefully down from the tree and landed on all fours. On the ground, the werjun didn't look simian at all, having the gait and something of the appearance of a gazelle—if a gazelle could have a rounded head, no neck, and an enormous tail.

As they passed the blue wagon, Riker called, "Doctor! Ensign! Reba and I are off to catch some fish. Care to join us?"

Dr. Pulaski and Ensign Greenblatt climbed out of the wagon and joined the unusual procession. They glanced back at the masked Lorcan, who never looked up from his fire.

"You wouldn't believe the junk he has in that wagon," whispered Kate. "He does, however, have some beautiful hand-woven cloth and two gorgeous masks, one of clay and feathers and another of wood and gemstones."

Greenblatt shook her head, obviously puzzled. "I suggested to the doctor that we wear the masks so we could come out of the wagon and help you make camp. But she said we could only wear the masks we were assigned."

"I'm sorry, Ensign, that there hasn't been time to fully brief you," said Riker, craning his neck to keep Reba in sight. She loped along the road for a few meters, then scurried up a tree to get a better view of the surrounding area. "The masks aren't just decorative or symbolic; they indicate a person's rank in the community. If you don't have the right mask on, somebody might challenge you to a duel."

The young woman made a low whistle. "So being this man's apprentice is fairly safe?"

"We hope so," answered Riker. "What is that beast doing?"

Above them, Reba chattered importantly and leapt down from the branches. The humans followed as quickly as they could in the fading twilight. They found her bent over a small knoll, intently combing through long brown blades of grass. Suddenly the werjun shrieked triumphantly and plunged her gangly arms into the blades of grass up to her skinny shoulders. Her head and upper torso soon followed, and Riker blinked with alarm.

"She's going into the ground!" he exclaimed.

But not all the way. The werjun's prehensile tail and powerful rear legs remained coiled around exposed roots at the top of the hidden hole. She obviously knew exactly what she was doing.

A spray of water shot out of the hole, like a small geyser. "She's found an underground spring," Pulaski observed.

"With those arms, I bet she could reach a couple meters deep," remarked Ensign Greenblatt, smiling for the first time since they had reached the planet.

Riker shook his head. "If she comes up with a fish, I'll really be amazed."

"Prepare to be amazed." The doctor smiled.

Almost immediately, the skinny haunches began wriggling, and Reba slowly emerged from the hole. Her shoulders followed her lanky torso, then her head, then her long arms, followed by the most remarkable sight—a squirming fish caught in her powerful three-fingered hands. She tossed it nonchalantly at the humans' feet, then plunged back into the bog.

Riker, Pulaski, and Greenblatt hovered over the

flopping fish. It was the ugliest water-dwelling creature any of them had ever seen. Huge near-sightless eyes bugged out on long tentacles from a cadaverous face. Nasty barbed spines radiated from the fish's snout and along its dorsal fin to its writhing tail. The fish's head and fins were milk-colored, and its body was transparent, revealing several internal organs which could be seen quivering inside a flabby torso. Its gills flapped like giant bellows, sucking in deadly air instead of water.

"I'm not sure I can eat that," Dr. Pulaski admitted.

"It looks like a larger version of cave-dwelling fish we have on Earth," said Riker. "Which stands to reason."

"There's more where that came from," said Greenblatt, indicating the busy werjun.

Reba tossed out another fish, even bigger than the first. This was a slightly different species, longer and sleeker, but no less ugly. In all, Reba caught six good-size fish before Will called a halt to the expedition.

"That's good, Reba," he commended her. "Now let's head back before it gets too dark."

The lanky sloth, her reddish pelt smeared with clay, looked up plaintively from the bog. She seemed almost disappointed, and Ensign Greenblatt instinctively reached down and scratched the pet's head. "That's a good girl, Reba," she smiled. "Thank you."

The werjun chattered happily.

The simple repast of underground fish cooked on spits over an open fire tasted surprisingly good, thought Kate Pulaski. She and Ensign Greenblatt sat close to the trunk of their tree shelter, bathed in shadows so as not to offend Day Timer, and finished their dinner. They were still close enough to the fire to enjoy its welcome warmth. Day Timer himself had eaten only a few bites, and he busied himself poking and prodding the clay masks, which he rolled in fireproof shavings of brown moss and stuck directly in the fire. He was obviously in a hurry to finish the masks and properly clothe his heathen visitors.

"Day Timer?" Riker asked respectfully, trying to stay in the shadows. "Before we came to this land, we heard of a great leader named Almighty Slayer. We have reason to believe our friends have gone to seek him. Do you know where we might find Almighty Slayer?"

The Lorcan, who was kneading one of the masks and gently curving it to offer a better fit and more protection, looked up from his work. "Almighty Slayer?" he mused. "I haven't heard that name in many a fortnight. Yes, he once was a great warrior."

"Is he still your leader?" asked Commander Riker.

"Yes," the old peddler said with a nod, "if he still possesses the Wisdom Mask."

"The Wisdom Mask?" Data repeated. "What is that?"

"The mask of the king." Day Timer shrugged. "Whoever wears the Wisdom Mask can demand obedience from every tradesman, serf, and nobleman in the land. Do you not have a king where you live?"

"We have leaders," Riker answered. "But they must earn their positions."

Although the yellow mask covered Day Timer's face, nothing could disguise the seriousness in his voice. "Believe me, the wearer must earn the Wisdom Mask. Only a true king, rich in wisdom as well as battle skills, can wear it."

"Who determines that?" asked Riker.

"The mask itself determines who its wearer shall be."

The small gathering around the campfire was still for a moment, digesting the peddler's solemn words. The campfire crackled and sputtered as Day Timer slipped the hardening clay mask back under glowing embers and pulled out another one. Reba dangled from the boughs above them, fast asleep. Even Data, who could be a bit too talkative for Kate's liking, seemed subdued by the majesty of night within the Lorcan woods. The visitors sat transfixed, staring at the fire, the palpable darkness all around them, and the deep purple sky above them, shot with stars.

Chapter Four

THE LEWIS AND PICARD EXPEDITION, as Fenton Lewis irritatingly insisted on calling it, got an early start the next day. There was no reason to sleep late, as no one, except possibly Worf, had gotten much sleep. Deanna Troi, in particular, hadn't slept well. She'd been tormented by a dream of a great cataclysm, in which a space vessel had literally been blown from space by a giant fireball, costing the lives of many unsuspecting souls. Of course, a fire in space wasn't even possible, and the dream hardly seemed to fit a planet like Lorca. Still, it had been troubling, and it had added to her unease.

The other reason no one had slept very much was that the three men had been unable to get a fire started. Even the next morning, Deanna still chuckled at the remembrance of her stalwart captain, the earnest Klingon, and the self-styled explorer, all slaving over a miserable pile of twigs.

They had tried everything to get it lit, from waterproof emergency matches to phaser fire. Every effort had failed spectacularly, accompanied by much colorful cursing. Deanna would have offered to help if she could have thought of a way. In the end, they had resorted to chemical heat packs to warm themselves during the frigid night. It seemed unnatural to have to squeeze plastic packs of chemicals for warmth when wood towered all around them.

They had been walking on the path for about three hours, in the by now familiar order: Ambassador Lewis, Captain Picard, Deanna, and Lieutenant Worf. The path was clearer now, etched in red clay, and they were all beginning to have some confidence in Fenton Lewis as a competent woodsman. Worf talked to no one and simply kept an eye on everyone. More than once, Deanna saw him feel his pants pocket to make sure his phaser was still there.

Sometimes Picard and Lewis would get involved in a historical discussion about ancient Celtic or American Indian civilizations. When the discussion became theoretical, as anthropology often did, both men hotly defended their positions. Deanna wanted to hear their lively debate and tried to keep up, but she was often slowed down by muddy stretches and fallen trees in the trail. Whenever she lagged behind, Worf gently hurried her along.

Ambassador Lewis was pointing something out to the captain. "Horses have trod this trail," he announced. "Small horses. See the hoofprints?"

"What I see is a road," Picard pointed out.

The captain walked past the ambassador and crossed several rain gullies to reach what appeared to be a similar trail, only twice as wide. The others caught up immediately and stood marveling at the rutted thoroughfare, as if it were the finest turbolift in the galaxy.

"Which way?" asked Worf.

"We've been going mostly south," said Lewis. "I suggest we take this road to the southeast and keep putting distance between us and those volcanoes."

"On the other hand," Picard began, "by traveling northwest, we'll be headed closer to our arrival point. The *Enterprise* will still be looking for us to the north."

"What do you think, Deanna?" Lewis asked, obviously hoping to win a vote for his plan.

"I think we should stay where we are," Counselor Troi answered. "We've found a road, so why don't we wait for somebody to pass us? They will sooner or later."

Worf stepped behind Deanna, visually reinforcing her position. "If we can make camp for a period of time, perhaps we can repair the communicators or find another way to contact the *Enterprise.*"

"That makes sense to me," said Picard. He bent down and studied the packed red clay. "These wheel ruts look fresh to me. What do you say, Ambassador?"

"I say you're crazy for just wanting to sit on your asses when there's a whole planet out there to explore!"

"Let *it* explore *us,*" Worf replied. The big Klingon had already sat down on a fallen log with his Starfleet insignia badge resting securely on one broad knee. He removed a small pouch of microtools from his pack and began selecting those necessary for the delicate disassembly.

Deanna smiled at the ambassador and tried to lessen the impact of the enforced stop. "On the *Enterprise,* we're basically very cautious," she explained. "We face the unknown constantly, and we have a deep and abiding respect for it."

Lewis snorted derisively. "I'm not normally so terribly impatient. But you see, Deanna, a diplomat's stock-in-trade is people. Until I've met all parties and decided how to approach them, I'm uncomfortable. I want to see a Lorcan right now, meet him mask-to-mask!"

Deanna nodded sympathetically. "I hope, when we do, we can all understand one another."

"If we can't," the ambassador said, "it won't be because of you. Your good humor and calm head are a real asset to this party." He thought for a moment. "You have too much going for you, Deanna, to be the shoulder-to-cry-on for a bunch of space jockeys. When we're finished here, you should think about entering the Diplomatic Service. I think your talents would be put to better use there."

"Thank you," Deanna said honestly. "But I don't think my talents could possibly get a better workout than they do aboard the *Enterprise*."

Worf suddenly twisted his neck to look toward the northern section of the road. His nostrils flared as he warned, "Someone comes. I smell them."

Lewis took a deep breath, too. "Horses! I knew I was right. Well done, Worf." He turned to Picard. "What do we do, Captain? We have time to hide."

"Let's greet them openly," Picard replied without a moment's hesitation. "We need their help if we're to find this Almighty Slayer and get back to the ship in a reasonable amount of time."

Deanna's olfactory senses were not as acute as Worf's or Lewis's, but she had her own early warning system—and it was flashing red. The life-forms headed their way were intelligent, all right, and full of anger. They were like a war party fresh from battle. Their primitive emotions frightened her.

The fear she suddenly experienced scared her even more than the approaching force. Fear, too, was a primitive emotion, necessary for survival in a harsh environment. For all its overt beauty, Lorca was as harsh and unforgiving a place as she had ever seen. The atmosphere was breathable, but it was under constant assault by volcanic ash, magnetic iron dust, and roaring fire. The ground was a soft shell over seething oceans; the entire planet was like an egg. It was a very new planet, still in its infancy, and the fact that humans clung to its fragile shell was amazing. But what kind of humans must they be?

They heard the horses' hooves and turned to meet the oncoming party. "Phasers ready," Picard ordered. "Set to stun!"

"Yes, sir," Worf replied, much relieved to be able to draw his phaser at last.

"Steady," said Picard, as flashes of color began to glimmer between the brown tree trunks in the distance.

"I'm putting my mask on," Lewis announced, pulling the ornate Ambassador's Mask from his pack. "I suggest you do the same!" he snapped at his comrades.

"Make it so," Picard ordered, nodding to Worf and Deanna.

Again the Halloween masks came out. The away team barely had time to put them on and straighten them before the road filled with colorfully garbed knights on tiny ponies. They pranced to a stop, and Deanna counted six masked riders astride six ponies, all snorting thick clouds of mist in the frigid air.

At first, the juxtaposition of ponies and armed warriors was incongruous and almost laughable. But the way the ponies pawed the clay and chomped at their bits made it clear they were eager to carry their masters into battle. The riders were faceless behind their startling masks, each one of which was a work of art to rival the Ambassador's Mask. But the riders' hands, gloved in chain mail, gripped the hilts of their sheathed swords as if the weapons, unrestrained, might leap into battle by themselves. Deanna didn't know exactly why, but she was glad to be wearing a mask during this confrontation.

At the front of the pack, a statuesque warrior sat astride a muscular roan pony. The curves in her bronze breastplate bespoke her femininity. But her mask was the largest and heaviest-looking of the lot, a jagged five-pointed star made of the same burnished silver metal as Fenton Lewis's. A lightning bolt of blue gemstones streaked from the star's highest ray, sent out sparks that formed irregular eye, nose, and mouth holes, and ended in a collision with a jewel-encrusted rainbow across the chin. No part of its design was symmetrical, and its overall effect was profoundly disturbing. To Deanna, the mask reflected the chaos, fury, and passion of unbridled nature.

Deanna could not read such powerful sentiments in the other masks, but they were no less startling. One wooden mask represented a snarling animal, with real fur and teeth pressed into service to form a snout over a sardonically grinning mouth. Another mask consisted almost entirely of brown, white, and lavender feathers on a wooden frame. Though beautiful, the feathered mask gave its wearer a slightly owlish look.

Two other masks were remarkably similar: bronze ovals with odd signs made of red jewels strewn haphazardly across cheek and forehead. One of the bronze masks was worn by a man and the other by a woman, leading Deanna to wonder if the two were personally or occupationally linked. The final mask featured twin snakes made of green jewels, intertwined in the center of a warlike face and separating to form stylized brows over the eyeholes. Each snake held a yellow-feathered bird in its mouth.

Unconsciously, Deanna found herself judging the status represented by each of the masks. The lightning-bolt mask worn by the female warrior was unquestionably the finest on display, followed closely by the Ambassador's Mask worn by Fenton Lewis. In fact, both displayed such a high quality of workmanship that they might have been fashioned by the same hand. The green serpent mask was the third finest, and the others would fall into line according to personal taste. Deanna preferred her ridiculous little Harlequin mask to the snarling animal and the startled owl.

The equestrians were equally curious about the pedestrians' masks, which must have looked just as exotic to them. Deanna thought the Halloween masks at least had humor, which was totally missing from the exquisite but solemn Lorcan masks. Deanna could feel the Lorcans' stares and wondered if this was how all meetings on Lorca began—with a mask scrutiny.

"Hello, Ambassador," said the woman in the lightning-bolt mask. "I am Piercing Blade. I recognize your mask, but the masks of your vassals are repulsive to me. I can't even tell their rank."

"We apologize," said Lewis smoothly, his voice amplified by the sound hole in his mask, which reverbrated like a fine guitar. "We are strangers to this land and do not know all the customs."

The lightning-bolt mask bobbed agitatedly. "I recognize your mask, because I have seen it before! It was made by the master, Fazool, for presentation to the Ferengi ambassador two summers ago. You are not Ferengi, so I must question your right to wear it."

Even hidden behind his mask, Fenton Lewis looked stunned by the accusation. As he weighed his response, Jean-Luc Picard suddenly remembered the one black spot besmirching the ambassador's record, his conviction in absentia for murder by the Ferengi. Lewis certainly wasn't denying that he had gotten the mask from them.

"I admit the Ferengi *sold* me this mask," he said forcefully. "But I am an ambassador in full standing of the United Federation of Planets. I have a right to wear the Ambassador's Mask!"

"I think not," seethed Piercing Blade, reaching behind the calf of her thigh-high boot and drawing out a short but deadly-looking double-edged sword. "I hereby publicly challenge your right to wear the Ambassador's Mask made by Fazool!"

"I don't understand this custom," cooed Lewis sweetly. "As I stated, and as the mask reveals, we are strangers here and do not claim to have mastered the etiquette of mask-wearing."

"Cursed jackal," growled the man in the smiling animal mask. "Lady Piercing Blade will have that mask from you—with or without your head in it!"

This was evidently a favorite joke, as the wearers of the emerald snake mask and the feather mask laughed heartily. Picard couldn't be sure how much of all this was a joke or a bluff, but he was determined to avoid bloodshed. Under the circumstances, he didn't think Fenton Lewis would mind a little diplomatic help.

"We are peaceful visitors," proclaimed the captain. "We will gladly wear whichever masks your customs dictate, but we are not of this society. We have come to this land only to seek an audience with your leader, Almighty Slayer."

Now the blue and silver lightning-bolt mask leaned forward interestedly. "Do you know where he is? We have sought him in vain for one full cycle. He must be dead or in hiding. Either way, his claim to the Wisdom Mask is ended."

"We can work together to find him," Lewis suggested hopefully.

"Yes, we can," Piercing Blade replied, "if that is my wish." She extended a sinewy arm wrapped in black chain mail and pointed to each member of the away team in turn, ending with Fenton Lewis. "Once you are my vassals, you will obey my every command."

The man in the serpent mask reached into a bag strapped to his pony and drew out a dirty burlap sack. He tossed it to the ground at the ambassador's feet. "Give us the Ambassador's Mask and clothe yourself in this."

Fenton Lewis stood immobile, his mask giving him dignity despite the challenge. Finally, he drew himself up to his full height, which was considerable, and tossed his lion's-mane head of hair. "I will defend my right to wear the Ambassador's Mask. I request a sword."

"No!" snapped Picard. He appealed to the tall woman warrior. "Piercing Blade, isn't there some other way to resolve this? We came here in peace."

"This one *is* a sniveling jackal," giggled the woman behind the animal mask, pointing to Captain Picard. "He will make an excellent wet nurse for my piglets."

The Lorcans laughed, except for Piercing Blade, who was assessing the slim man in the horned devil's mask. "We won't insult the rest of you by demanding your masks," she said, "because we do not recognize them. But the Ambassador's Mask by Fazool is a great treasure, and we cannot let an impostor wear it!"

Her glistening mask swiveled toward another of her comrades. "Spider Wing, hand the impostor your short-sword."

The man in the feathered mask reached into his boot and pulled out a sword similar to the one wielded by Piercing Blade. In a scabbard fastened around his waist, a long double-edged sword waited its turn. He plunged the short-sword into the ground at Lewis's feet. "Don't disgrace it," he snapped.

"I shan't," promised Fenton Lewis, seizing the weapon. As soon as his hand touched it, Piercing Blade leapt down from her pony and assumed a crouching position. She pointed her sword at Picard. "Let your own entourage bear witness—this is a fair challenge, fairly met!"

Picard appealed to Lewis. "For God's sake, Fenton, give her the mask. It's not worth dying over."

"I don't intend to die, Captain," said the man in the winged Ambassador's Mask. "I deserve to wear this mask!"

The conflict had degenerated into violence so swiftly that the *Enterprise* crew members were slow to react. As the two masked combatants circled each other at swordpoint, it was difficult to remember that one of them was from a space-traveling society thousands of light-years away. Here, in the Lorcan woods, they were equals.

Finally, Worf edged up behind Picard. The big Klingon was gritting his teeth with anger. "Let me stun them, Captain," he growled. "They haven't the right to accost strangers this way."

"They don't feel Lewis *is* a stranger," observed Counselor Troi, "because they know his mask. They feel he is a usurper and that they are perfectly justified in their actions."

The two continued to circle each other warily, trying to find safe footing in the muddy rutted road. The riders sat immobile on their ponies, watching the duel as if such events were an everyday occurrence hardly worthy of comment. Picard, Worf, and Deanna, their faces hidden by the Halloween masks, stood frozen, astounded by the primitive spectacle before them. Suddenly Lewis lunged, and Piercing Blade parried skillfully. Metal had clashed against metal, and the duel was on.

Picard drew his phaser. "Set to stun, Worf. Fire only to safeguard the ambassador's life."

"Aye, sir."

The duel reminded Picard of fencing matches he had seen between participants as skilled as these. There was none of that lengthy and tedious banging of blades one so often saw in old Earth movies. Instead, there were lightning-fast lunges, whiplike reactions, and a series of strokes so swift that one could barely follow them.

Fenton Lewis mounted a valiant defense, but he was clearly outclassed. Within seconds, the ambassador was reeling backwards, off balance, struggling to parry the woman's slashing blows. Worf raised his phaser to fire, but Picard steadied his hand. "She's toying with him," Picard whispered.

Indeed, the statuesque warrior seemed to have no intention of killing Fenton Lewis, only of embarrassing him to death. He finally stumbled over a fallen log and wound up flat on his back, his sword stuck in the ground several meters away. Piercing Blade lowered her sword and pressed its point against the panting man's throat.

"Enough!" barked Picard. "Spare his life!"

"I will," answered Piercing Blade, who sounded only slightly winded. "I need all the vassals I can get." She held out her hand to the fallen foe. "Give me the mask."

Fenton Lewis slowly stripped the gleaming mask from his face. He stared defiantly at her. "You'll pay for this," he vowed.

"Have you no decency?" she shrieked, turning away in disgust from his naked face. She speared the filthy burlap bag with her sword and tossed it at him. "Cover yourself!" With a gulp, Fenton Lewis lowered his head and pulled the bag over his head.

Piercing Blade turned to her comrades, triumphantly holding the Ambassador's Mask over her head. "We now have an ambassador in our band! Who shall it be?"

"Let me be the ambassador!" the man in the animal mask shouted. "I am silver-tongued, as all the women know."

"No, Cold Angel," she laughed. "The only ones who listen to you are the animals, and I need you to build me a great herd of war ponies. Keep the Trainer's Mask, for it suits you best."

She turned to the man with the mask of emerald serpents. "You, Medicine Maker? Do you wish to be an ambassador?"

"I will gladly add that prize to my collection,"

Medicine Maker replied, "but I won't forsake the Herbalist's Mask."

"Then Spider Wing will be our ambassador!" the woman declared, proudly presenting the glistening silver trophy to the man in the feather mask. His comrades cheered, and, from his startled movements, Spider Wing seemed to be genuinely surprised. He took the proffered mask in both hands.

"Thank you, my lady," he said, his mask tilting forward in a bow. "I pray I am worthy of this promotion and your trust."

"What about the others?" asked the woman in the bronze oval mask. "Their masks are strange to us."

Piercing Blade shrugged. "Whatever their rank, they are now my vassals. They will join my entourage."

Deanna and Worf were helping the stunned Lewis to his feet. Now Worf drew himself up to his full height, put his hands on his hips, and glared at the Lorcans through his jolly pig mask. "A Klingon is no one's vassal," he declared.

Jean-Luc knew they could make quick work of the Lorcans with their phasers, but the Prime Directive bound him. He also knew he had to gain control of the situation as quickly as possible.

"It's against our principles to meddle in the affairs of others," explained the captain slowly. "Therefore we cannot become your vassals or join your entourage, although we are honored by the request."

"You refuse Piercing Blade?" asked the man in the bronze oval mask, sounding incredulous. "Do you not recognize the mark of her nobility, the Thunder Mask?"

"We recognize her nobility," Picard replied. "And we recognize her right to *have* vassals, but we came here as visitors and don't plan to stay. We merely request safe passage in our search for Almighty Slayer."

The woman took a couple of threatening steps toward Picard. "I don't recognize your mask, but you seem to think that your nobility is greater than mine. Is that what you're saying?"

The red devil shook his head. "Nobility has nothing to do with it. Where we come from, we believe in freedom of choice. We serve only those whom we choose to serve. We have an allegiance to our Federation and cannot accept the offer to join your entourage."

"It isn't an offer," said the Lorcan leader. "You *must* join my entourage, or I must join yours." Reluctantly she drew her sword.

"Captain!" Worf called with alarm.

The captain motioned Worf to keep calm as he backed slowly toward Deanna and the big Klingon. Fenton Lewis sat dejectedly at the side of the road several meters away, the burlap bag draped over his face like a veil.

Piercing Blade bent down to retrieve the sword Lewis had used unsuccessfully. She tossed it to Captain Picard, who surprised himself by catching the weapon in midair. The sword, which reminded him of a Roman short-sword, felt surprisingly light and well balanced in his hand.

"We are fighting for the mask of greater nobility," the woman explained, "and for the right to lead this band of warriors."

"Do I have any alternative to fighting?" Picard asked.

"You can join our band," Piercing Blade replied. "We will give each of you the rank of page, which is very generous. As you can see, the Page's Mask is quite handsome." She motioned to the man and woman wearing the bronze oval masks.

"We would be honored to travel with you," Picard responded. "But as comrades, not as vassals."

"Then you leave me no choice," she said sadly,

dropping into a crouch and leveling her sword at the captain.

Jean-Luc whispered quickly to Worf, "I hate to cheat, but if you see me point my sword straight up, stun her."

"With pleasure," Worf replied.

Now it was Jean-Luc's turn to warily circle the crouching female warrior in her spectacular Thunder Mask. He hated to order phaser fire on an inhabited planet, but he and his crew couldn't serve any power other than the Federation.

Aware of his reluctance to fight, Piercing Blade jabbed playfully at the captain with her sword. "You don't even handle a blade as well as the impostor," she observed. "Throw down your weapon and join us."

Timing was going to be crucial, thought Picard. He wanted the Lorcans to think he had bested their Amazonian leader in battle, but he didn't want to risk harming himself or her. He could be sure of Worf's aim, so he worked himself closer to his foe. She responded with a few crisp flicks of her sword, which he was barely able to parry. That was just a preview, he thought.

Worf wished the sword were in his hand, as well as the fate of the away team. The captain hadn't a prayer against the towering long-limbed warrior. She was toying with him blatantly now. Worf envisioned his own battle strategy against the more skilled opponent: he would use brute force, gladly absorbing a blow or two in order to smash his sword into that ludicrous lightning bolt.

The battle was only seconds old, and already Jean-Luc felt as if his heart would pound its way out of his chest. Piercing Blade parried the captain's best stroke with such force that the sword was nearly ripped from his hand. And she was only half trying. What a woman! But this wasn't a time for idle gawking—he had to gain the upper hand. From the corner of his eye, he saw Worf maneuvering for a clear shot. The Klingon had wisely palmed his phaser, keeping it out of sight in his mammoth left hand.

Piercing Blade slashed at his legs, barely missing his knee, and Picard decided that the match had gone on long enough. He brought his blade crashing down on top of hers, momentarily driving both blades into the ground. Then he grabbed the Lorcan's other arm, feeling nothing but youthful muscle under the links of chain mail, and pulled her toward him. She was surprised by the sudden wrestling tactics and tried to pull away, but Picard held her still long enough to raise his sword in the air.

The flash of light lasted less than a second, and Piercing Blade slumped to the ground as if she were a marionette whose operator had dropped her strings. Her entourage bolted upright on their ponies, stunned and amazed. They had been watching the two combatants and had no idea where the flash of light had come from or what it meant. All they knew was that their leader lay motionless on the ground with a stranger in a horned mask holding a sword to her throat.

"Don't move!" Picard shouted to them. He was panting so heavily his shoulders were heaving and he felt light-headed. "We want no more trouble."

"You have no more," said Medicine Maker. "We recognize your mask of nobility."

The man in the emerald snake mask bowed his head and climbed down from his pony. The others, slowly, numbly, did the same.

"I didn't even see the blow," wailed Cold Angel, shaking his hairy Trainer's Mask.

"Is she dead?" muttered the woman in the Page's Mask.

"No, no," said Picard. He glanced at Worf, and the Klingon nodded, signaling that the phaser had been set to stun briefly. Nevertheless, the captain kept his swordpoint on her throat, just under the jewel-encrusted chin of the dazzling Thunder Mask.

The eyeholes of her mask remained blank, and nobody knew Piercing Blade had regained consciousness until she tried to sit up. Feeling the cold metal swordpoint at her throat, the noblewoman quickly lay back on the damp clay.

"I have been bested," she admitted, "for the first time in my life. I know not how, but the blow was sudden and telling. The Thunder Mask is yours, our ponies are yours, and we are yours to command."

Picard removed his sword from her throat. His victory felt hollow, and he truly regretted having cheated. Besting such a magnificent woman in a fair battle would have been a glorious achievement; tricking her was unfair and beneath him. He hoped one day to give her a second chance in a more even contest.

"Stand up," he said, offering her his hand. "I prefer that you keep your mask. It suits you."

The woman stood, towering a few centimeters over Picard, but he could see her quizzical green eyes through the eyeholes of the Thunder Mask. Having seen only the mask until now, he found the sight of her eyes incredibly intimate and thrilling. He stared into their uncomprehending depths.

"You refuse to take my mask?" she asked incredulously.

Picard nodded. "I refuse to take anything that is yours or your party's. We offer you the same friendship and respect that we were seeking. We're not here to collect masks or money or vassals; we're here to talk to your leaders about establishing relations between our two worlds."

"Then you are like the Ferengi," she concluded. "From the sky?"

"Yes," said Picard. "You understand about space travel?"

"I do," replied Piercing Blade, "for all life comes from the sky."

"That's right," echoed Medicine Maker. "Our ancestors came from the sky, but we were forbidden sky travel by the dragon who lives inside Lorca."

Picard shook his head, not wishing to get involved in some sort of quasi-religious discussion. Worf and Deanna Troi had joined him now, and he looked in vain for Fenton Lewis.

"What do you know about Almighty Slayer?" Worf asked. "Is he dead?"

"Who knows?" Cold Angel asked from behind his animal mask. "They say he was seen at the Dragon Ceremony on Redding Mountain. None of us have seen him for two cycles or more."

The Thunder Mask shook with anger. "One who hides his mask is no king!" spat Piercing Blade. "The Wisdom Mask is the greatest of masks, but where is it? If the Wisdom Mask isn't seen by all at the fair, then I will claim the throne for the Thunder Mask."

"Hear, hear!" chimed the other Lorcans, echoing Piercing Blade's bold proclamation.

"Lady Piercing Blade deserves to rule!" shouted Spider Wing. He was still clutching his newly acquired Ambassador's Mask, and Jean-Luc wondered how he was going to tactfully arrange to have the mask returned to Fenton Lewis. Or if he should.

"Where is this fair?" asked Deanna Troi.

"In Cottage Meadow," answered Spider Wing. "It's about ten days' ride. But," he said with sudden realization, "you have no ponies."

The captain shrugged. "We can walk."

"Perhaps," Medicine Maker suggested, "you can trade those unusual masks for ponies. We have never seen anything like them."

Picard laughed, stroking the plastic goatee of the devil's mask. "Whom can we trade with?"

"You can start with us," exclaimed Cold Angel, reaching a tentative finger toward Worf's jovial pig mask. "I must have this fine mask."

Commander Riker tried on his Apprentice's Mask and was amazed that it fit so well. Day Timer took hold of the leather thongs, one on either side and a third at the top, and tied them at the back of Riker's head in an intricate slip knot. "You can adjust that later," he said.

The mask curled around Will's face, touching his cheekbones, forehead, and nose. The clay was cool against his skin, but his steamy breath kept his face warmer than it had been since coming to Lorca. He was amazed at how perfectly the holes in the mask lined up with his eyes and nose. He couldn't see the mouth hole and had to speak in order to know his voice was audible.

"How do I look?" he asked self-consciously.

"The same as the rest of us," answered Dr. Pulaski.

Riker had been fitted last for the mask and only had to look around to see what a Lorcan apprentice looked like. Except for differences in height and body type, he was surrounded by clones of himself. The second away team now looked like a collection of slightly dirty pennies. The masks were circular and convex, like Day Timer's, but they were innocent of paint, except for a few haphazard yellow markings across the cheeks and foreheads. They looked unfinished, thought Riker, but pleasantly organic in their natural color. Being the same color as the soil, they would make excellent camouflage gear, concluded the first officer.

"What do apprentices do first?" asked Data enthusiastically.

"Do you know how to make anything of value?" asked Day Timer.

The apprentices looked dumbly at one another.

"Do you have anything we can sell?" Day Timer asked.

Again he was greeted by silent masked stares.

"I was afraid not," grumbled the peddler. "Start digging more clay, then, and start gathering feathers, bones, pebbles, and anything else you can find. I'm going to teach you how to make masks."

Chapter Five

THE HALLOWEEN MASKS proved so popular among the Lorcans that Captain Picard almost wished he was on a trading mission. With a few dozen devil, Harlequin, and pig masks, they could probably own half the planet. As it was, they now had one pony, two Page's Masks, a feathered Messenger's Mask, and an unsightly Trainer's Mask.

No amount of bargaining, however, was able to secure the return of the Ambassador's Mask. As soon as the fighting was over, Spider Wing had slipped off into the woods and had emerged a few moments later wearing the dazzling silver mask. He graciously gave his old feathered mask to Picard, but it was evident that he enjoyed his new post and wasn't going to relinquish the Ambassador's Mask, except at swordpoint.

Now every member of the away team had a genuine Lorcan mask to wear, making them less conspicuous, Picard hoped. But the captain was faced with the unwelcome task of assigning masks, and thus status and rank, to his own people. He gave the Page's Masks to Worf and Deanna. From an aesthetic point of view, Worf probably deserved the Trainer's Mask and Deanna the lovely Messenger's Mask, but he saved those two higher-ranking masks for Fenton Lewis and himself.

First he had to find Lewis, who hadn't been seen since Picard's "victory" over Piercing Blade. The Lorcans appeared to harbor no grudges. In fact, they seemed to be delighted with the results of the chance encounter between the two parties. To celebrate the almost doubling of their ranks and the acquisition of new masks, the Lorcans decided to make camp early and relax. While the Lorcans were doing the chores, Jean-Luc instructed Worf and Deanna to be alert and stay friendly while he sought out the ambassador.

As he walked along the road, the captain removed the feathered mask he'd been wearing and rubbed his clammy skin. There would be no soothing showers for any of them tonight. But a bigger concern was the absence of the man who had brought them there, Fenton Lewis. The ambassador had a tremendous ego and didn't take defeat lightly, that much was evident. Perhaps he had immersed himself so deeply in Lorcan lore that the loss of his high-ranking mask was a blow to his self-esteem. Jean-Luc hoped Lewis was professional enough to forget personal setbacks and keep his attention on the mission.

The captain thought that they had gotten a lucky break by meeting Piercing Blade and her band. If Almighty Slayer couldn't be found, they might already be in the company of the next ruler of Lorca. On the other hand, there could be scores of similar bands, all promoting themselves in what was an obvious power vacuum. Lewis's expertise as a diplomat would be invaluable if they were going to sort this out.

But what kind of man was Ambassador Lewis? Just because he had been widely acclaimed and decorated in his field didn't mean he was a decent or dependable person. Selfishness and ambition accounted for great works as often as altruism did. Also, there was the question asked by Piercing Blade: Where had he acquired the Ambassador's Mask? From the Ferengi, that much was certain, but had they sold it to him, as he claimed, or had they lost their lives along with the mask? Back on the *Enterprise,* Lewis had said that the mask hadn't come cheaply. But would a man kill for such an unusual artifact? Knowing the Ferengi and their greed, Picard guessed that the mask could have been bought, sold, and stolen many times before landing in Fenton Lewis's hands . . .

Even now, the mask was in other hands. Lorcan masks, thought Jean-Luc, thinking of the owlish feather mask and the toothy animal mask, evidently changed hands fairly often. What an extraordinary culture they had fallen into, he marveled. Molded by harsh environment, born of the theater, these hearty survivors had developed into a society built around masks. They hid behind the masks but drew strength and purpose from them. And the masks, by changing hands, bestowed instant recognition upon the wearer and allowed him to try out as many different occupations as he chose. Imagine the freedom—every day one could present a new face to the world.

"Seductive" was the word for such a society. An ambitious person could go far, providing he or she could handle a sword.

"Lewis!" called Picard, remembering his purpose. "Ambassador Lewis!"

"Shut up, Picard, and quit your bellowing," came the reply. Picard looked up and saw Fenton Lewis sitting high up in a tree only a few meters from camp. "Wait there, and I'll be right down."

Deftly, Fenton Lewis shinnied down the dark pine. His clothes were smeared with the brownish moss, but he was grinning broadly.

"Good job, Picard!" he said, slapping the captain on the back. "Where I failed, you succeeded! Of course, you had that big Klingon and his handy phaser on your side."

Jean-Luc reddened with anger. "I wouldn't have used a phaser unless it was a life-threatening situation!"

"You know damn well that girl could've taken either one of us without breaking a fingernail. But you had Worf blast her."

Picard was so angry he was stammering. "You rushed into that fight without consulting us!"

Fenton Lewis cocked a sly eyebrow. "I didn't have much choice, now, did I? But I'm not mad at you, Picard, or jealous—I'm just glad you succeeded in getting her on our side. That's where I want that tigress."

Picard simmered down, realizing that Lewis was making perfect sense, even if he was being undiplomatic about what had happened. The captain had to keep telling himself that he shouldn't be ambivalent about using phaser fire. The technology remained a secret to the Lorcans, and no facet of their natural evolution had been compromised. After all, they already knew about space travel; it was simply ancient history to them. In the end, all that had happened was that the away party's autonomy had been preserved.

"So what is all this about Almighty Slayer and the Wisdom Mask?" asked Lewis. "I couldn't hear everything that was said."

Picard shrugged, unsure himself. "Apparently whoever has the Wisdom Mask rules Lorca. But the Wisdom Mask hasn't been seen in some time, and people are beginning to suspect that something has happened to the mask or to its most recent wearer, Almighty Slayer. These Lorcans are headed to a fair, where they plan to promote Piercing Blade as ruler."

"Sounds like quite a party," Lewis said with a smile. "I see you've got new masks for us."

The captain nodded, holding out the two wildly dissimilar masks, one as beautiful as the other was ugly. "You can have whichever one of these you want, but I couldn't get the Ambassador's Mask back."

"Not to worry," scoffed Fenton Lewis, taking the hairy-beast mask and studying it closely. "The Ambassador's Mask is more trouble than it's worth. It served its purpose. Now we're better off with something a little less controversial, like this." He wrinkled his nose. "Although this one smells bad."

Jean-Luc sat on the skeletal remains of an ancient fallen tree and wiped the moss off his pant leg. Trying to sound matter-of-fact, he wondered aloud, "How did you happen to come by the Ambassador's Mask?"

Lewis gritted his teeth and shook his fist. "My big mistake was in going to an auction alone and without proper clearances. I don't have any witnesses to testify in my defense, Captain, so you'll have to take what I tell you at face value. It wasn't an officially sanctioned art auction; Ferengi auctions seldom are. I knew there would be some rare articles there, but I didn't know how rare they would be."

He sat on the log beside Picard and looked earnestly at the starship captain. "One comes across a treasure like the Ambassador's Mask only once in a lifetime. It is a priceless work of art that represents a living, breathing culture which is unique in the galaxy. Do you think I would have had the courage to come here without it? I had to have it. My bid was the highest; there was no doubt that I deserved to own the mask. But there was some disagreement over the method of payment."

"What sort of disagreement?" Picard asked warily.

"Patience, Captain," Lewis cautioned. "You have to hear this whole story if you are to judge my actions.

Remember, I have no witnesses; no one from the Federation was present."

"Are you in the habit of attending illegal art auctions?" asked Picard.

The ambassador smiled. "I often find myself in unusual places at opportune times," he admitted. "I knew the Service was planning a diplomatic initiative toward Lorca, so I responded. I didn't plan to hide the mask away in a closet or add it to my private collection. I wanted to use it for its intended purpose."

"But you bought it before clearing it with the Diplomatic Service," Picard concluded, "and they wouldn't foot the bill?"

Lewis shrugged. "They wanted to, but you know the bureaucracy. They didn't move fast enough for the Ferengi auctioneers. I was in danger of losing the mask and my deposit as well, so I sold interests in the mask to two Ferengi traders. After we left the auction, they tried to kill me and steal the mask."

The long-haired civilian stood and stared into the hushed Lorcan woods. "I killed them in self-defense."

"And took the mask," snapped Picard, bolting to his feet, "which wasn't really yours!"

"Please, Captain," the ambassador said softly. "I know my career is almost over. The whole sordid mess will come to light if we ever resolve our differences with the Ferengi. In the meantime, you are the only one who knows the entire story—knows that I tried to do the right thing and was caught up in my desire for the mask." He snorted. "How ironic! I destroyed my career to acquire a Lorcan mask, then lost it the day after I came to Lorca."

"Under the circumstances," grumbled Picard, "I almost feel like calling the mission off."

"But you can't," the ambassador pointed out, "because the future of the Lorcan people may be at stake and you've been sucked into the politics of this crazy planet just as I have. I don't mind, because I meant to end my career here. I never intended to return to Starfleet but planned to make myself indispensable here on Lorca. Now the double irony is that I may have company in my exile."

Picard shook his head, unable to think of a word to say. Their lives were in danger, the *Enterprise* was in limbo, and the mission had nearly been compromised —all because of one man's fascination with a work of art. What about the mission? The Ambassador's Mask was gone, but they had met and won over at least one member of the nobility. They had guides and Lorcan masks and were headed toward a gathering where the question of leadership would be decided. To turn back now would render meaningless all the hardships they had endured to get this far.

Jean-Luc felt instinctively that Lorca was worth every effort needed to protect it. These people were of Earth stock. To desert them now was to deny them a heritage they themselves acknowledged with their talk of "coming from the sky." Without disrupting their natural evolution, the Federation could give them a safety net in case the planet became too volatile to support life. If the Ferengi were making frequent visits to the planet, the Lorcans were already in real danger of being subjugated economically.

"Lewis," said the captain finally, after mulling over his responsibilities, "I am not a tribunal. I have no interest in determining whether or not you're guilty of murder. We've been sent here to establish diplomatic relations with the Lorcans, and you *will* help me fulfill that mission. If you don't, I'll have you returned in irons to the nearest starbase."

"A threat, Captain?" replied Fenton Lewis, arching an eyebrow. "I thought that was beneath you. Of course I'll fulfill my mission. I didn't come here under false pretenses. Until the day I'm relieved of duty, I'm still an ambassador from the Federation."

"See that you don't forget it," Picard ordered. "Put your mask on, and let's return to camp."

"Wait," said Lewis. "I haven't made up my mind yet. You said I could have my choice." He pointed to the feathered mask. "What flavor is that?"

Jean-Luc hefted the wooden mask adorned with lavender, brown, and white feathers. Despite its size, the mask was surprisingly light. "It's called a Messenger's Mask," he said, handing the creation to Lewis. "It's really not much different from the Trainer's Mask, except for the decorations."

Lewis nodded, running his fingers over the lavender plumes that curved out from the temples of the mask to form small horns. "The Lorcan who wore this is now wearing *my* mask, so I guess that's a fair trade." He pulled the mask on, and his height and long hair combined with the striking visage to make him look strangely godlike. Picard was reminded of Ra, the Egyptian half-man, half-bird sun deity.

"I'm ready to show my face again," declared the ambassador.

"Just a second," Picard insisted, as he untwisted the straps of the Trainer's Mask and slowly pulled it on. Whether it was the fur and teeth or the general uncleanliness of its former owner, Jean-Luc didn't know, but the mask did possess a distinct musky scent. Otherwise, the well-worn mask molded smoothly to the structure of his face and was ten times more comfortable than the awkward Halloween mask. For one thing, the snarling snout afforded him unrestricted mouth movement, and he could be sure his voice would be plainly heard.

Fenton Lewis chuckled. "You have one thing in your favor, Picard. Nobody will challenge you to a duel for that mask, because nobody would want it!"

Will Riker was growing increasingly impatient. They had wasted most of the morning being fitted for their new Apprentice's Masks, and now Day Timer wanted to spend all afternoon teaching his new charges how to make masks for the fair. Will had acquiesced at first, because he still hoped that Geordi would locate the captain with the ship's sensors, or the captain would find a way to contact the *Enterprise*. Riker feared charging off in the wrong direction and making his task even harder. But, dammit, this wasn't an arts-and-crafts class at summer camp!

He activated his communicator. "No word, Geordi?" he asked for the fourth time that day.

"No word, Commander," came the response. "Are you ready to beam up?"

"Not a chance," Riker replied. "We're staying here until we find the captain."

"We'll keep all frequencies open," Geordi assured him. "By the way, the sensors indicate an increase in volcanic activity around the equator."

"Great," muttered Riker. "Keep me informed. Out." He stuck the communicator in his inside pocket and zipped it shut. The sun was going down behind the trees, and Riker slapped his hands together to keep them warm. Damn, he had never seen a place where the days were so short. Of course, being in the middle of a towering forest didn't help.

Will heard the voices of the other away-team members behind him, and he adjusted his mask before turning around. Oddly, after only a half-day, he was getting used to the mask. It kept his face warm, if nothing else. With all of the *Enterprise* crew wearing the same mask, it was beginning to seem like part of the uniform, and Riker was comfortable with uniforms. He might have enjoyed this strange sojourn on Lorca if he had been sure of the safety of the captain's away team.

He saw Data sitting at Day Timer's knee, soaking up instructions on how to find the right kind of wood for carving a mask. Dr. Pulaski sat nearby, listening to the old peddler and watching Reba, the werjun, hanging upside down from a tree branch, sucking on a fish head. Whiff and Greenblatt flanked the small gathering, guarding the road from both directions. No one had appeared on the rutted thoroughfare all day, only adding to the party's feeling of isolation.

"Are you well known as a maskmaker?" Data asked the Lorcan, as Riker approached.

"Oh, no," scoffed the peddler. "I always say my masks are made by so-and-so, the great maskmaker from such-and-such. I make very basic masks and sell them at fair prices. No one complains."

"Those two masks in your wagon certainly aren't basic," Kate Pulaski observed.

"I didn't make those," said Day Timer, with obvious respect in his voice. "The one of clay and silk is my Proprietor's Mask, which I shall wear at the fair, surrounded by my dutiful apprentices. The jeweled mask is a family mask of nobility. It is called the Forest Mask."

"Can you wear that mask?" asked Data.

The peddler reached under his sunflower mask to scratch his chin. "Perhaps I could, if I had twice as many apprentices and a dozen ponies."

Data sat forward intently. "Do you mean somebody would challenge you if you wore it?"

"Absolutely." The Lorcan nodded. "I should have to keep my sword sharpened all the time." He added hopefully, "Unless all of you would be so kind as to defend me."

That request seemed to Riker to mark a fitting time to end the fun. "I'm sorry, Day Timer," he said, "but we can't stay here any longer. Unless you agree to take us to a village or someplace where we can seek news of our comrades, we shall have to leave you."

The Lorcan leapt agitatedly to his feet. "No! You can't go. You owe me for the masks. And you can't just roam around—a party of apprentices. Whoever you meet will claim you for his vassals." Reba began to chatter in agreement with her master.

"We'll take our chances," answered Riker, gesturing to Data and Pulaski to get to their feet.

"All right," sighed Day Timer. "If I take you to a village, even though it's out of our way, will you agree to come with me to the fair?"

"This fair is very important to you, is it not?" asked Data.

The yellow disk nodded. "Yes, very important."

"As long as we keep moving," said Riker, "and find people to talk to about our friends, we'll stay with you."

"Then let's go!" exclaimed Day Timer, waving his arms. "Time waits for no man, as we say."

Returning to the Lorcans' camp with Ambassador Lewis, Captain Picard was startled anew by the diversity of masks on display. So much else was going on in the camp—the catching of fish, the pitching of what resembled a miniature circus tent, the tethering and feeding of ponies—that Jean-Luc was annoyed at his fascination with the masks. But he found that he couldn't take his eyes off them.

The mixture of Halloween masks with Lorcan masks had given the gathering a Mardi Gras atmosphere. Medicine Maker, in his artistically wrought twining-serpents mask, was tethering the ponies with Cold Angel, who proudly wore the pig-in-a-top-hat mask.

Then there were the two truly spectacular masks, the Thunder Mask and the Ambassador's Mask, worn by Piercing Blade and Spider Wing, who were doing the bulk of the fishing with crude hand-drawn lines. Even an uninformed eye such as Picard's could tell that the two objects d'art had been wrought by the same skilled craftsperson, Fazool. From the burnished metal to the bold sapphire streaks to the jutting chins, both masks bespoke the majesty of their owners and the artistry of their maker. Had either of these masks been seen in a gallery, thought Picard, only the maker would have been honored. Here the genius of the artist was complemented by the bearing of the wearer, who strove to embody the spirit of the mask.

Again, Picard felt the seductiveness of this civilization, which was simple on the surface but sophisticated underneath. Who was the woman in the Page's Mask, for example? She had spoken only once but very forcefully. Was she really a warrior-in-training or was someone else hiding behind that mask? Was Picard the captain of the U.S.S. *Enterprise* or was he a Lorcan trainer? Where he came from, didn't people make masks of their own faces?

Now Jean-Luc had a new face. He couldn't see it, but he could see other people's reactions to it. Nobody looked at his snarling animal face for very long. Of course, even as Captain Picard, no one had stared at him for long. What was remarkable was the ease with which they all accepted him, and he them. Didn't they realize he would never have chosen this coarse wooden mask for himself? The mask had, in an odd way, chosen him.

"Captain," said Worf, approaching him. The well-built Klingon looked even more formidable in his full-face armor. He pointed to the man in the pig mask. "Cold Angel, I think his name is, said that they passed a village yesterday. If we ride all night, he says we can get back there by daylight."

"That's right, Captain!" echoed Cold Angel, strolling over from the makeshift pony corral. He fondled the pig's top hat. "This mask is very lovely but not strong enough for battle. I will ask the maskmaker in that village to fortify it with wood or metal."

"If there's a village," said Fenton Lewis, "I'd like to go, too. We'll ask about Almighty Slayer and the Wisdom Mask."

"There aren't enough ponies for all of us to go," Worf added.

"Don't worry, Captain," Cold Angel exclaimed, putting an arm around Worf's shoulders, "this lad will be okay with me." He pointed to Lewis and his feather mask. "I don't trust that one."

Picard wouldn't be swayed. "We should all go."

Cold Angel lowered his voice and pointed toward Piercing Blade. "The problem is, I don't think our lady will agree to that. She's determined to get to Cottage Meadow in eight days. But she won't mind if we catch up with you."

"I'd better talk to her," Picard concluded.

"We've already done that, sir," Worf interrupted. "She's given permission for Cold Angel and I to go, but no more. That will leave you only four ponies among the eight of you. We will return as quickly as possible with news."

With a nod, Picard relented. "Be careful, Worf. And get back to us sometime tomorrow."

"Just stay on the road," Cold Angel advised Picard. "Don't wander off."

Klingon and Lorcan rushed back to the corral, where Medicine Maker held two saddled ponies with very light packs. The ponies had eaten a meal of mixed natural grains and had rested most of the afternoon, so they looked fresh and eager. Worf and Cold Angel mounted and rode off at a trot that was none too stately, since their feet were nearly scraping the ground.

"I guess I'm odd man out," grumbled Fenton Lewis.

"We're all just feeling our way," Picard assured him. "Stay observant. I need to talk with Counselor Troi."

Picard strode purposefully toward the tent, glad to get away from Fenton Lewis. He didn't blame Cold Angel for being distrustful of the dashing explorer, who seemed more desperado than diplomat.

83

The two female pages were buttressing the tent stakes with logs. At first, Jean-Luc wasn't sure which of the two women in the oval bronze masks was Counselor Troi. Even their clothing was similar—dark functional trousers, boots, and drab parkas. None of the pages wore chain mail or breastplates, as did the higher-class Lorcans. Picard didn't regard this as any great disadvantage, since the armor looked more decorative than functional. But he did recognize that the two women had very quickly formed an efficient team for pounding tent stakes.

The tent hung from a gaily striped center pole in strips of red, blue, and yellow oilskin. Picard touched the material and was reminded of eelskin. Like eelskin, this waterproof fabric had been stitched together from various sized patches, then oiled and treated. He ran his hand over the sturdy twine of the guy ropes and was reminded of the catgut strings of an antique violin he had once seen. Perhaps this substance was made of fish or fish by-products. He was mulling this over when one of the female pages approached.

"Captain?" queried a familiar lilting voice.

"Yes, Counselor." Self-consciously, he rubbed the snout of his animal mask. "I seem to have gotten the booby prize of masks."

"It is striking, Captain," the Betazoid remarked. "Also a little frightening."

"Lewis says I won't have to worry about anybody challenging me to another duel."

"How is the ambassador taking his demotion?" the counselor responded.

Picard shook his head to show his discouragement. He glanced around the tent to make sure no Lorcans were in earshot. "We have to watch the ambassador carefully," he said. "He has things to hide, and I'm not exactly sure why he came here."

"He is very secretive," Deanna agreed. "I haven't

been able to read him at all, except to see that he rarely lets his guard down."

The captain switched to a less troubling topic. "Worf has gone with one of the Lorcans to a nearby village. They will try to catch up with us by tomorrow night."

"I hope Worf learns something," Deanna replied.

The captain touched her elbow. "How are *you* holding up?"

She shrugged. "Well, I think. Shining Dagger—that's the Lorcan woman in the Page's Mask—has been helpful and considerate. She is not a young woman, and I sense that she was once a member of the nobility. But she is very pleased to be in Piercing Blade's company. She and the entire group are very loyal to their leader."

"Yes, they are." Picard nodded thoughtfully. "Counselor, do you think we're safe in joining them, even temporarily?"

Deanna hesitated. "They live in a volatile environment, and they are prone to violence. We may never be safe in their presence."

"But would we be safer without them?" Picard wondered. "By ourselves, we might run into other Lorcans who are more dangerous. Do you think there is safety in numbers?"

"Our safety depends upon Piercing Blade," concluded Deanna Troi, "and your relationship with her. I firmly believe that. The others won't disobey her and will treat us well as long as she does."

"Very well," said Picard through his grotesque Trainer's Mask, "then I had better attend to public relations. Try to gather as much information as you can."

"I will, Captain," Deanna said, then added sympathetically, "And if it's any consolation, I believe meeting Piercing Blade was fortunate."

"As do I," Jean-Luc agreed. "I'll try to talk to her."

The captain nodded to Troi and gave her a smile she didn't see.

Piercing Blade had removed her breastplate and chain mail but she still wore the commanding Thunder Mask. Even stripped of her armor and dressed in a plain brown woven garment, she was an imposing woman. Picard saw the muscles in her forearms ripple as she hauled in the fishing line from the hidden hole. It was an extraordinarily long line with several crude hooks. Incredibly, each hook held a squirming fish of the ugliest, spiniest, and palest variety Picard had ever seen.

Spider Wing, still wearing the awesome Ambassador's Mask, deftly grabbed each fish by the gills—the only safe place to grab it—and tore it from its hook. Despite the brutal treatment, the fish continued to flop on the ground, clutching to life. Picard marveled at the number and variety of fish strewn on the red clay. For a fishing expedition that hadn't been in progress more than two hours, this was an incredible catch. Lorca might not be an agreeable place to live, thought Jean-Luc, but there was no doubt of its ability to support life.

He almost felt Piercing Blade and Spider Wing were being greedy. "How many fish do you intend to catch?" he asked.

"Enough to feed us for a few days," Piercing Blade replied. "We will eat some tonight and smoke the rest for our journey." She turned to Spider Wing. "That is enough. Start gathering wood for the fire."

"Yes, my lady." Spider Wing tore the last fish from the line, tossed it into the squirming pile, and strode off.

"What do you use for bait?" asked Picard.

The warrior swung her jagged star mask toward him. Even though the mask couldn't change expression, her pause expressed her puzzlement. "Dirt. The smaller underfish eat the worms and decay from the dirt, and the larger underfish eat the same thing, plus the smaller fish."

She picked up a hook where the bait was still intact, and Jean-Luc saw a ball of clay impaled upon a hook with a couple of frozen worms clinging to it.

"How is it your people can be so ignorant?" she asked.

"We come from a long distance away," he replied. "Our world is much different from yours."

"But you do wear masks," she remarked with a tone that gave the visitors credit for displaying some culture. "Your masks are not fit for battle, but they have a certain allure. We've never seen anything like them."

"We do not wear masks all the time," Jean-Luc admitted, "only on special occasions."

"Such as . . .?"

The captain shrugged. "For certain holidays, festivals, and parties."

She sounded shocked. "And the rest of the time you expose your naked faces?"

"Yes," said Picard. "We think nothing of it."

Piercing Blade shook the marvelous mask in wonder. "And men and women see each other's faces?"

"All the time. We appreciate the beauty and expressiveness of people's faces."

"So do we," Piercing Blade answered softly, "but we see only the faces of our most intimate companions."

Picard knew he was on dangerous ground, but curiosity about this fascinating woman forced him to plunge ahead. "Have the others in your band ever seen your face?"

She stiffened and her voice was as cold as the metal in her sword. "You are lucky you're a stranger," she seethed. "If you were a Lorcan, your effrontery would be punishable by death!"

"I'm sorry," Picard said quickly. "I meant no

disrespect. I didn't understand what you meant when you said 'intimate.'"

He thought he heard her laugh behind the impenetrable mask. "Picard," she cooed, dropping her forbidding tone, "there is much I could teach you."

She brushed past him, and the momentary nearness of her stately body made Picard catch his breath. When he turned around, she was striding purposefully away from him, toward the tent.

"Night comes," she announced, turning to face the camp and pointing skyward to where the treetops were just beginning to disappear into the red mist. "Pages, gather and fillet the fish. Everyone else, gather and strip wood for the fire."

She stopped and turned back to Picard. "Are these orders acceptable to you?"

"Certainly," the captain replied. Then he picked up a dead limb at least a meter long. Remembering the trials of the night before, he wanted to see how they managed to get a fire going on Lorca.

But none of the Lorcans moved. Instead, they lowered their masks and waited for their noble leader to speak.

Piercing Blade held out her arms and spoke as if making a familiar benediction. "Great Dragon, sleep in peace tonight and allow us to sleep in the glow of your breath. Give us the stars to guide our dreams and the morning flame to follow our path."

After the benediction, they built a huge fire inside a living tree and hung the blind fish, mercifully filleted from their unsightly carcasses, on the branches to cook. The lower fillets cooked quickly and were eaten as soon as they were retrieved, while those on the higher branches were left to smoke all night. The aroma filled the camp and more than made up for the tedious job of stripping of moss from the firewood.

As soon as the meal was over, Piercing Blade retired to her tent. Medicine Maker and Spider Wing bedded down just inside the tent door, leaving their two pages to stand guard in shifts. The captain suggested to Deanna Troi that she sleep inside the tent, but she preferred to sleep outside, by the fire. The crackling flames and natural warmth appealed to something primal inside the Betazoid's soul.

The muscles in Deanna's shoulders, arms, and legs ached from the strenuous activities of the day, and she had a hard time getting comfortable on the thick bed of evergreen needles. Everyday life on Lorca made the Starfleet fitness regimen look like a stroll on the holodeck. At least cold wasn't a problem, Deanna mused; if she covered herself with enough moss, she could probably sleep right *inside* the fire. It was not the lack of creature comforts that was keeping her awake.

Nothing was keeping Captain Picard and Ambassador Lewis awake, she noticed. They were snoring peacefully on the other side of the flames. Deanna saw their masks lying on the ground beside them, and she wondered if the Lorcans slept with their masks on. With no light in the tent, masks probably weren't necessary. The male and female Lorcan pages kept to themselves, obviously nervous about sleeping at all with so many strangers in camp. But it wasn't their subdued conversation that was keeping her awake.

What deprived her of the sleep she so desperately needed was a disturbing impression. Someone among the quiet sleeping figures was planning a deception. She couldn't tell who it was or what it was, but the feeling was unmistakable.

Despite her apprehension, the Betazoid finally gave in to sleep, knowing she could do nothing to prevent a mind from scheming. The situation would become clear soon enough.

It did, sooner than she thought it would. Deanna bolted awake, confused and groggy, a short time later.

She rolled out of her makeshift bed and crouched beneath the overhanging boughs of the tree. She counted the bodies around the fire. One of the Lorcan pages was sleeping with his mask on, and Captain Picard was curled in a fetal position, dozing peacefully. But where was Fenton Lewis?

Instinctively, she knew he was gone.

Chapter Six

DEANNA TROI gently shook Captain Picard awake, keeping her voice low so as not to attract the attention of the Lorcan pages, one of whom was on guard by the tent.

"Captain," she whispered, "please wake up."

He responded to her urging by rolling off his pallet and blinking at her. "What is it?"

"Fenton Lewis is gone."

"Lewis?" he asked, still groggy. He glanced at the spot where the ambassador had bedded down beside him. Now there was nothing but an indentation in the brown needles. Most tellingly, the feathered Messenger's Mask was gone. "Are you sure he's not somewhere nearby?" Picard asked.

The Betazoid shook her head with certainty. "He's gone. I don't sense his presence anywhere in camp."

The captain grabbed his mask and moved out from beneath the tree. Away from the snapping fire, his breath came in vaporous bursts, and he shivered with the chill of the gloomy night. No stars shone above the gigantic trees, thanks to the clouds that blanketed the planet, but the mist itself seemed to sparkle with a faint luminescence. Surely Fenton Lewis wouldn't be foolish enough to have dashed off into the unknown darkness of Lorca by himself. To what purpose would he have done so? Had he been so humiliated by Piercing Blade that he couldn't face another day in her band? Could some harm have befallen him?

Deanna touched his shoulder, and he turned to see her impassive Page's Mask. "The guard approaches," she whispered.

Jean-Luc barely had time to pull his snarling Trainer's Mask over his face before the male Lorcan page emerged from the darkness into the faint circle of light surrounding the tree. "Is everything all right, Sir Trainer?" he asked.

"Quite all right." Picard nodded. "Please return to your post."

The page started off, and Picard called softly after him, "Wait. Have you seen our companion, the messenger?"

The bronze oval swung back and forth. "No, not since our lady retired." He glanced suspiciously over Picard's shoulder. "Is he not with you?"

"Not at the moment," the captain answered. Thinking quickly, he added, "Perhaps he's gone to deliver a message for me. I asked him to get an early start."

The page shrugged and motioned to the black woods. "I hope he keeps to the road. In the dark, it's easy to fall into a bog."

"He knows he will have to be careful," Deanna remarked soothingly. "Thank you."

The page nodded and disappeared into the darkness surrounding Piercing Blade's tent.

Jean-Luc turned to Deanna, lowering his voice but failing to hide his anger. "What's the matter with that fool? Where could he have gone?"

"Lewis is a strange man," Deanna admitted. "A headstrong man. I sensed he was disturbed about something."

"He had reason to be," Picard answered, refusing to elaborate. Instead, the captain paced for several moments, trying to recollect everything he knew about Ambassador Fenton Lewis. "Deanna," he said finally, "do you think Lewis is capable of deserting us in an attempt to stay on the planet by himself?"

She shrugged. "Why not? What have we to offer him now that we're out of contact with the ship? And he doesn't have much faith in Piercing Blade's ability to further his aims."

"What are his aims?" he asked, afraid he already knew the answer.

Deanna shook her head, puzzled. "At one time, I would have said his aims were the aims of the Federation. But here"—she gestured toward the vast primeval forest all around them—"so much is possible. If he found the Wisdom Mask, he could be king."

Jean-Luc nodded, suddenly reminded of a Rudyard Kipling story he had read in a twentieth-century literature course. It told of another "civilized" man who journeyed to a primitive land in the hope of being a king. He achieved his goal, Jean-Luc recalled, but was separated from his head.

Deanna took her captain's silence for a request for suggestions. "We could go after him," she said, without much conviction.

"No," the captain replied. "He's an experienced woodsman, and we're hardly that. Besides, we must continue on the road with Piercing Blade if Worf is to rejoin us tomorrow. We have no choice but to leave Ambassador Lewis to his own devices."

After the third branch whipped across his face, Worf was thankful for the Page's Mask he wore. Of course, not many Lorcans would be riding at break-neck speed on a murky dirt road in the dead of night. Or would they? He was following Cold Angel, whose pony kept kicking clay clods back at him. Occasionally one would strike his face, and he had yet another demonstration of a mask's usefulness.

Despite the Klingon's weight, Worf's pony remained strong and surefooted under him. Cold Angel had a system for conserving the animals' strength while making good speed: first, twenty minutes at a full gallop, then twenty minutes of walking to cool the equines, then a drink of water and a five-minute rest before going back to a gallop. Worf had no idea how far they'd come, but Cold Angel was evidently pleased with their progress. Several times he had said they would eat a sunrise breakfast of fish stew and moss muffins.

Ahead of him, Cold Angel slowed to a trot, and Worf assumed they would dismount and walk for a spell. He pulled on the reins of his pony, but the beast didn't want to stop; it nearly collided with Cold Angel's mount.

"Hold up!" ordered the Lorcan.

The Klingon grabbed a single rein and tugged the pony's head around. When the pony stopped its struggling and pawed the ground anxiously, Worf reached down to stroke the animal's stiff mane and matted coat. "Slow down," he cooed soothingly. "Time for a rest."

"He's in a rush," explained Cold Angel, "because he smells the hay and the well water. The village is just ahead."

"Where?" asked Worf doubtfully, peering into the gloom. Endless trees masked any hint of civilization.

"You'll see it at first light," answered the man in the plastic pig mask, dismounting from his pony. "I don't want to enter the village in darkness. The people might mistake us for a raiding party."

Worf cocked his Page's Mask. "Are raiders and thieves a problem?"

"Not to me, no." The brawny animal trainer shrugged. "That rabble usually haven't got the stomach for a fight." He fingered his flimsy Halloween mask. "But sometimes I have to do combat. That's why I've got to get this mask fortified."

"Do thieves wear a certain type of mask?" Worf asked sarcastically.

"Of course," said Cold Angel. "They wear the Raider's Mask, which is painted red and is often armored and sturdy." He fingered the little green top hat of his pig mask. "This represents an animal, doesn't it?"

The Klingon nodded. "I believe it does, but I am no expert on human masks or human livestock."

"You're not a human, then?" asked the Lorcan matter-of-factly, loosening his saddle cinch.

Worf wanted to avoid conflict with his guide, so he chose his words carefully. "I am *humanoid,* which is very close. But there are differences."

Cold Angel slid the saddle—little more than a wooden sawhorse with oilskin stretched over it—off his pony, which was protected by coarse blankets. "Worf," he observed, "I can tell you don't understand our masks. You probably see them as a form of vanity."

"At first I did," admitted the lieutenant, removing his own pony's saddle and blanket. "In other human cultures, masks *are* a form of vanity. But here on Lorca, the masks have practical applications. The mask indicates a person's profession and social status."

Cold Angel again fingered his pig's mask. "Because it bears the likeness of an animal, this *is* a Trainer's Mask, isn't it."

"Of course." Worf nodded.

He could almost imagine the Lorcan smiling behind

his ridiculous mask as he spread his blankets on the ground and lay on them. "Get some sleep now, humanoid. We have about an hour before daybreak."

Night was but a rumor aboard the *Enterprise.* Not a single light was dimmed during the yellow alert called by Acting Captain Geordi La Forge. Geordi had called the alert mainly to keep the transporter rooms at full readiness, but he hoped the extra activity would keep the ship's population too busy to worry about the captain. By now even the children had heard that the captain and his party had lost contact with the ship. The adults went about their increased duties stoically, forming bulkhead safety crews, helping out in sickbay and engineering, and suspending normal scientific pursuits to study the mysterious red planet.

As intensely as they studied Lorca during fifteen orbits, its swirling magnetic clouds did not divulge any secrets. The whereabouts of Captain Picard, Counselor Troi, and Lieutenant Worf remained unknown. Geordi's frequent contact with Commander Riker offered some comfort, but their mutual efforts on two separate fronts had turned up nothing. Lorca remained an enigma, and the first away team remained lost. Geordi could sit in the captain's chair and stare at viewscreens and readouts, but nothing was going to make him relax until he heard the captain's voice.

Wesley Crusher had the conn for two straight shifts without a break. *At least* two straight shifts, thought Geordi, remembering that he had been on duty longer than that and hadn't seen anyone else at the console. The young man had the stamina of, well, a sixteen-year-old, but that didn't mean he should be worked to exhaustion.

Had the yellow alert gone on too long? the engineer wondered. The crew had passed the point of readiness and reached the state of edginess. Unfortunately, the quick return of either away team did not seem likely. They could orbit this planet for weeks before finding the captain. Perhaps the captain and the ambassador were engaged in sensitive negotiations and didn't want to be found or forced to return immediately. Worse possibilities entered Geordi's mind, and none of them would require the continuation of the alert.

"Lieutenant La Forge to all hands," he announced. "Yellow alert is now canceled. Transporter rooms, maintain ready status until further notice. Repeat, yellow alert is canceled."

He glanced at Wesley and saw the boy looking back at him with the trace of a smile on his lips. "It's night for the away teams," Wesley observed. "This would be a good time for you to take a break."

"What are you, ship's doctor now?" grumped Geordi, managing a weary smile himself. "We both need a break."

He peered around at a full complement of relief personnel, judging them not by the outward appearances others saw but by the electromagnetic impulses and brain activity revealed by his visor. One ageless Vulcan woman had a nervous system that was particularly composed and balanced, despite the highly charged mind that ran it. She was only an ensign, but he knew instinctively he could depend on her.

"Ensign, you have the bridge," Geordi said with a sweep of his hand from the woman to the captain's chair.

The Vulcan didn't bat an eyelash as she stepped down from her aft station into the command area.

Geordi strode to the turbolift. "If there's any communication from the planet, patch it to me immediately in the Ten-Forward lounge."

"Aye, sir."

"Ensign Crusher, I have a special request for you," he added.

Wesley looked up eagerly. "Yes, Lieutenant?"

"Accompany me to Ten-Fore. Your shift is over."

The ensign joined Geordi, and the two of them stood silently in the turbolift, letting waves of exhaustion sweep over them. Both of them would gladly have served two more shifts in a row if it would have helped to bring their missing comrades back. But they both knew that staying on the bridge was akin to watching a pot boil. It simply wasn't going to help.

"Where are they?" muttered Wesley in exasperation.

"On that planet somewhere." Geordi shrugged. "We lost contact with them so quickly that I have to assume they had equipment failure."

"Or else the volcanic eruption . . ." The young ensign didn't finish the thought.

The turbolift doors opened, and they found themselves staring into the deserted Ten-Fore lounge. The furnishings and lighting were tasteful and subdued, but an angry red planet was visible beyond the window ports, demanding their attention. Even here, thought Geordi, there was no escape from anxiety.

At first he was confused by the deserted recreation center. Then he remembered that the yellow alert had been rescinded only a few moments earlier. The place would begin filling up in no time. He and Wesley collapsed into the first chairs they came to, their backs to the planet they had been staring at for days.

"My first customers," said Guinan, emerging from behind the bar. She was draping dark gray fabric around her head in the shape of an outlandish hat.

"Hi, Guinan," said Wesley, managing a weary wave.

"Hi, Wesley."

Geordi sighed. "I'm afraid you have me to thank for the drop in business."

"I know." Guinan leaned over them with a warm smile.

"You can get the captain back," muttered Geordi. "And Worf and Counselor Troi."

She clucked her tongue. "I thought that ambassador was supposed to know his way around down there."

"It's not his fault the sensors won't give accurate readings," Wesley said. "We know there are life-forms down there, but they're so scattered that we can't get a fix on them."

Geordi quickly added, "There's no reason to believe the away team is in any trouble. Equipment failure would account for all of this."

"I still wish we would hear from them," Wesley said with a sigh.

Guinan wiped some dust off their table. "Don't they have an expression on Earth—'No news is good news'?"

"That's right." Geordi nodded decisively. "They're probably having the time of their lives."

Worf was in a netherworld between sleep and wakefulness when he felt wetness all around him, accompanied by an unpleasant tickle. He had lain on dry ground, but he was now slipping head first into a pool of slime. He instinctively touched the ground, but it oozed through his fingers.

Icy water lapped about him as he slipped forward into the morass. He was about to shout for help when a wave of muddy water and worms swirled under his mask and around his mouth, choking him. He sputtered and coughed as he clawed at the slippery clay.

"Stop kicking!" ordered a forceful voice from behind him, and he felt powerful hands gripping his thigh.

Worf stopped his futile efforts and concentrated on gripping first a clump of grass, then a vine, and finally a root. The hands now seized him around the waist, and he knew he was no longer sinking, but he still couldn't breathe. He dug his long fingernails into the roots and clumps of grass and slowly pushed himself out of the sucking quagmire. The muck clung to his shoulders, but the brackish water began to drain from his mask, allowing him to gasp for air.

A tense moment later, the Klingon rolled up onto wet but solid ground, and Cold Angel dragged him farther from the treacherous spring. Worf struggled to his knees and wheezed for breath.

"That bog almost got you," the Lorcan remarked. "It may get bigger. Let's grab the ponies and get out of here."

Watching their footing in the faint dawn light, the two travelers untied their ponies and led them up the road, not stopping until they were on dry clay. Worf dropped his saddle and bent over, his shoulders still heaving.

"Can I take my mask off?" he asked hoarsely.

"Go ahead," answered Cold Angel. "I'll turn away."

In reality, curiosity made the Lorcan turn only halfway around, but Worf didn't mind. He just wanted to wipe the crud and squiggly things off his face. Had it been possible, he would've shed his muddy clothes, too.

"Does that happen often?" he muttered.

"Sure," the Lorcan shrugged, stealing a look at the Klingon's massive brow and deep-set eyes. "The road gets worn thin, and the undersea swamps it."

Worf dried his face with his sleeve and pulled his mask back on. "I don't suppose I could get a bath in this village?"

"A bath?" laughed Cold Angel. "You just had one!"

They walked their ponies the rest of the way, keeping a careful eye out for new bogs. By the time dawn had advanced to a cold misty gray, they began to see smoke curling through the trees ahead of them. They heard happy voices, and the first villagers they saw were three children dressed in identical brown smocks and gaily painted wooden masks and wooden shoes. The crude squiggles on the masks suggested that children were allowed to decorate their own masks. Childhood was evidently its own rank.

They stopped their play and stared at Cold Angel in his plastic pig mask. They barely acknowledged Worf in his Page's Mask and filthy clothes.

"I knew this mask would demand attention," Cold Angel whispered proudly. "I will be the most famous animal trainer on Lorca."

But Worf's attention was riveted to the tidy rows of thatched huts that lined a widened section of the road. The cylindrical huts were red, from the clay used as binding, and ranged in diameter from a few to as many as twenty meters. All of them stood on stilts a meter off the ground. After his recent experience, Worf could well imagine why.

Every building had a chimney, and the larger ones had two, suggesting more than one room. No building was over one story high, and the village reminded Worf of a farm on Khitomer, with the huts looking like grain silos and mounds of grain. There were rows of cultivated soil between some of the huts, and the main crop seemed to be a fibrous brown pod, probably grown for fabric rather than food. In the center of the community, a half-dozen masked villagers were milling around a low roofless structure.

"That's the well," Cold Angel explained, noticing the direction of Worf's gaze. He pointed out other buildings, each of which had a distinctive mask painted on its crude wooden door. "There's a smithy. That one's a woodcarver. There's a tanner, and this one's a tailor who can make you new clothes, if you wish. At the far end of the street is a baker and, of course, the maskmaker. This town isn't big enough to have an inn, but the maskmaker is a friend of mine. He'll feed us."

"Then why do we wait?" asked the Klingon.

They continued through the center of the village.

The colorfully masked inhabitants were too busy drawing water or fish from the well to pay them much attention. When they did glance up from their work, they stared at Cold Angel, who obviously relished the attention. The three children they had met outside the village now followed them in, and they had picked up a full entourage of gawking children by the time they reached their destination.

The maskmaker's shop was one of the largest in the village and three masks were painted on the door. "Why three?" asked Worf.

"The one at the top is the Maskmaker's Mask," explained Cold Angel, pointing to a stylized representation of a human face. How ironic, thought Worf, that the maskmaker's own symbol would be the face he took such pains to hide.

"The others are family masks," continued Cold Angel. "They show the maskmaker's lineage." He rapped on the door. "I hope it's not too early. Trim Hands is not a young man."

An older woman answered the door. She was wearing a white mask with so many delicate inscriptions painted across it that she looked like a living parchment.

Cold Angel bowed respectfully. "Please tell the master that his humble servant Cold Angel is here."

"I don't recognize your mask," she said.

"Nor should you," replied the jovial pig, bowing lower. "It's a Trainer's Mask from another land, far away. The master will recognize it."

The woman disappeared behind a shimmering curtain without inviting the visitors inside. Cold Angel turned to Worf and shrugged.

Seconds later a small man in a human mask appeared from behind the curtain. His mask was of a young man with a close-trimmed beard, but his gnarled hands and stooped gait belied the youthful disguise. He reached immediately for Cold Angel's Halloween mask and stroked its flimsy pink surface.

"What material is this?" he asked haltingly.

"I don't know." Cold Angel shrugged. "Ask my friend."

"It's a synthetic substance," Worf answered.

"Do you have more?" asked the maskmaker.

Worf knew the transporter could make kilos of it, if necessary. Trade wasn't his primary mission, but it could be a means to an end. "Perhaps," he said. "We must make arrangements with your leader. Do you know where to find Almighty Slayer?"

"Slayer?" scoffed Trim Hands, shaking his head. "He must be nearly as old as I am." He turned irritatedly to Cold Angel. "Is this why you awoke me?"

"No," the Lorcan said quickly. "My new mask is lovely to behold but not fit for battle. I would ask you, with your great skill and wisdom, to fortify it."

The maskmaker nodded. "I could make a cast of it, but you will have to leave the mask for a fortnight. Come inside."

They were ushered into a spacious room that was part living quarters and part studio. From the thatched ceiling hung masks in various stages of completion, as well as bolts of fabric, strips of leather, chunks of wood, sets of feathers, strands of jewels, and other shiny odds and ends. A fireplace pumped sooty heat into the room, and Worf noticed a bellows, clamps, hammers, and other smithy tools. Trim Hands was obviously prepared to fashion masks that were functional as well as beautiful.

"Do you wish some food?" asked the maskmaker.

"Yes, please," answered Cold Angel. He turned to Worf, and the Klingon could almost see him winking.

The maskmaker went into an adjoining room, and the visitors heard muffled but spirited voices. When

Trim Hands returned, he was carrying a light green mask with exaggerated puffed cheeks, heavy-lidded eye sockets, and gossamer fringe.

He showed the mask to Cold Angel. "What do you think of this Fisherman's Mask?" he asked proudly.

Cold Angel nodded noncommittally. "Good workmanship."

"The finest!" snapped the maskmaker. "I will trade you this brand new Fisherman's Mask for that grotesque thing *you* are wearing."

The pig mask shook forcefully. "No. I don't seek a new mask. I seek repairs."

"Very well," muttered the maskmaker, handing Cold Angel the Fisherman's Mask. "Wear this until you return for your mask. I can't quote you a price now."

"I understand," said Cold Angel. He turned away from them and deftly replaced the pig mask with the Fisherman's Mask, moving so quickly that Worf couldn't even catch a glimpse of his companion's face.

"Remember, I'll need a fortnight."

"You'll have longer than that," said Cold Angel, looking and sounding strange in the pale fish mask. "We are going to the fair at Cottage Meadow."

With his companion's business out of the way, Worf decided to press for more information. "Trim Hands," he said respectfully, "are you sure you know nothing more about Almighty Slayer?"

"I know he wears the Wisdom Mask," answered the old artisan. "And a magnificent mask it is, worthy of a king. But I haven't seen it for many, many cycles." His voice took on an angry edge. "Perhaps if we had a real king, the raiders would not be so brazen!"

"We will have a *queen* soon," promised Cold Angel. "When I return from the fair, it will be with great news!"

"Great news would be no more raiders," snarled the maskmaker.

The uneasy silence that followed was broken by the entrance of the woman in the Scholar's Mask, carrying a tray with two steaming bowls.

"Ah! Fish stew!" exclaimed Cold Angel in triumph, rubbing his dirty hands together.

Piercing Blade rose to her full impressive height, and her voice snapped like the lightning bolt on her Thunder Mask. "What do you mean, you don't know where he is!"

Captain Picard wished he could take off the snarling Trainer's Mask and appeal to her face-to-face. "I want to be honest with you, Piercing Blade. During the night the man we call Fenton Lewis, who came here as an ambassador, left the camp. We don't know where he is or where he went."

Piercing Blade swept her hand in an arc to encompass her whole troupe. "My page told me you sent the messenger away. You lied to him?"

"I did," Picard admitted. "At the time, I didn't want to arouse the entire camp. I was wrong to lie, and I admit it. I wish to enlist your help in finding Lewis."

She stepped forward, her huge chrome mask looming before his face. "I defeated him in battle, and he has the right to hate me. Do you think he has gone to aid our enemies?"

"He's a stranger here," the captain answered. "He doesn't know who your enemies are."

"Then forget him," the warrior said, dismissing the whole subject with a wave of her hand. "We must reach the meadows before the fair begins. We can't concern ourselves with renegades." She turned back to Picard, her piercing green eyes gleaming in the sockets of her mask. "But you, Picard, do you wish me ill?"

"No," answered the captain forcibly. "I respect you and wish you well."

The woman gripped his shoulders. "Then we remain comrades, Picard. I will not judge you by the actions of one of your vassals."

As exasperated as he was, Jean-Luc didn't want to endanger the genuine bond he had formed with this imposing woman. Despite the masks, the duels, and the hardships, the two of them had connected on a primal level that was real, more real than anything else on the planet. He couldn't lie to her, and he knew she couldn't lie to him. Though both of them were leaders in their own right, they seemed to need each other. He reached across her robust arms and gripped her shoulders in return.

"You can trust me," he said simply.

Will Riker sat beside Day Timer in the peddler's wagon, watching the endless parade of trees pass by. Data, Dr. Pulaski, and the security personnel, Greenblatt and Whiff, strode behind and to one side of them. Day Timer's pony kept a leisurely pace, and no one had a hard time keeping up. In fact, Will had resisted taking a seat in the wagon, but Day Timer had insisted on his company.

"These comrades for whom you are searching— they must be very important," the peddler observed.

Riker nodded his clay Apprentice's Mask, hardly noticing its weight or clammy warmth anymore. "They're more than comrades. They're my friends."

"I'm a nosy old man," said the Lorcan, "but I would guess that one of your missing friends is a woman."

The commander swiveled to look at his benchmate, but, of course, the implacable mask told him nothing. For once, Will was thankful that his own emotions were hidden behind a mask. He had been so busy worrying about the away team as a whole that he hadn't confronted his concern for Deanna Troi.

The loss of Captain Picard would be devastating, but he was mentally prepared for such an eventuality.

He had to be—it was part of his job. But never to see Deanna again? Will didn't think he was prepared for that.

"We'll find them," he said, more to himself than to anyone else.

"If they've been to the village, we'll find out about it," the peddler assured him. He pointed toward the top of the trees, where the sun was just beginning to peek through. "That's not mist; that's smoke. We should be there in a few minutes."

"How should we behave?" asked Data.

"Behave like apprentices," the peddler urged. "Don't handle anything that isn't yours, don't appear too inquisitive, and let me do the talking."

"That sounds easy enough," remarked Data.

"Still," Riker said grimly, "be ready for anything."

Chapter Seven

AS THE PEDDLER'S WAGON and the small band of apprentices neared the village, Day Timer handed the reins to Riker. "Take over for a moment," he said.

Quizzically, Riker took the reins and watched as the peddler ducked back into his wagon. The swaybacked pony paid no attention to the change in drivers and continued plodding ahead. A moment later, Day Timer emerged wearing a different mask.

This one was also made from clay but was finely crafted, with eye, nose, and mouth holes that were molded into a haughty expression. Bloodred feathers formed sweeping eyebrows, and rich blue brocade adorned the edges of the mask. The strange markings were more numerous than on the Peddler's Mask and had been skillfully applied in sparkling gold paint.

"My Proprietor's Mask," said the Lorcan proudly. "Please don't disgrace me by telling anyone that you aren't my apprentices."

"We won't," Kate Pulaski answered. "It's a beautiful mask."

"Yes, it is," Day Timer agreed. "I had to trade two

ponies to get it, and this is the first time I've worn it." He lowered his head bashfully. "Until today, only Reba has seen me in it."

Data looked around with concern. "Where is the werjun?"

"She hates villages," Day Timer explained. "Some townspeople eat werjuns."

"Will she rejoin us later?" the android asked.

"She always does," replied the new proprietor.

The road widened, and the first stilt-huts became visible. Will Riker handed the reins back to the peddler and jumped down from the wagon. He debated whether to retrieve his pistol phaser from the back of the wagon. When he saw a handful of children in brightly painted masks dashing between the huts, he decided not to carry it.

"No phasers," he whispered to his crew. Then he turned back to Day Timer. "We're putting our trust in you."

Day Timer nodded. "I came here on your behalf. I have no reason to betray you."

Day Timer stopped the wagon in front of the first large hut. The children clustered around them, and the adults put down their hoes, water pails, and fishing lines long enough to take note of the new arrivals. Others emerged from their huts, and a crowd slowly approached the garishly painted wagon. Uneasily, the apprentices backed up until they stood shoulder to shoulder against the wagon, staring at the sea of colorful masks.

"Do you have any candy?" asked one small child.

"No," said Day Timer sadly. "I'm sorry."

An adult waved at him with a crude rake. "I know that wagon! Are you Day Timer?"

"I am he," answered the peddler with a regal bow.

"I like your new mask," exclaimed a woman whose own mask was little more than a piece of burlap stretched over a wooden frame.

"I'm a proprietor now," bragged Day Timer. He pointed to the row of clay masks. "These are my apprentices."

"Where is your store?" a villager asked snidely.

"I am opening my store at the fair in Cottage Meadow."

This announcement drew an appreciative murmur, and many masks bobbed in approval. Day Timer leapt down from the wagon and pointed to the man with the rake. "Friend, if you will feed and water my pony, I will give you a new fire starter."

"Done," said the man, reaching for the pony's bridle.

Day Timer motioned to Riker. "Come with me to the maskmaker's hut. He will know if any strangers have passed through."

Riker glanced at his identically masked companions, unsure which one was Katherine Pulaski. Finally, he recognized her medical equipment belt. "Doctor, will you please come with us?"

"Certainly. What about the others?"

Day Timer made it a point to issue the order. "You others, stay with the wagon! Data, you may take orders for goods, but don't sell anything until I return."

"I will do as you have instructed," Data said dutifully.

Day Timer headed for a large hut with three masks painted on the door, as Will Riker and Kate Pulaski followed close behind. "The maskmaker is discreet and reliable," he whispered. "These other villagers would say whatever we wanted to hear, in the hope of getting some free goods from us in return for information. This is a very poor village."

They stopped at the door, and Day Timer knocked forcibly. A woman in a pale mask answered the knock.

"Proprietor"—she bowed respectfully—"please enter. The maskmaker will be glad to see you."

They were ushered into the maskmaker's studio. The maskmaker apparently sold most of his handiwork, Kate Pulaski decided, because only half-finished masks and raw materials were on display. The woman who had admitted them shuffled off through a curtain into an adjoining room, and they heard muffled voices.

"Trim Hands was once very famous," Day Timer whispered. "But now he is slow, and his work is not what it was."

Pulaski fingered a plumed visor intended to protect a warrior's forehead and cheekbones. By itself, the armored headgear would be a prized museum piece in most parts of the galaxy, and she wondered what additions the old artisan would make to turn it into a full mask. Maybe leather would complete the nose, mouth, and chin. Perhaps more feathers would be added, or some of those dazzling green gems.

She was still gazing at the treasures around the room when a stooped man in a lifelike human mask shambled through the curtain. He bowed to Day Timer, ignoring Dr. Pulaski and Commander Riker.

"Noble Proprietor," he said, "I am honored to receive you and your apprentices. Unfortunately, I have few creations at the moment to grace the shelves of your establishment."

Day Timer held up his hand. "Never mind, old friend. I am only seeking information. It is I, Day Timer."

The impassive face mask reared back. "Day Timer, it is you! I see your fortunes have improved."

The peddler nodded. "Immeasurably. I have five apprentices and am on my way to the great fair."

"Everyone is going to the fair," Trim Hands groused. "To me, it's just another opportunity for raiders and bandits."

Day Timer glanced at Riker, sensing his impatience. "Old friend, we have been looking for some comrades of ours. They are strangers to this land and may not be familiar with our customs." His voice plainly revealed his disgust. "They may not even be wearing masks. Have you seen any such travelers in the last few days?"

The maskmaker shook his head. "The only ones through here have been Piercing Blade and her group. Just this morning, two of them came back to drop off an unusual mask for repair."

"An unusual mask?" asked Commander Riker.

The two older men glared at him, and he remembered suddenly that apprentices were supposed to be seen and not heard.

"Yes," said Trim Hands, addressing himself to Day Timer. "This mask is made from a material I have never seen before."

"May I see it?" Day Timer asked.

"Why not?" The maskmaker shrugged. "They said it's a Trainer's Mask, but it's not like any I've ever seen. Maybe you can tell me more about it." The old man shambled back into the other room and returned a moment later.

In his gnarled hands he held the Halloween pig mask.

Kate Pulaski sensed that Commander Riker wanted to leap through the thatched roof, but he restrained himself admirably. He merely held out his hand. "Please, sir, may I see that?"

Day Timer nodded his consent, and Trim Hands gave the jolly pig mask to the tall apprentice. Will held it for several moments before reluctantly handing it back to the old maskmaker. "Who did you say gave that to you?"

"One of the warriors who follows Piercing Blade. Cold Angel is his name."

Riker leaned forward intently. "You're sure it wasn't a stranger?"

"Cold Angel was here only the day before, with Piercing Blade and her entire band."

Will turned to Day Timer. "Who is this Piercing Blade?"

The peddler spat his words. "She claims nobility, but she's little better than a raider. I hope your friends haven't fallen afoul of her."

Kate felt like sitting down somewhere, but there was hardly enough room in the cluttered hut to breathe. Or perhaps it was her dread and the dread she felt from Commander Riker that made breathing difficult. She knew Will had dozens of questions he wanted answered, and so did she. But she knew equally well that the two Lorcans wouldn't be able to help even if they wanted to. On a planet where survival was a day-to-day struggle, the problems of a few strangers were of minimal concern.

She looked again at the happy Halloween mask. As the full significance of its presence sank in, Dr. Pulaski began to understand the necessity of masks on Lorca. They hid the tears and anguish.

Kate's grim reverie was suddenly broken by shouts and cries from outside. The shouts turns to screams, and something crashed into the side of the hut. Riker, galvanized into action, bounded out the door. Day Timer grabbed a sword from Trim Hands's workbench and rushed after him.

The old maskmaker dropped to his knees, wailing, "Raiders! Raiders!"

By the time Kate Pulaski reached the door, the main street of the village had turned into a chaotic melee of villagers running in every direction and sword-wielding horsemen charging after them. Whiff, the giant Antarean, had single-handedly knocked one of the ponies off its feet into Trim Hands's hut and was grappling with a man in a red mask. She watched in horror as the raider slit Whiff's shoulder open with his blade. But the cut wasn't serious enough to faze the big Antarean; he gripped the man by a hank of hair and twisted his neck into an obscene angle. Red Mask slumped to the ground on top of his kicking pony.

Everywhere, similar scenes of violence assaulted her senses. One villager stood to fight, and a raider promptly skewered him with a deadly lance at full gallop, then dragged his body at least ten meters before it tore loose. Wounded villagers crawled between the stilts of their huts, and raiders chased them, cutting down the slowest ones. In the center of the melee, a clay-masked figure plunged a sword into one of the raider's legs and through the rib cage of his pony. Man and animal shuddered to the ground in a clump, and the clay-masked figure rammed his sword into the fallen rider's stomach clear up to its hilt.

Kate realized with a start that the victorious figure was Day Timer. He didn't even bother to retrieve his own sword but simply grabbed his victim's. He whirled around just in time to parry the blow of a red-masked attacker on foot. The spry peddler dropped into a crouch and, with one sweeping blow, severed the man's legs at the knees.

Pulaski watched Commander Riker duck between two huts as the raider with the lance lunged after him. The lance missed him by centimeters and stuck in the clay-encrusted thatch, giving Will the opening he needed. He grabbed the man and pulled him off his skittish pony.

They wrestled to the ground. But the agile raider broke away and rolled to his feet. He drew his sword, but Will grabbed his wrist before he had a chance to use it. Now it was a matter of brute strength, as the two big men grappled for control of the weapon. Riker used his T'ai Chi training to toss the raider over his shoulder, wresting the sword from him in the process. The raider was on his feet again in seconds and was reaching for his lance when Will plunged the sword into his armpit, through his clavicle, and out the other side of his neck. Riker stepped back, aghast at his actions, as the raider slumped against the wall.

Then a red mask blurred in front of Kate's face, and she saw a raised sword poised to strike her. Before the raider could complete his stroke, a blinding flash of light struck him and froze him in mid-swing. His frightened pony reared and dumped him head first on the ground. He lay there, unmoving.

Still gasping from her narrow escape, the doctor looked up and saw Ensign Greenblatt standing by the wagon. The security officer gave her a thumbs-up sign, then leveled her phaser at another raider. This one, though, had seen enough; he spurred his pony and galloped out of the village.

The doctor finally spied Data protecting a group of children who were huddled under a hut. One of the raiders came at the android on foot and lunged at him with his sword. Data astounded his attacker by grabbing the swordpoint with his bare hand and stopping it centimeters from his stomach. No matter how much the brigand twisted and pulled, the sword stayed motionless, as if rooted in cement.

"I will not give it back," Data said.

The man in the red mask looked around and, seeing that most of his comrades were dead or gone, let go of the sword and tried to escape. Unfortunately for him, a handful of villagers, emboldened by the apparent victory, caught him and finished him off with harvesting tools. Kate averted her eyes.

She sought Ensign Whiff to see how badly he was hurt. An instant later, she was joined by Riker, Greenblatt, and Data.

The Antarean was still conscious and was sitting up, but blood was streaming from his shoulder.

"I may be able to stop the bleeding," said the

doctor, "but we really should send him to sickbay, in case an artery's been severed."

"Anybody else injured?" asked Commander Riker.

The *Enterprise* crew members shook their heads, still too dazed to do much talking.

"Many of the villagers are injured," said Data. "At least four of them are dead."

"Dead," Riker repeated numbly, glancing back at the raider he had killed.

"I saw it all," said Kate. "You had no choice."

"That doesn't make me feel any better," Will murmured, trying to block out the sight of the crumpled body.

Though he felt only remorse, the villagers were laughing with delight as they plundered the bodies of the slain raiders. Their wounded were being attended to, and their own dead had been respectfully covered, but much fuss was made over the five dead raiders. With great ceremony, the villagers were stripping the raiders of their masks and ridiculing their faces. Some of them danced around the bloody heaps.

Riker shook off his guilt and stepped to a neighboring hut to look inside. It was empty. "Data, have you got your communicator on you?"

"Yes," replied the android.

"Take Ensign Whiff inside this hut, call Geordi, and have him beam Whiff up to sickbay."

"Yes, sir." Effortlessly, the android lifted the wounded officer and carried him inside the hut.

Wearily, the commander put his arm on Kate Pulaski's shoulder. "Come on, Doctor, let's see what we can do for the wounded. Later on, I'll worry about how to explain this in my log."

For the rest of the day, Katherine Pulaski efficiently patched up the wounded villagers. Only one of them was in serious danger, and he would probably lose a leg even if she could take him back to the *Enterprise*.

The Prime Directive discouraged that, as it did intervening in the affairs of any planetary population, but it didn't prohibit Federation personnel from defending their lives during a wanton attack.

Though the others had helped her with the seriously wounded, Kate was now by herself in the empty hut, treating her final patient, a woman with superficial cuts on her back and arms. Commander Riker was outside with Data and Ensign Greenblatt, seeking opinions about what the discovery of the Halloween mask in the maskmaker's shop might mean. At the very least, it meant that Picard's party had come into contact with a band of Lorcans led by someone named Piercing Blade. Kate could only hope that Day Timer had been wrong when he said that Piercing Blade's followers were little better than a band of raiders!

There was a rap on the door. "Come in!" Kate called.

Commander Riker stuck his head in. "Doctor, are you about finished? Day Timer says that the maskmaker and leaders of the village want to thank us for our help. This may be our chance to get going."

"I'm done," answered Dr. Pulaski, smoothing down the last of the bandages. "Change those twice a day," she told the woman, handing her a package of medicated bandages that had been beamed down from the ship.

"Thank you, Healer," the woman said reverently. She nodded to Riker on the way out. "Thank you, too, sir."

Riker nodded his clay mask. "I'm glad we could help."

"You did more than help," the woman replied. "You freed us."

After the woman had left, Riker turned to Pulaski and lowered his voice. "I had to tell them that Whiff was dead and that Data went off to dispose of his body. There's no other way to account for his absence without explaining more than we want to."

"I understand," the doctor replied. After the commander left, she carefully straightened the hut and packed up her equipment. She didn't want to leave clues to their true identity.

When Kate stepped outside, she saw that most of the villagers had gathered around Day Timer's wagon. She joined the clay-masked apprentices, who now numbered four, as they stood in a line facing Day Timer, Trim Hands, and the assembled villagers. She hadn't seen the peddler or the maskmaker since the attack began, and she wondered what they'd been up to.

Trim Hands cleared his throat importantly and stood as straight as his aged spine would allow. "Today is a great day in the history of our beloved village," he announced. "Never have we repulsed a band of raiders so successfully, killing over half of them."

The crowd murmured its approval, and some cheered lustily. Kate glanced at her shipmates, but their simple masks betrayed none of their curiosity and puzzlement.

"In deep gratitude for your assistance in our time of need," the maskmaker continued, "your benefactor has allowed us to honor you with masks that reflect the esteem in which we hold you."

Trim Hands glanced at Day Timer, who nodded his approval. He stood straight and proud and was probably beaming, Kate thought, under his Proprietor's Mask.

"To the one called Doctor," said Trim Hands, "we present the Herbalist's Mask, the mask of the healer." He raised his hand ceremoniously, and one of the younger villagers rushed back to his hut and emerged a moment later, carrying a yellow mask with twin green serpents coiled in the center of its face. Carefully handling the mask by its edges, he passed it to Trim Hands, who presented it to Katherine Pulaski.

As soon as she took the sturdy bronze mask, she realized why they were handling it by its edges: The paint on the yellow face and around exquisite emerald serpents was still wet and gleaming. She looked with astonishment at Day Timer.

"You do not need to wear the mask now," he explained. "This morning, it was a red mask worn by a killer. Now, fittingly, it is an Herbalist's Mask to be worn by a healer."

"Thank you," she said, her voice choking slightly. "This is an honor."

Trim Hands nodded, and the villagers murmured their approval. "Now," intoned the maskmaker, "we honor the one called Data, who protected our children, by presenting to him the Teacher's Mask."

He repeated the ritual of holding up his hand and waiting as one of the village youths retrieved a white mask from his hut. This mask looked something like the one worn by the maskmaker's female assistant. It was adorned with strange writing and signs, but it had been given a benevolent smile and a tender expression. It was the first smiling Lorcan mask that Kate remembered seeing.

Data took the mask. Although his features were hidden, Kate could tell that the android was pleased with the honor. "I will cherish this always," he said.

"To the one called Greenblatt," said the maskmaker, "who stood her ground and protected her master's wagon, felling one of the raiders with a fire arrow, we present the Archer's Mask."

Another freshly painted mask was brought forth, this one with surrealistic blue and white arrows streaking from the nose hole, across a jet black background, to the edges of the mask. The black coloring of the mask and its substantial construction gave it the appearance of a formidable piece of armor.

The young blond woman accepted the prize graciously. "May I be worthy," she said.

Next, an unaltered Raider's Mask, still the color of blood, was handed to Trim Hands. "This mask," he said reverently, "is presented in honor of the one called Whiff, who is no longer with us. Take it in your travels to be reminded of him."

He gave the Raider's Mask to Day Timer, who held it in both hands and stared at its somber visage. "The raiders stand for all that we despise about our land," he declared. "We are, by birthright and custom, a violent people, but we don't need to indulge that blood lust by senseless killing and preying upon peaceful villages. We can direct our energies toward making this a better place to live."

"I accept this mask for my followers and friends in the hope that we will never see another one." He motioned to his astounded apprentices. "Had I a dozen more like these, I would wear the Avenger's Mask and rid our fair land of all bandits and brigands. Perhaps, at the fair in Cottage Meadow, peace-loving Lorcans will finally band together to put an end to these scavengers who prey upon innocents."

The crowd erupted with cheers, and Katherine Pulaski was again amazed at the talents of her "master." First a peddler, then a maskmaker, then a lethal swordsman, and now a speechmaker and politician. Was there any end to the number of hats, or masks, Day Timer could wear?

Of course, she agreed with every word he had said. The question remained, was he or anyone else on this planet capable of bringing order to a society where might made right and the sword was the ultimate arbiter? Were the Lorcans ready for peaceful coexistence?

Before she could consider the question further, Day Timer held up his hands to quiet the crowd and then began to speak: "Your esteemed maskmaker has given me the honor of presenting the next mask to the man called Will Riker, who has demonstrated true leadership and bravery. Upon him I bestow a special honor."

Day Timer then went to his own wagon to fetch a mask and returned with the stunning wood and jewel creation known as the Forest Mask. A high polish showed off the wood's beautiful black and red grain, and the eye, nose, and mouth holes were natural knots in the wood. The mask flowed upward in sculpted boughs, simulating the growth of a tree, and widened into an incredible array of green, yellow, and red gems, arranged like tiny leaves. It was a breathtaking mask, which Kate could imagine seeing in an airtight museum case.

Day Timer held the mask up for the entire assembly to see. As they cheered, Commander Riker shrank back, as if he couldn't believe the immense honor was for him. Kate Pulaski couldn't believe it either.

"I know I am losing an able apprentice when I do this," Day Timer said, "but I can think of no one I would rather see wear this mask. Will Riker, wear the Forest Mask and let all the world know that you are nobly born."

He held the stunning mask out to Will, who took it with trembling hands. "I . . . I don't know what to say. This is an extraordinary honor."

Trim Hands, the maskmaker, clapped with delight. "Only one who is deserving could be so reverent. I praise our new nobleman, our herbalist, our teacher, and our archer. I mourn the passing of our dead. But from the masks of the dead, new masks are born. Let us celebrate all of them with a feast."

Now the cheers were really deafening, and Kate felt

caught up in the joyful rush of the villagers, each straining to congratulate her and the other honorees personally. Merrily jostled back and forth in a sea of colorful masks, she momentarily forgot about the missing away team, the *Enterprise,* and the reason they had all come to Lorca.

For that moment, she was a Lorcan.

Chapter Eight

CAPTAIN PICARD LOOKED BACK over his shoulder for the hundredth time that day, wondering where Worf and his Lorcan escort were. Even with half of their party on foot, Piercing Blade had encouraged them to make good time; they had probably covered fifteen kilometers of rugged road since breaking camp that morning. But darkness and amber clouds were creeping down the branches of the great trees, and the forest would soon be shrouded in nightfall. Picard didn't worry about Worf's ability to take care of himself, but he wanted to know the big Klingon was safe.

Perhaps they had run across Fenton Lewis, who had to be somewhere between the larger party and the village. He still couldn't believe that a Federation ambassador had deserted them. And "desertion" was the appropriate term; there was no doubt about that. Picard harbored the faint hope that Fenton Lewis thought he would be more effective on his own and had every intention of returning. But the captain's mind kept replaying the conversation in which Lewis had admitted his career would be over when the facts of the two Ferengi deaths became public knowledge. In reality, Fenton Lewis had little incentive to return to the Federation fold.

"Picard," said a husky voice beside him, "I cannot see your face, but your gait looks troubled."

Jean-Luc whirled to his right to see Piercing Blade striding beside him. She had walked the entire way, graciously allowing Counselor Troi and her own followers to ride the ponies. Of the group of eight, only Picard and Piercing Blade had traveled on foot the entire day.

"I'm worried about Worf and Cold Angel," he answered. "I expected them to join us before now."

"You worry too much, Picard," she said. "Both men are loyal and will join us as soon as they can. They have the fastest ponies. Perhaps they stopped to dally with the women in the village."

Picard tried to imagine Worf "dallying" with the neighborhood women. The image brought an unseen smile to his face, "I'm sure they're all right. Maybe I do worry too much."

"Just in case they were delayed," she said, "we shall make camp soon and give them a chance to catch up. I know of a bog farther along where the fishing is good. We'll stop there."

The Thunder Mask swiveled away from him and he caught a glimpse of Piercing Blade's copper-colored hair curling around the nape of her neck. For such an athletic woman, she had a surprisingly slender and feminine neck. She was a tall woman, six or seven centimeters taller than Picard, and in amazing physical condition. Nevertheless, he wondered how muscular she really was and how much of her imposing stature was armor and mask.

Then Jean-Luc chided himself, feeling ashamed. Here he was, mentally undressing the woman. A starship captain acting like a lovesick teenager. He had to curb his unseemly curiosity and concentrate on the mission.

But what was the mission anymore, except to survive? The prospect of finding the mythological Almighty Slayer and pounding out diplomatic agreements now seemed ridiculously remote. They were cut off from the ship, missing two of their complement, and marching in the wrong direction. What a botched job this turned out to be.

Nevertheless, he couldn't feel totally inept marching alongside the majestic Piercing Blade. Their mission had been partly successful, in that they had won the faith and trust of a local leader. They were on their way to what was apparently the biggest gathering of Lorcan notables ever held. Somehow, Picard vowed to himself, he would see this mission through to its conclusion.

When he turned to look again, he found the noblewoman gazing at him instead. Blade's green eyes sparkled in their jeweled frames. "I would like you and your female page to dine with me in my tent tonight," she said.

He nodded, glad for once that his emotions were hidden behind the grim animal mask. "It will be our pleasure."

"Good," she said emphatically. "Now I must look for that bog, if we are to have anything to eat."

The warrior strode to the front of the queue, her long legs carrying her effortlessly past those mounted on ponies. The captain debated whether to follow her and learn more about the hidden passageway to the underground sea, but he decided against it. He would see her at dinner that night, and that would be enough.

Too much of Piercing Blade could be intoxicating.

Cold Angel and Worf stopped near a bog to water their ponies and give them some grain. Under normal circumstances, they would have camped there for the night, but Cold Angel was convinced they weren't very far behind the main party. For proof, he pointed out several sets of fresh hoofprints and footprints in the damp clay ahead.

Lieutenant Worf looked at his brave little steed with sympathy and concern. Even with frequent stops, they were riding the animals to sweat-soaked exhaustion. But Cold Angel insisted that the ponies could take it, and Worf took the Lorcan trainer at his word. Despite the amber clouds of approaching darkness, the equines remained spirited and ready to take to the trail again, as they pawed the ground and playfully tossed their feed bags.

"These are young mounts," Cold Angel assured him, inspecting his pony's bridle. "Mine has teeth like a hatchet. Look at the way he has chewed through this new bit."

Worf massaged his aching haunches and did a few deep knee bends. "Maybe we should walk the rest of the way."

Cold Angel chuckled. "Don't you have ponies where you come from?"

"Uh, no," the Klingon answered. "I'm more accustomed to riding horses."

Cold Angel cocked his stylized fish mask questioningly. "Horses?"

"Like these animals," Worf replied, stroking his pony's sweaty mane, "only bigger."

The Lorcan shrugged, as if conceding that such a thing might be possible. "I've heard many stories about ponies in the old times, before the dragon breathed. The storytellers say that ponies are not native to Lorca, that they came here with our ancestors. But those ancient ponies were different. They were as smart as people and knew how to dance and do tricks. Do you believe such a thing, Worf?"

"Yes." The lieutenant nodded, remembering that

the Lorcans were descended from a theatrical troupe who might have used trained ponies as part of their entertainment. Certainly, ponies would have made better space travelers than full-size horses. "There's no telling what might have been in the past," he observed. "But I doubt if ponies were ever as smart as people."

"Perhaps not," agreed the Lorcan. "I breed ponies, and I don't think they're smart at all."

"But these are brave and steadfast," said Worf sincerely, staring into the eyes of his plucky mount.

Cold Angel nodded. "Thank you. I raised these two from foals."

"Do you have a farm somewhere?" the Klingon asked. "A ranch?"

"Lady Piercing Blade has a wonderful home, far to the west," he said proudly. Then his voice became wistful. "We've seen too little of it in the last months. She has a dozen serfs who manage the land and grow the crops. They probably think they own the place by now."

"Then you have been a long time searching for Almighty Slayer?"

"A long time," growled the Lorcan, "searching for a dead man, seeking followers and warriors, trying to persuade people to accept Piercing Blade as queen. But change is hard on Lorca. People prefer the old stories and traditions, such as this mindless devotion to Almighty Slayer."

"What did he do?" asked Worf.

"He wore the Wisdom Mask," the trainer answered, as if that were enough. "I know Slayer was a great warrior who settled many disputes, but his time is past."

"How important is it for the ruler to have the Wisdom Mask?"

Cold Angel paused to scratch under his mask. "I can't believe how ignorant you strangers are. A ruler who didn't wear the Wisdom Mask might be accepted by some, but not by all. As soon as someone else showed up wearing the Wisdom Mask, *he* would be accepted as king. It's harder for Piercing Blade, not knowing where the Wisdom Mask is."

"So the right to rule is always in question," Worf concluded, "unless the ruler possesses the Wisdom Mask. It's a form of validation."

Cold Angel deftly pulled off his pony's feed bag and slipped the bit into his mouth. "I don't know that word—'validation'—but many Lorcans believe that the Wisdom Mask *chooses* the ruler of Lorca. Don't ask me how. This kind of ignorance is hard to overcome."

The Klingon agreed, slipping the bridle over his own pony's head.

Cold Angel suggested, "Why don't we walk the ponies for a bit, let them digest their food?"

The Lorcans made camp in record time, eager to rest after so strenuous a march. Fish had been caught in the bog and were starting to sizzle over a fire erected inside a huge fir tree. Captain Picard and Counselor Troi waited until the first fillets were plucked from the branches before approaching Piercing Blade's tent.

The night was dark, with heavy opaque clouds, but it was the warmest of the three nights the away team had spent on Lorca. As Picard and Deanna approached the tent, they were startled when the flap swung back and the gleaming Ambassador's Mask loomed in front of them. Since his promotion, Spider Wing was everywhere, screening callers for Piercing Blade, issuing opinions, and in general making a nuisance of himself.

"Did you want something?" he asked.

"We were invited to dine with Piercing Blade," Picard answered, grimacing in irritation. How easy the mask made it to conceal one's feelings. As captain, Jean-Luc was accustomed to hiding his emotions. Now he was free to contort his face into any expression he chose. The mask would maintain an appearance of civility.

"Our lady made the invitation herself," Deanna added.

The mammoth silver mask nodded, and Spider Wing held the tent flap open, revealing oil lamps beyond. "Now I remember her mentioning the invitation. Please enter and go straight ahead. Our lady has dressed for dinner."

Indeed, Lady Piercing Blade had dressed for dinner. She was wearing a gown of white feathers that flowed from her shoulders to her feet, giving her the appearance of a shimmering pillar. The Thunder mask topped off the apparition, and Jean-Luc Picard felt as if he were staring at an angel.

"Please be seated," she said with a sweep of her hands. "I'm sorry I have nothing better than saddles to offer you as chairs."

Jean-Luc noted that the pony saddles did not look all that uncomfortable after so many hours of walking. He took a seat, and so did Counselor Troi.

"That is a lovely gown," said Deanna.

"Thank you, Page." The Thunder Mask nodded. "Do you have a name you would prefer to be called by?"

"Deanna is sufficient," the oval mask answered.

The two Lorcan pages entered with metal plates of steaming fish, accompanied by a thick gruel made from the same grain eaten by the ponies. They gave each of the three diners a cup of water, a plate, and a wooden spoon, then hurried off to their own dinner.

Piercing Blade sat cross-legged on the floor, with her plate balanced between her thighs. "Eat," she commanded.

Picard smiled under his mask at her unregal pose. She was a would-be queen who had never been trained for the job. To her credit, she was the same person all the time, whether she was covered with burlap and mud or wearing jewels and an evening dress.

"I can't tell you how pleased I am to have you here with me," she said effusively. "But I have one question. When we get to the fair, will you support me as queen?"

"We cannot take sides in your internal affairs," Picard said candidly.

"Why not?" asked Piercing Blade, leaning forward. "Do you support someone else?"

Picard and Deanna looked at each other, and Deanna took the initiative. "We come from a place far away in space, and we are forbidden to involve ourselves in your culture. But we would like to be friends and assure you that you are not alone among the myriad worlds out there." Her sweeping gesture was meant to indicate the galaxy.

"Yes, the stars," said Piercing Blade, sitting back. "You and the Ferengi are equal in that regard. You remind us that our ancestors came from the stars. Unfortunately, we don't know very much about them."

"What *do* you know about your past?" asked Jean-Luc.

"We know that they survived a terrible cataclysm," answered the Lorcan. "That's what all the storytellers say. In the olden times, before they settled in this place, our ancestors traveled around in a huge airship. But after they came here, the dragon who lives at the center of the world breathed a monstrous column of fire, and it engulfed the airship."

Deanna Troi bolted upright. "That would explain it. It explains my dream. Captain, I believe the theatrical troupe's spaceship was orbiting the planet when a huge volcanic explosion tore through the planet's atmosphere and destroyed the ship. It also put a perpetual cloud around the planet that lowered the temperature and made life arduous.

"Ever since then, the survivors on the planet have been left to fend for themselves without technology, all of which was destroyed in the cataclysm."

"But their masks and vestiges of their theatrical heritage survived," replied the captain.

Piercing Blade sounded puzzled when she replied, "The two of you would make good storytellers if anybody could understand you. The past is the past. We know very little about it, and we don't concern ourselves with it. My concern is the future. How can I persuade my fellow Lorcans to stand behind me? Lorca needs leadership."

The captain shook his head. "We can't help you consolidate your power. We are on a mission to open communications, nothing more."

Piercing Blade squared her impressive shoulders. "Then you aren't as valuable to us as the Ferengi. When they come here, they offer trade—manufactured goods we don't have. They offer synthehol, which many of our people have grown to like."

"What do they want in return?" Picard asked.

"They are interested in the moss that covers the trees."

Picard nodded. "A cheap natural flame retardant. They could strip your trees of it. Then where would you be? Your forests would burn. The Ferengi always want something. We offer friendship, and we ask nothing in return."

"I've seen your friendship," Piercing Blade countered. "You came here with a mask stolen from the Ferengi. Is that an example of your friendship?"

Jean-Luc waved his hands at her. "Let's start over. You invited us for dinner, not a political discussion. As far as I'm concerned, you should be free to deal with the Ferengi, the Federation, or whomever you choose. We've come here to accept and appreciate your hospitality, nothing more."

"That's better." Piercing Blade nodded. "Politics is too dull a subject to discuss at dinner. We must be grateful to have encountered each other." She stared directly at Captain Picard.

"That's the way I feel," he answered intently.

Assuming her presence would soon be superfluous, Deanna Troi swallowed one last mouthful of fish. She had already eaten enough of what was, for her, very rich food. "Thank you for the delicious dinner," she said. "I must be going."

Neither Picard nor Piercing Blade tried to stop her. "Sleep well," said the noblewoman.

"Will you be by the tree?" asked the captain.

"Yes," answered the Betazoid. "I will stay on the alert for Lieutenant Worf and Ambassador Lewis."

"But get some sleep," ordered Picard.

Deanna stood and nodded. An instant later, Picard and Piercing Blade were alone in the flickering lamplight. The night was quiet and warm all around them, and no light or prying eyes invaded the oilskin tent.

Blade put her plate aside and stood to her full imposing height. Her feathered gown glistened in the lamp glow, enhancing her sumptuous figure. "I have something to show you, Picard."

"What is that?"

"My face."

"I would like to see it," Picard rasped, rising to stand facing her.

"And I would like to show you my face," the warrior queen breathed, "but I am unaccustomed to such behavior."

"Is it so rare," the captain asked, "to show one's face to a trusted companion?"

"For me it is."

Picard struggled to find the right words. "I don't

wish to make you feel uncomfortable. Our customs are not yours. On my . . . home, I would have seen your face at our first meeting."

Her voice was soft and contemplative. "I find that unthinkable, but, in a way, pleasant."

"Let me show myself first, then," said Picard. He removed the Trainer's Mask and waited, giving her a reserved smile. He remembered her reaction to Fenton Lewis's naked face, and he didn't want to startle her.

Piercing Blade's eyes widened inside the jewel-framed sockets of her mask, and she stepped closer to Picard. He gazed into her haunting eyes, as she tentatively reached out with a trembling hand to touch his face. When he didn't flinch, she became emboldened and began stroking his cheekbone and caressing his jawbone to his chin. With the back of her hand, she smoothed his stubbly three-day-old beard. She curled the fingers of both hands around his slim patrician nose and stretched them into his eyebrows.

Her fingers lingered in his eyebrows, driving him to distraction. As she raked her fingers over his forehead and into his scalp, she pressed her body into his.

Picard was not thinking clearly. He wanted to put his hands everywhere at once, but they were drawn to the Thunder Mask. The mask was like a distorted mirror, shooting back reflections of gold lamplight and fractured images of his own face. He reached for the bindings of the mask.

"Let me," she said, reaching behind her head. "There's a trick to it." Her hands cupped the mask as it fell away from her face.

Picard gasped. He was not prepared for such a pale and innocent face, so totally devoid of corruption and deceit. The warrior's face was incredibly youthful, and Picard was shocked into thinking she might be a child. But no, he thought, as he stroked her fine cheekbones and creamy complexion, only her skin was childlike. Having never been exposed to harmful ultraviolet rays, Piercing Blade's facial skin was perhaps twenty years younger than she was.

However, the warrior's face wasn't entirely without character. Running diagonally from her hairline across her forehead and to the bridge of her nose was a jagged scar.

Jean-Luc reached out to touch the scar, and Piercing Blade flinched. But he kissed her hand, and that soothed her. She melted back into his chest, allowing him to touch her one imperfection. It was an old scar, scarcely darker than her extraordinary skin, but it had the proud contours of a mountain range on a relief map. She was obviously self-conscious about the scar, and Picard drove those fears away with a kiss.

He was cast into a deep tunnel of forgetfulness as he explored her warm and trembling lips. Nothing else in the world mattered but those lips. So deep was he in the pleasurable abyss that he didn't hear the voices calling. Piercing Blade reluctantly pulled herself away from him.

She picked up her mask and motioned to him to do the same. "What is it?" she called.

"Cold Angel and the new page have returned!" announced Spider Wing. "The other new page felt the trainer should be informed."

"Thank you," answered Piercing Blade.

She smiled wistfully at Picard and pulled the mask over her head. Like the curtain falling on a memorable stage production, the mask again hid Piercing Blade's angelic countenance. "You have to go, Picard."

He heaved a sigh of profound disappointment. Before pulling on his own mask, he managed to say, "I have been honored tonight."

"As have I," she countered. "I am so glad you are with us."

Jean-Luc left the tent before he could say anything stupid.

Once Captain Picard, Counselor Troi, and Lieutenant Worf were far enough away from the Lorcans to be out of earshot, Worf immediately pulled off his mask and started to shake clumps of dirt out of it.

"Nothing, Captain," he said grimly. "We learned no more about Almighty Slayer than we already knew. But whoever possesses the Wisdom Mask will command more followers and vassals than anyone else."

"That much is certain," Picard agreed.

"What was the village like?" asked Deanna.

"Primitive," the lieutenant answered, wiping caked clay from his face and neck. "The huts are built on stilts, and the maskmaker is a most revered person. Even the children wear masks."

"How did you get so dirty?" asked Picard with some amusement.

"I fell into a bog," the Klingon admitted. "This is an infernal planet."

Deanna paced nervously. "We have some bad news. Ambassador Lewis has disappeared."

"To be more precise," snapped Picard, "he's run off."

Worf cocked his chin at the captain and lowered his ponderous brow. "That is most unfortunate. I personally didn't care for the man, and it doesn't surprise me to hear that he's unreliable, but I valued his skills."

The security officer shrugged and dug some clumps of clay from his beard. "It is possible to argue that without the ambassador our mission is ended and we can return to the *Enterprise* as soon as possible."

"Our mission would seem to have been a failure," Picard admitted. "At least the part about delivering Ambassador Lewis to qualified Lorcan representatives. But who are the qualified representatives on this planet?"

"Piercing Blade," Deanna suggested. "I think her followers believe in her nearly as much as she believes in herself."

Jean-Luc waged a mental battle trying to evaluate that extraordinary woman objectively. *He* was enamored of her, but were the Lorcans? Did she command enough allegiance to rule Lorca without the hallowed Wisdom Mask?

"We'll find out soon how important Piercing Blade is," he predicted, "at the fair. In the meantime, we're discovering more and more about the planet, its history, and its social structure. I believe we're safe at the moment with Piercing Blade's band, and we can only hope Fenton Lewis is safe, too."

"The *Enterprise*, sir," Worf reminded him. "They don't know we're safe, and they must be extremely worried."

Jean-Luc bowed his head and sighed. "I know how worried they must be aboard the *Enterprise*. But they can't fail to detect a gathering as large as this upcoming fair. They'll find us. I have faith in Commander Riker and the rest of the crew."

With the ease of an old habit, Worf and Troi affixed their bronze masks and walked toward the fire. Jean-Luc looked at the fearsome animal mask in his hands and marveled at the ease with which the away team had been assimilated into a culture of masks. Remembering how gorgeous the fair face of Piercing Blade had been, he wasn't sure anymore that the Lorcans were wrong to love masks.

Day Timer, mindful of the days needed to cover the distance to Cottage Meadow, wanted to travel that night instead of celebrating in the village. Not that the celebrations were particularly memorable. The villagers opened their coffers for the feast, but they were poor and had only the essentials, some fresh fish but mostly dried, and a barleylike grain. One hunting party went to catch werjuns but returned empty-handed, much to Day Timer's delight.

Many of the villagers, instead of celebrating, spent the afternoon praying to the dragon and other gods. Of course, they had lost four of their own people, and a score had been wounded, recalled Commander Riker. In a village of maybe a hundred people, those were sizable casualties. The music had been subdued, too, provided by a couple of stringed instruments.

Now Day Timer and the second away team were strolling in soothing darkness, the trees providing a friendly environment. Concerned about potholes and bogs, their benefactor insisted on maintaining a slow pace for the health of his pony. Will Riker, too, was content to dawdle and avoid any excitement. The din of the brief but bloody battle still roared in his ears, and he wished it would go away. Violence was so close to the surface, he thought, on the planet or within the person. He was still blocking out the sight of the man he had stabbed to death.

He reached up and felt the polished wood of his Forest Mask. Its cool bulk was comforting. Will resolved to keep the mask, if possible, as a memento of Lorca. Though he hadn't wanted to come here—hadn't wanted anything but to find the captain—Will felt he had been accepted by the Lorcans. So had the entire party. They had all received the equivalent of a field promotion. But the awarding of the masks was more than an honor; it was a way of welcoming new people to the neighborhood.

The Lorcans had simply observed what each member of the party could contribute and had assigned each of them a profession. To their credit, the Lorcans did not worship money, although some crude coins seemed to possess some value. But the masks carried intrinsic value, expressing each person's worth to the community. Will was almost sorry that he wasn't wearing a vassal's mask anymore. He missed the simplicity of being an apprentice.

He didn't fully understand what wearing a mask of nobility meant. He tried to tell himself that it made him an officer, one who commanded, and nothing more, but there was a reverence in the way the villagers addressed him after he started wearing the mask. Or was it fear?

"Whoa," breathed Day Timer, pulling the reins and halting the slow-moving wagon. His voice stayed at a whisper. "Riker, there is someone ahead of us."

Will rushed to the peddler's side. Lieutenant Commander Data, Dr. Pulaski, and Ensign Greenblatt froze on the trail, listening. The shadows at the base of the great trees were deep enough to hide an army.

Will strained his eyes and ears to detect something, but couldn't. "Maybe it's Reba," he suggested.

"Reba wouldn't wait to greet me," said the old peddler. "She'd jump on the wagon and give me a hug."

Riker glanced at Ensign Greenblatt and saw her holding to her pistol phaser, still in its holster. He nodded, and she discreetly drew it out.

"We mean no harm," announced the commander.

"The road is wide enough for all of us to pass," Day Timer replied.

In the shadows, surprisingly close to the wagon, stood a lone figure. It waited for a moment, then walked toward them, arms swinging slowly and deliberately.

"I mean you no harm either," said a pleasant male voice. "I am alone."

The stranger remained invisible until he stopped a scant two meters away, and Will could finally see his mask, an elaborate creation adorned with white, brown, and lavender feathers.

"Good evening, Sir Messenger," called Day Timer

with relief. "You must have an urgent message to be traveling so late at night. But you have no reason to hide from us."

"Forgive me," said the man in the owlish mask. He bowed, and his hair tumbled over his shoulders. "I have had . . . misfortune. I was afraid, because I didn't know who you were."

"Wait a moment," said Data suddenly, stepping forward. "I recognize that voice. You are Ambassador Fenton Lewis, are you not?"

The man stumbled back a step out of shock, stared at the masks confronting him, then doubled over with laughter. "This is rare!" he howled. "I didn't recognize a single one of you. Is that the android?"

"Ambassador?" said Riker, rushing around the pony. With his back to Day Timer, he tore off his mask.

"Riker," exclaimed the befuddled owl. "I never thought I would be glad to see *you*."

"Where is the captain?" asked Kate Pulaski. "And the others?"

"You've heard nothing?" asked the ambassador.

Several masks swiveled from side to side.

Ambassador Lewis touched his feathered mask and hesitated before removing it. "Ironically," he said, "I must live up to the rank of this mask and be the bearer of bad tidings."

"What is it?" asked Riker.

"Captain Picard and the others are dead."

Chapter Nine

"WHAT?" GASPED KATE PULASKI. She ripped off her Herbalist's Mask. "The captain's dead?"

Will Riker lowered his head, almost wishing he could put his mask back on. "What happened?"

"We were attacked," Lewis answered, "by a band of thieves. They were led by a woman."

"Piercing Blade," said Data glumly.

Fenton Lewis shrugged. "That might be her name. We weren't given a chance to get to know them."

"You're the only survivor?" Riker asked, not bothering to hide the doubt in his voice. "How did you manage that?"

"And how did you come by that mask?" asked Dr. Pulaski.

Lewis held up his hands. "One question at a time, please. I know all of this comes as a terrible shock to you and you want to know every detail. I'll be happy to write a complete report, but for the moment, let me give you the short version."

"Please," urged Riker.

"After we survived the volcano eruption," the ambassador continued, pacing thoughtfully, "we found that all of our equipment had been knocked out by the volcanic dust. It is highly magnetic."

"We are aware of that," Data remarked.

Lewis gestured at the immense trees. "We headed toward these woods in search of safety. Unfortunately, there are other dangers on this planet besides the volcanoes. We were ambushed and taken by surprise."

"Your Ambassador's Mask didn't help?" an incredulous Kate asked.

Fenton Lewis paused dramatically. "It saved my life. The others were killed outright, and I was captured. The Lorcans took my mask, but they didn't want to leave me unclothed, so they gave me this mask." He pointed to the feathered mask, and the tone of his voice implied that it was vastly inferior to the mask made by Fazool.

"Not possible," growled Day Timer.

The others whirled around, having all but forgotten the Lorcan peddler sitting atop his wagon. He was shielding his eyes because all except Data and Greenblatt had removed their masks.

"Piercing Blade is uppity and devious," Day Timer explained, "but she isn't one to attack from hiding." He cocked his mask before admitting, "She might kill one or two in a duel—"

"One or two!" snapped Fenton Lewis, glaring at the haughty Proprietor's Mask. "She's a murderer, I tell you." He whirled back to Riker. "I have been through a great deal, Commander, and I don't like having my word questioned."

Will Riker was consumed by worry and shock. He tried to put his mind on the more immediate problem: whether to take Fenton Lewis's story at face value, as truth. Riker didn't like or trust the man, but he couldn't deny having seen that ridiculous Halloween mask in the maskmaker's shop. And he had experienced the violence of Lorca firsthand. Will hoped, if all of it was true, that Worf had put up a good fight.

"Can you find the place where this happened?" Riker asked hoarsely.

"I . . . I'm not sure."

"You'd better think about it," said the commander. "I can't report the captain or anyone else dead until I find their bodies."

"Your story is unsubstantiated," Data told Lewis.

The ambassador shrugged and pulled on his mask. "Very well. I'm not promising anything, but I'll do my best to lead you to the scene of the ambush."

"You came from the south," said Data. "Shall we go that direction?"

"All right," Lewis said, turning and marching off into the darkness.

"Are you coming with us?" the commander asked Day Timer.

"As long as you stay on the road and travel south, I am with you."

Conversation was rare during the slow walk before dawn. Even Day Timer was quiet, sensing his companions' grief. Kate Pulaski hadn't known Jean-Luc, Deanna, and Worf as long as the others had, but she could not conceive of them being dead. It was too much to absorb, too devastating. All she could feel was emptiness.

She found Commander Riker walking beside her. He glanced at her and then looked down. The shipmates were not in a hurry to take their masks off now.

"Are you going to let Geordi know?" she asked.

"I don't want to," Will replied, "until we find . . . As far as I'm concerned, they're still missing."

"I understand," Kate said. Noticing that Ambassador Lewis was far enough ahead of them to be out of earshot, she added, "You think he could be lying?"

"Don't you?" asked Riker.

"I agree with your decision to search for them" was all Kate could manage in reply. In reality, she wasn't sure she really wanted to know the whole truth. She wanted to keep some hope, even if it was just a form of denial.

With his amplified hearing, Data couldn't help hear the anguished conversation between Commander Riker and Dr. Pulaski. So that was grief, he thought. Data could only observe the emotion, because he didn't believe that Captain Picard, Counselor Troi, and Lieutenant Worf were dead. The android had evaluated both Ambassador Lewis and Day Timer as reliable sources and had decided that Day Timer was far superior.

For one thing, the Lorcan was objective in the matter and had no vested interest. While he had exhibited a dislike for Piercing Blade, he had not wanted her to be misrepresented as a thieving murderer. This indicated a balanced view, and the peddler knew his countrymen far better than any of them. Although Lorca was a violent society, it was not without rules and conventions: even the raiders had observed the convention of wearing red masks. The Lorcans often behaved violently, but they were not savages.

The biggest doubt in Data's circuits stemmed from Ambassador Lewis's new mask. It was a well-worn Lorcan mask of respectable workmanship. Though not on a par with the missing Ambassador's Mask, the Messenger's Mask was surely of value. Why would cold-blooded murderers spare one life out of four if they were going to steal the Ambassador's Mask anyway? And why give their victim a valuable mask in its place?

Data had observed the frequency with which masks were exchanged on Lorca. They were almost a unit of barter. Each member of their team had, for example, been granted a new mask. But it was in exchange for services rendered. Day Timer had given each of them an Apprentice's Mask in exchange for behaving like his apprentices. But nobody received a mask for nothing. Two undisputed facts—that a Halloween mask had shown up in a village mask shop, and that Lewis's original Lorcan mask had been exchanged for another—only indicated business as usual.

In fact, the fact that Fenton Lewis was alive and well strongly suggested to Data that the entire party had managed to survive.

"What are we going to do at this place called Cottage Meadow?" Deanna Troi asked Medicine Maker.

The jeweled green serpents angled in her direction, and the healer continued walking. "There will be many people there, every citizen and subject of importance. Piercing Blade has won a rank of nobility second only to that of the king. But where is the king? Where is Almighty Slayer and where is the Wisdom Mask?"

The two walked in silence for the moment through the Lorcan dawn. They were at the end of the procession, having given up their ponies to Captain Picard and Piercing Blade. Apparently the band was approaching a well-known crossroad where they were likely to meet other travelers, and it was deemed necessary for the leaders to have mounts. Deanna welcomed the walk.

Medicine Maker trailed behind a bit to gather some sprouts and herbs. He stuffed the cuttings haphazardly into a leather bag slung over his shoulder, then caught up with Deanna.

"Our task won't be easy," he admitted. "We have to convince everyone we meet that Lorca can have a ruler who doesn't wear the Wisdom Mask. In my opinion, Almighty Slayer has been absent so long that he has abdicated the throne."

"What if he is at the fair wearing the Wisdom Mask?" she asked.

Medicine Maker clenched his fists. "All the better. Then Piercing Blade will challenge his right to wear it."

Deanna nodded solemnly. "What if somebody else has found the Wisdom Mask and is wearing it?"

"The same," answered the Lorcan.

"So we may be marching into battle."

The Herbalist's Mask turned toward her. Beneath the serpent eyebrows, a pair of very dark eyes glared at her. "You are free to do whatever you wish. Let's hope the others are easier to convince than *you.*"

"I'm sorry," Deanna admitted. "I shouldn't be critical. I know you believe in the rightness of your cause and I respect that."

Medicine Maker's big shoulders heaved as he sighed. "You are not going to make a very good page. We should get you a different mask. What skills do you have?"

How could she explain her job in terms the Lorcan would understand? Deanna wondered. Finally she shrugged and said, "I play cards very well."

The Lorcan chuckled, and his voice echoed warmly within his mask. "Then we'll get you a Gambler's Mask. But be careful, or Cold Angel will win it from you."

"How many masks can a person have?" she asked.

"We have a saying," answered Medicine Maker. "'A person can have a hundred masks, but he can wear only one.'"

Deanna nodded appreciatively and they walked in comfortable silence for a few moments.

"Is it true," he asked, "that where you come from, people go without masks?"

"That's right," she replied.

"Don't your faces get cold?"

The Betazoid laughed out loud, enjoying the spontaneous release. "Yes, they do."

"Then it's absurd not to wear masks."

"But it can't be cold like this all the time," Deanna insisted. "What are the summers like on Lorca?"

It was Medicine Maker's turn to laugh. "This *is* summer."

"Oh."

"At least you knew enough to bring masks with you."

"We've adapted to your ways," she answered, "because we want to be friends. We don't believe in the people from one place trying to change how another people live."

"If you could change the way we live," said the healer, "then I'd be impressed."

"Why?"

His voice hardened. "Because this violent seizure of power has got to stop. Only the very strongest survive on Lorca. I don't blame Almighty Slayer for hiding. *I* certainly wouldn't want to fight duels all day long. He used to have a band of followers who defended him, but eventually they were all killed. Almighty Slayer has fought his share of duels and should step down."

"I agree with you," said Deanna. "So why are we marching off to fight? How will another battle change anything?"

"I need some of that sedge," he remarked, bending to pull up a scrawny sprig from the soil on one side of the road.

She waited for him, wondering what Medicine Maker looked like behind his elegant mask. Was he elegant, or was he a brute? Why should surface beauty matter to her? His mask expressed the person he was perceived to be by all who knew him, and that was good enough for her. She remembered how he had refused the sumptuous Ambassador's Mask to retain the simpler Herbalist's Mask. It must mean a great deal to him.

"Go on," he said. "You don't have to wait for me."

"I want to," she answered, bending down to help him collect cuttings of the sedge.

"This is very good for stomachache," he commented, twisting a sprig between his fingers. A shaft of sunlight spilled down through the tree limbs and illuminated his jeweled mask and the tiny plant he held. Medicine Maker truly had a healing presence, and Deanna felt relaxed for the first time since arriving on Lorca.

"Don't any of you have spouses and children?" she asked.

"That's the life of a villager," he scoffed. After a moment, the herbalist reconsidered. "Maybe, after Piercing Blade is safely crowned ruler of Lorca, I'll take the time to think about such luxuries."

She nodded, wishing she could show him with her face how much she sympathized with him.

Suddenly the Lorcan bolted upright and froze. His mask swiveled slowly, like a radar dish.

"What is it?" breathed Deanna.

"Come," he said, grabbing her arm with one hand and snatching his short-sword from his boot with the other. "Let's join the others."

She jogged beside him up the road, glancing behind her but seeing nothing. They quickly caught sight of the ponies and the rest of the entourage, and Medicine Maker slowed to a brisk walk.

"What did you see?" she asked.

"I heard whispering voices," replied the Lorcan. "Worse, I thought I saw a glimpse of red between the trees."

Deanna was puzzled. "Red? What does that signify?"

His mask swiveled toward her, and she saw his dark eyes widen with surprise. "You've never heard of the raiders? Bandits in red masks?"

"I've heard of bandits," she answered. "I didn't know Lorca was troubled by them."

His mask bobbed up and down. "Very much so. Travelers are their special prey. That's why you are safer traveling with us, in Piercing Blade's entourage."

"What can be done about them?"

He glanced nervously over his shoulder, then grabbed her arm. "While Lorca has no ruler, nothing. Let's keep up with the others—no more straggling behind."

Geordi La Forge caught himself drumming his fingers on the arm of the captain's chair. He stopped immediately. He watched the unchanging view of Lorca below, an endless vista of curving horizon and swirling salmon-colored clouds. He almost felt like asking Wesley Crusher to turn the viewscreen off, but then there would be nothing at all to watch.

If only the planet wasn't so damned inhospitable, Geordi thought to himself. Normally, in a long orbit like this, the captain would send scientific teams to the planet's surface, and nonessential personnel could take recreational leave. With nothing to do but maintain a standard orbit, *everyone* was nonessential, mused the engineering officer. The transporter rooms remained on full alert, but all of the other crew members were just waiting, going about their daily routine as usual. Unfortunately, there was nothing routine about all the key officers being gone and the captain, the security chief, and the ship's counselor being missing.

"Mr. Crusher," he said, "how long has it been since we last heard from Commander Riker?"

"Almost fourteen hours, sir," answered the teenager. "When we last talked to him, his party was having dinner in a Lorcan village. Now it's midmorning where they are."

"That's a long time," Geordi agreed. "See if you can raise them."

"Yes, sir," Wesley answered. He checked the communication channels, then announced, *"Enterprise* to Commander Riker. *Enterprise* to Commander Riker."

"Riker here," came a weary voice. "What is it, Wesley?"

The ensign glanced at Geordi, who stood and stepped forward. "This is Geordi, sir. I asked Wesley to contact you because we hadn't heard from you in fourteen hours."

"Sorry," Riker said hesitantly. "We've been very busy."

"Any news? Any word about the captain?"

A long pause did nothing to allay their fears. "Nothing substantiated," said the commander finally. "Geordi, if you'll go into the captain's ready room, I'll talk to you privately."

The engineering officer glanced at Wesley Crusher, who bit his lower lip and looked down at his console. "I'll patch you in," said the boy.

Lieutenant La Forge walked slowly across the bridge and stepped into the ready room. As the door whooshed shut behind him, he announced, "I'm in the ready room. What is it, Commander?"

"First of all," sighed Riker, "we found Ambassador Lewis, alive and well."

"That's great," exclaimed Geordi.

"No," answered Will. "According to Lewis, every other member of the original away team was killed by bandits."

"What?" asked Lieutenant La Forge numbly.

"I wish you hadn't heard me correctly, but you did. According to the ambassador, the captain, Worf, Deanna . . . they're all dead."

Geordi sat down heavily. "This is . . . I can't believe it."

"But we haven't seen any bodies," Riker went on with a trace of hope in his hoarse voice. "And certain parts of Lewis's story are not logical. I won't go into it now, but these death reports are *not official* and are not to be repeated. Is that understood?"

"Yes," Geordi croaked.

"The first away team is still missing, and we are still looking for them. That's all you're to tell anyone. And you must keep looking, too."

"We will."

On the surface of the planet, Riker watched Day Timer's wagon vanish around a stand of cane. A figure in an ivory-colored mask stopped at the bend in the road and waited. Riker motioned for Data to stay where he was.

"Riker out—" he started to say, but before he could finish, the ground started to shudder, coinciding with a bizarre explosion that threw Riker off his feet.

At first he was certain they had been fired upon, but the ground continued to jostle him. Even the giant trees swayed to and fro in rhythm with the eerie rumblings coming from deep within the planet. Ten meters away, a plume of steam shot twenty meters into the air, dousing Riker with scalding water.

"Aaagh!" he screamed, but strong arms were pulling him away and lifting him up.

Within a matter of seconds, he was safe. Not only had Data's quick actions saved him, but the phenomenon had ended just as suddenly as it began. The plume of steam had shrunk to about three meters before turning into a picturesque bubbling spring.

Data set him down on his feet. "Were you injured, sir?"

"No, no," answered Will. He took off his mask and wiped his face. The mask was still smoldering from the first blasts of scalding water. He looked for his communicator insignia, but he had lost it when he fell.

"Contact Geordi," he told Data. "Find out what that was."

"Yes, sir." The android unzipped an inside pocket of his parka and pulled out his insignia. He touched it gently. "Data to *Enterprise.* Come in, Lieutenant La Forge."

"Data!" answered Geordi. "Is the commander all right?"

"Yes, he is." With his peripheral vision, Data glimpsed Dr. Pulaski and Ensign Greenblatt running toward them. "We are all fine. What was the cause of that temblor?"

Geordi had returned to the bridge and was standing over Wesley Crusher's shoulder. "Ensign Crusher has a fix on it. He'll tell you."

"What you got was nothing," proclaimed Wesley. "Four hundred kilometers to the north of you there has been a major volcanic eruption."

Riker and the others turned to the north and could see the orange canopy above the trees darkening with bloodshot streaks.

"Shall I beam you up?" asked Geordi.

"Negative," said Riker. "We can't lose any time, and I don't think the air around us is going to get any worse. But what are the chances of that happening again?"

"We can't give you any predictions. But I would say, Commander, the chances of more eruptions and earthquakes on that planet are very good."

"I thought as much," muttered Riker. "Geordi, stand ready to beam us up."

"Yes, sir," snapped the acting captain. "Sir, may I talk privately with Data?"

"Go ahead," grumbled the first officer, "I don't have a communicator, anyway."

"You can borrow mine," offered Ensign Greenblatt, tilting her distinctive black Archer's Mask in his direction.

"Thank you, Ensign." As Riker put out his hand to take her insignia, he saw the solitary figure of Fenton Lewis waiting on the road ahead of them. "I wish everyone were as cooperative as you are," he complimented Greenblatt. "I wonder if the earthquake jarred the ambassador's memory?"

He pulled his mask back on and sloshed up the road as Greenblatt and Dr. Pulaski hurried to catch up.

On the bridge of the *Enterprise,* Geordi was headed back to the captain's ready room. "Patch it in, Wesley, and keep it confidential."

"Aye, sir."

As soon as the door breezed shut, the lieutenant called, "Data, do you read me?"

"Yes, Geordi."

"Data, what's this about the captain, Deanna, and Worf being dead?"

"Unsubstantiated," answered the android. "Ambassador Lewis has absolutely no corroborating evidence. We are looking for the alleged remains now."

"What's your gut instinct?" asked Geordi.

"I do not have a gut," Data reminded him. "But if I did, I would say that some masks have changed hands, as they often do here, but there is no proof that anyone has died."

"All right," breathed the engineer. "Nothing's official, and that's the way it stands. But do me a favor, Data . . ."

"Yes, Geordi?"

"If things get hot, let us get you out of there."

"We will. This is an intriguing culture, Geordi. I will have many interesting anecdotes when I return."

"I just want to hear one anecdote," said Geordi, "about how you rescued the captain."

"I will remember every detail. Out," Data replied.

"Out," muttered the chief engineer.

As he strode out of the ready room and headed for the center chair, Geordi knew all eyes on the bridge were upon him. His fellow officers would never pump him for information, but they would watch his every move and reaction, waiting for him to slip up and offer a clue as to what all the secrecy was about.

"The captain's away team is still missing," he announced. "We've been requested to step up our efforts to find them. What about those scanners, Wesley?"

"With a fresh layer of dust and ash circling the area," the boy sighed, "it's up to Commander Riker to find them."

"Keep trying," replied Geordi, sinking into the center chair. The red globe of Lorca kept revolving in the viewscreen, and within moments he was nervously drumming his fingers on the armrest again.

Jean-Luc Picard tried to calm his frightened pony by petting her mane and talking soothingly to her, but the animal remained skittish after the earthquake. He finally gave up and dismounted.

"Picard," barked Piercing Blade, still bouncing back and forth on her jittery pony. "We can't let a little boggle slow us down."

"With all due respect," said the captain, "I think the ponies need a rest. They seem to take the boggles more seriously than you do."

"They are dumb animals," said the warrior.

"They probably think the same about us," remarked Deanna Troi, joining the two leaders. She indicated Medicine Maker, who was rushing to catch up with her. "Captain, the earthquake isn't our only worry at the moment. Medicine Maker thinks he has seen bandits behind us."

The Thunder Mask confronted the Herbalist's Mask as Medicine Maker approached. "What did you see?"

"Only a glimpse of red, my lady," answered the healer. "But I heard voices."

Piercing Blade rose in her saddle, gripping her pony's mane to get its attention and make it stand still. Intently, she surveyed the forest behind them, as Worf, Cold Angel, Spider Wing, and the two Lorcan pages joined the conference.

"Cowards," she muttered. "They won't dare to show themselves. My guess is that we're not their intended victims. They probably hope to catch some unsuspecting travelers at the crossroads."

"What can we do, my lady?" asked Spider Wing.

"We can lie in ambush," suggested Cold Angel.

"No," the noblewoman said. "As much as I would like to teach the raider scum a lesson, we can't jeopardize our cause. We'll need everyone healthy when we get to the fair."

She jumped down from her pony, tied the reins together, and handed them to the man in the delicate Fisherman's Mask. "Cold Angel, see what you can do to calm these animals. Lead them to the crossroads, if you have to. I don't want the raiders to get a single pony of ours."

"They won't, my lady," vowed the former trainer. Within seconds, he had formed the ponies into a caravan by looping the reins of one mount over the saddle of the one in front of it. Clucking his tongue to get them moving, Cold Angel led the ponies away.

The Thunder Mask swiveled ominously as Piercing Blade scrutinized every member of the band. Jean-Luc felt as if he were back in Starfleet Academy, about to receive a particularly unpleasant assignment from a tough instructor.

"We need volunteers to guard our rear," she announced. "It will be dangerous work, because the rest of us must hurry to reach the crossroads. I think we can leave our red shadows there."

"I'll take the rear," said Picard immediately.

"I, too," replied Worf.

Spider Wing scoffed, "You don't know what to look for."

"I think we'll know if someone tries to attack us," the Klingon countered.

"We haven't time to argue," snapped Piercing Blade. "Picard and Worf, good luck to you. I welcome your valor." She made a circular motion with her arm. "Everyone else, at a run."

Piercing Blade jogged after the ponies at an easy pace. Deanna glanced at Captain Picard, and he motioned to her to follow. The other Lorcans needed no encouragement, and Worf and Picard were soon left alone on the trail, glancing uneasily over their shoulders.

"I think I know what you intend to do," said the Klingon.

The captain nodded. "We can't pass up an opportunity to talk with other Lorcans, no matter how warlike they might be. One of them could be Almighty Slayer, or they may know something about him."

"What if they really are 'raider scum'?" asked the Klingon.

"Phasers set to stun."

Geordi took his visor off and set it on the small round table. Suddenly the subtle lighting in the Ten-Forward lounge blinked out and the room was plunged into blackness as Geordi massaged his aching temples.

"This waiting is driving me crazy," he moaned to Guinan, who was delivering his chamomile tea.

"I shouldn't tell you this," she replied, "but the scuttlebutt has it that you know more than you're letting on."

"I do. But none of it's official, and scuttlebutt is the exact reason why I have to keep quiet." The engineering officer grimaced in pain as he replaced his visor. "At least, there was some news and some activity going on down there today. A huge volcano blew."

"Was anyone hurt?" Guinan asked.

"Not as far as we know."

"It doesn't sound as if the away teams are bored," she remarked.

Geordi thoughtfully stirred his tea. "Do you know what a taxicab is?"

"No," the humanoid answered.

"It's an ancient Earth conveyance, totally dependent upon a driver. Variations of it existed all over the galaxy. Basically, the driver is at the beck and call of his passenger, and he spends some of his time sitting in his vehicle waiting for his passenger to return. That's called 'keeping the meter running.'"

"Well," he sighed, "I feel like a taxicab driver who's been keeping the meter running for four days. There is absolutely nothing we can do from here, except to keep the transporter rooms ready. Each new eruption on the planet makes the cloud cover more impenetrable. Each day that passes makes *me* feel more helpless."

Guinan sat down in the chair opposite him and regarded him sympathetically. "Geordi, you are in command of the starship *Enterprise* in the middle of an emergency. Nothing you will ever do in your whole life is as important. Waiting is not inactivity—it's waiting, which can be much harder than taking direct action. The time for action will come soon, and when it does, you'll be ready."

"Thank you." The lieutenant smiled. "I know that what I'm doing is important. I needed someone to tell me that it was also hard work."

An excited voice broke through the hum of conversation in the lounge. "Ensign Crusher to Lieutenant La Forge. Urgent! Bridge to La Forge."

Geordi bolted upright in his seat and slapped his communicator badge. "Lieutenant La Forge here. What is it, Wesley?"

"Sir," gulped the teenager, "we're not the only ones interested in Lorca. A Ferengi ship has just warped into our sector and is establishing orbit around the planet."

Geordi and Guinan exchanged raised eyebrows. "Have you tried to hail her?"

"No, sir, I was waiting for you."

"I'll be right there."

Geordi stood up and took a hurried sip of tea. "You were right," he told Guinan. "Things are about to get interesting."

Chapter Ten

THE AFT TURBOLIFT DOOR whooshed open, and Lieutenant La Forge charged onto the bridge. "What's happening, Wesley? Do the Ferengi know we're here?"

"They must," answered Ensign Crusher. He punched some keys on his console, and a distinctive Ferengi vessel filled the viewscreen.

"Why would they be here?" wondered Geordi.

Ensign Crusher shrugged. "Shall I go to yellow alert?"

Frowning, the acting captain scratched his chin. "What are *they* doing?"

"Just establishing orbit. No alert, no shields, no weapons being armed. This close, we're not going to hide many secrets from each other."

"We're not at war with the Ferengi," said Geordi, "and Lorca is nonaligned. We have no reason not to be friendly."

"Yet," added Ensign Crusher, remembering unpleasant encounters with the profiteering Ferengi in the past.

"Scanners show that the Ferengi vessel has just

beamed personnel down to the planet," announced a third officer stationed at the Ops console.

"Open a hailing frequency," said Geordi, shifting nervously in his seat.

"Hailing frequency open."

Geordi finally decided to stand up. "Lieutenant Geordi La Forge, in command of the Federation Starship U.S.S. *Enterprise,* addressing the Ferengi commander."

"We know who you are," cooed a voice.

"On the screen," Geordi ordered.

At once, the viewscreen filled with the image of a short humanoid with tremendous ears. His longish nose, beady eyes, and snaggleteeth gave him a distinctly feral appearance. He was sitting at a large desk and appeared to have been interrupted during a consultation with another Ferengi, who was leaning over his shoulder. He shut off his computer terminal, and the second Ferengi abruptly left.

"Excuse me," he apologized, "for not contacting you as soon as we arrived, but I had some urgent business to attend to. I am Karue Nobnama, first officer of the Ferengi Alliance trading vessel *Lazara.* Our captain is indisposed at the moment, and I am in charge of this mission."

"And what is your mission on Lorca?" asked Geordi, trying to sound nonchalant.

The Ferengi smiled and leaned back in his overstuffed chair. "I could ask you the same question. This is a trading vessel, whereas the *Enterprise* is a famous warship. I think we can draw our own conclusions."

"Every Ferengi vessel is a trading vessel," Geordi remarked. "And the *Enterprise* is designed for exploration."

Karue Nobnama nodded, as if conceding the point. "'Exploration' is as good a term as any for what we are doing here."

"Perhaps we can pool our efforts," Geordi suggested.

The purser smiled, showing more crooked teeth. "No, I think not. Ultimately, your aims and our aims are different. The Federation wishes to expand its military dominance over the entire galaxy, whereas we wish to conduct mutually agreeable trade, nothing more."

Geordi let the remark slip by in the hope of coaxing at least some information from the Ferengi merchant. "You mean," he suggested, "you wish to develop raw resources on Lorca?"

"I mean," said the purser, his huge ears twitching, "that I am not providing more information to a competitor. Good afternoon."

The screen went blank.

"Transmission ended," a bridge officer added unnecessarily.

Geordi pounded his fist into his hand and shook his head. "Why are they so obstinate?"

"The Ferengi see nothing but the bottom line," answered Wesley Crusher. "They're concerned only about how much profit they can make. Because the Federation doesn't think like that, they don't trust us. They think we just *pretend* not to want to be like them."

"Let's look on the bright side," said Geordi, managing a weak smile as he sank back into the captain's chair. "The more eyes and ears on that planet the better. If we don't run across the captain, maybe the Ferengi will."

Commander Riker stared bleakly at the red road snaking among endless kilometers of tall brown trees. He turned his eyes skyward, and his face contorted into a look of frustration no one would ever see, thanks to his formidable Forest Mask.

"Blast the stars, Lewis! Don't you have any idea where this attack took place?"

The studious feathered mask bowed low, and Fenton Lewis kicked a clump of wormy clay off the road. "I'm sorry, Commander. One stretch of forest looks like another."

"That is not entirely true," Data said. "The road has varied in width from one meter to six. The vegetation may appear constant, but I have counted over four hundred different species. After having climbed uphill for three kilometers, we are now traveling downhill at a ten degree angle—"

"All right, Data," interrupted Katherine Pulaski. "To you, maybe it all looks different. But for us humans, this forest is incomprehensible. If it wasn't for the road, we would be lost."

Will Riker was far from satisfied with either explanation. "Lewis, you're an experienced woodsman, are you telling me that you can't even find your way back to a place where three-quarters of your party was massacred?"

The long hair shook slightly, and the wiry shoulders rose and fell as Lewis heaved a sigh. "I'm sorry you are so reluctant to believe me, Commander Riker. But you'll have to take my word for what happened."

"Starfleet regulations," said Data, "require a period of five years before a missing crew member is reported dead without positive identification of his remains. We have no choice but to continue looking."

"As I said before," countered Lewis, "Captain Picard isn't missing. He's dead. I saw him get killed. Now, if all of you want to go back to the ship, I'll continue looking."

"Not on your life," growled Riker. "If it takes five years, we'll *stay here* five years."

His communicator beeped softly from within his breast pocket, and Riker snatched it out, reminded of

Ensign Greenblatt. He glanced at her ebony Archer's Mask and gave her a smile she couldn't see. Greenblatt had lent him her communicator badge, and Data had done the code conversion to make it respond as his own. "Riker here!" he answered.

"Lieutenant La Forge," came the response. "For once, Commander, I have news for you. A Ferengi ship has just established an orbit around the planet."

"Ferengi," exclaimed Will. He glanced at Fenton Lewis, who looked away. "What do they want?"

"I hailed them," Geordi replied, "but all they would say is that they're engaged in 'exploration.' They have already beamed at least one team down to the planet surface."

Ambassador Lewis shrugged. "They've come here before. It's probably just a coincidence that they're here now."

"What have you told them about us?" asked Riker.

"Nothing," Geordi answered. "As usual, they think we're competitors for the same market."

"All right," said Riker. "Keep them under close scrutiny. I'm not thrilled about this complication."

"I don't think they are either," Geordi answered.

"Out," said Riker, putting his new communicator back into his pocket and zipping it tight.

He turned to the feathered Messenger's Mask. "Shall we catch up with Day Timer's wagon?" he asked. "Or head off in some other direction? It's up to you, Lewis. We're not leaving this planet until we find those bodies."

Jean-Luc Picard tried to get comfortable in his treetop roost, but the stump of a broken bough kept prodding him when he leaned back to rest. Also, he kept jarring moss off the branches around him, and the brown powder trickled down his collar and into his clothing.

Worf, on the other hand, looked as if he had been

born in a tree. Despite his size, he had settled comfortably into a crux of branches over Picard's head, and there he sat with his arms folded, apparently dozing. His mask hung from his belt, and his breath swirled in the frosty air.

The captain turned his attention back to the forest floor, some twenty meters below them. They had decided to observe the raiders before making contact with them, so they had selected the stoutest tree and had climbed as high up into it as they could without risking life and limb. Now the captain perched uncomfortably and Worf dozed far above the red road meandering peacefully below them.

Picard had expected the Lorcan bandits to come along much sooner, if they were really as hot on their heels as Medicine Maker had said. But something had delayed them. Maybe they wanted no truck with Piercing Blade and her band and were happy to put some distance between them. Maybe not as much time had passed as Jean-Luc thought. In the cathedrallike forest, shafts of light sneaked through the boughs like beams from a stained-glass window, and time seemed suspended.

Picard had spent most of his adult life cooped up in one type of space vehicle or another. Here, lost in the majesty of a planet still in its formative stages, his previous experiences didn't seem to matter. On Lorca, life was as intense as the cold and as real as the stump sticking into his back. On the *Enterprise*, the vastness and emptiness of space was the master. Here on Lorca the primeval force once known as Nature prevailed.

A twig cracked, snapping him out of his reverie, and Jean-Luc stared down at the rutted road snaking between the trees. From the brush, at least five red-masked Lorcans emerged on foot, stalking cautiously onto the road. Their swords were drawn and ready.

He tugged Worf's pant leg, and the Klingon stared

down at him, instantly awake. Picard put his finger to his lips and pointed toward the ground. Worf acknowledged the instructions with a silent nod.

The half-dozen raiders moved warily on, followed by another four on ponies. They moved with the precision of a crack military outfit, long accustomed to working and fighting as a team. They were followed by two more riders who looked different, alien. These riders had the bearing of generals and wore imperious silver masks, which were wider than any Lorcan masks Picard had yet seen—wide enough to accommodate tremendous ears.

Picard and Worf looked at each other, and Worf mouthed the word "Ferengi."

Jean-Luc nodded. But he was more puzzled than ever. Why were two Ferengi traveling with Lorcan outlaws? He remembered Ambassador Lewis's account of how he had come by the Ambassador's Mask. Could these Ferengi be looking for Lewis? No, that didn't seem likely, even if they had somehow gotten word that Lewis was coming to Lorca. The planet was too vast a place to conduct a manhunt, and yet the Ferengi appeared so at ease with their Lorcan escorts that they had to be allies, not prisoners.

Picard was tempted to reveal himself to the offworlders, knowing they might be able to help his party get back to the *Enterprise*. But something stopped him; some nameless instinct froze him to the tree limb until the procession of raiders and Ferengi had passed.

After they had been out of sight for some moments, Picard turned to Worf. "Those *were* Ferengi, weren't they?"

"Yes, Captain," answered the Klingon. "Do you suppose the Ferengi are helping one of the factions on Lorca?"

"They would, if they thought they could get something out of it—like the fireproof moss on these trees, or more masks for their auctions. But the Ferengi have no equivalent to our Prime Directive. They'll subvert the government, do whatever it takes, to achieve their aims."

"There isn't any government on Lorca," Worf observed.

"Except for the Wisdom Mask," Picard reminded him. "That's all the Ferengi need to rule the planet."

The Klingon stretched his long legs. "We have a more immediate concern. Do we approach the Ferengi and ask for their help in getting back to the Enterprise?"

"I think we have to try," Picard said.

The two clambered down from the gigantic tree and walked slowly along the road in the direction the raiders had taken. Without thinking twice about it, they pulled on their masks, and Picard again drew his phaser from his pocket. "Phasers set to stun."

"Yes, sir," answered Worf.

"And keep it out of sight."

"Yes, sir."

"Also, Lieutenant, if something goes wrong and we have to make a quick retreat, try to get past them and head toward Piercing Blade."

The Page's Mask nodded gravely.

Their voices carried in the hushed forest, and they could hear shouts and frantic movement ahead of them. As he strode determinedly forward, Picard's heart pounded as loudly as the horses' hooves. The initial meeting with Piercing Blade's band had resulted in violence, and these raiders were said to have fewer scruples than the average Lorcan. Would they challenge his right to wear the Trainer's Mask?

What would the Ferengi do? They hated the Federation and everything it stood for. But they had to have a ship nearby, and maybe they hadn't lost contact with it.

By the time Picard and Worf rounded a bend in the road, the raiders' party had been noisily deployed into a battle line, with those on foot in the front row and the riders behind them, all with swords drawn. The Ferengi remained in the rear, as they had in marching order.

"Peace," said Picard, palming his phaser. "We wish only to talk and to share the road with you."

The wall of red masks stared at them, as if nobody had ever before dared to stroll up to a band of raiders. They looked around nervously, as if suspecting that this was a trick.

Nothing happened for a few seconds, which seemed interminable. Worf and Picard glanced at each other, trying not to appear nervous. Finally, one of the mounted raiders waved his sword at them.

"You are brave, Trainer, I'll give you that much," he declared. "So we'll allow you to state your business before we kill you."

Picard shrugged as if death was the least of his concerns. "Is this the way the kindhearted Ferengi greet their trading partners?"

One of the silver-masked Ferengi spurred his pony past the raiders to the front of the battle line. "Who are you?" he demanded.

"On Lorca I'm an animal trainer," Jean-Luc replied, indicating his mask. Then he pointed toward the sky. "But up there, I am Captain Jean-Luc Picard of the U.S.S. *Enterprise*."

The second Ferengi urged his pony forward. "We saw your ship. We had no idea that the Federation had become so fully integrated into Lorcan society."

"It was not intentional," the captain admitted. "We came here several days ago on a diplomatic mission, but we've lost contact with our ship. To put it bluntly, we need your help to get back."

"Ah," murmured the first Ferengi. Picard could well imagine the toothy grin behind his mask. "Then you want something from us. What do you offer in return?"

"These masks," answered Jean-Luc, indicating his and Worf's facial armor. "And our gratitude."

Both Ferengi shook their heads. "Not enough," said one. "Your masks are very ordinary, and so your gratitude is worth nothing."

Most of the raiders had relaxed and lowered their guard, despite the fact that Picard and Worf had been walking steadily toward them. They were now only a few meters away from the mounted Ferengi.

"What about ponies?" Worf suggested.

"No," the other Ferengi replied. "Our friends here can get us all the ponies and Lorcan goods we need. They're very resourceful."

"Then what *do* you want?" asked Picard.

The Ferengi leaned forward and stared at the *Enterprise* officers. "We want the Wisdom Mask."

"If I knew where that was," scoffed Picard, "I wouldn't need to talk to you. The whole planet would be at my feet."

The Ferengi dealer straightened up in his saddle. "That's our price for helping you. I doubt if you have anything else of value."

"What about the Ambassador's Mask?" asked Picard innocently.

Now both Ferengi leaned forward in their saddles, and one of them motioned violently at him. "You stole that mask from us."

"Not I," said Picard. "We know all about that now. Ambassador Fenton Lewis stole the mask, an action that we gravely regret. But he wasn't acting on behalf of the Federation."

"Then why are you here?" he asked.

"Why are *you* here?" Picard replied.

The other Ferengi held up his hand. "All of this is getting us nowhere. Picard, we will supply you with transportation to your ship in exchange for either the Wisdom Mask or the Ambassador's Mask *and* Fenton Lewis."

"I might be able to secure the Ambassador's Mask," answered Picard, "but Lewis's whereabouts are unknown. Will you at least contact the *Enterprise* and tell them we're all right?"

"You've heard our offer," said the other. "Now be on your way."

"Wait," growled the raider who had spoken to them first. "We can't just let these two werjuns go. Piercing Blade's force is right ahead of us."

"They know you're here," growled Worf, matching the Lorcan in snarling fury. "You haven't fooled anyone."

The Lorcan spurred his pony and jostled the men in front of him out of the way. His mask was one solid sheet of bloodred metal with long crude wings. His eyes were hooded by the thick armor.

He flashed his sword in Worf's face. "No *page* speaks to me in that tone."

Picard expected to see the raider stunned off his mount by a sudden ray, but Worf restrained his temper and his trigger a moment longer. Jean-Luc could see his grip tightening around the phaser.

"No, Skinner, let him be," snapped a Ferengi. "They're no good to us dead."

But the Lorcan wasn't listening to reason, only to the battle lust in his adrenaline. "They must die," he screamed, lunging at Worf with his long-sword.

Before Worf had even ducked out of the way, one of the Ferengi lashed out at the raider with a slender whip. The weapon was extremely accurate, and its glowing tip struck the raider square in the chest. His entire torso lit up with an unholy charge. He screamed and his mask flew off as he toppled from his pony.

"The effect is temporary," one of the Ferengi remarked. "He'll be good as new soon."

"Minus a few million brain cells," Worf added.

A Ferengi nodded, taking the remark as a compliment. "This is quite an effective disciplinary device on some of our mining colonies."

"Undoubtedly," agreed Picard. "We'll be going now. Will you make sure we're not attacked by the others?"

"They'll be docile," the Ferengi assured him.

Most of the raiders had slunk off to the side of the road, making it easy for Worf and Picard to slip past them. They headed down the road at an easy jog, glancing often over their shoulders.

"Remember our terms," a Ferengi called. "The Wisdom Mask alone or Fenton Lewis *and* the Ambassador's Mask together."

Deanna Troi watched Piercing Blade as the warrior peered back over her shoulder one more time. Night was melting into the forest, and there had been no sign of Captain Picard and Lieutenant Worf. Piercing Blade had pushed her company to make good time and put distance between themselves and the raiders. They had rushed through the crossroads, not waiting to meet any fellow travelers. Now, thought Deanna, the noblewoman seemed to be regretting her decision.

Should she have sent her own people to guard the rear? Should she have stood her ground and fought the raiders? Deanna could sense the warrior's concern with no problem, because the same questions haunted the Betazoid. On one level, the captain and Worf had been successful: no raiders had followed them closely enough to be spotted. But that success didn't explain their long absence. Until the trainer and the page returned to camp, neither woman would be content.

The imposing figure in the Thunder Mask pulled up her pony. "Halt," she called. "We'll make camp here."

No one argued with Piercing Blade, although they easily had half an hour more of fading daylight. Cold Angel gathered up the ponies as the others dismounted. The two pages began to unpack the tents and utensils while Medicine Maker scouted for a bog. As always, Spider Wing attended to Piercing Blade, and the two of them surveyed nearby trees, deciding which one would harbor that night's campfire. The Lorcans went about their routines with practiced efficiency, but they spoke in hushed tones and displayed none of their usual joviality. Like Deanna, they sensed their leader's concern.

Counselor Troi wanted to get away from them, not to avoid work—they were all so skilled in their routines that she was superfluous anyway—but to be by herself. So she strolled north up the road, back over a small stretch they had just traveled. Personal safety was the last thing on Deanna's mind. If the Lorcans were on their heels, then the captain had failed and was probably dead. She preferred to find out sooner rather than later.

She pulled off the Page's Mask and let the chilly wind hit her face. It felt bracing, and the way things were going here on Lorca, she needed some bracing. The raw emotions on the planet, experienced by everyone including herself, were draining her. Abject fear was immediately followed by exhilaration, then the emptiness of loss. No sooner had she recovered from the stunning blow of being cut off from the *Enterprise* than Ambassador Lewis had disappeared. Now it was the captain and Worf.

Of all the emotional states, worry had to be the most unpleasant and least useful. Deanna hated succumbing to it.

Twigs crackled to her left, and she whirled around, half expecting to find that Medicine Maker had followed her. But the healer wasn't there. She heard subdued voices in the distance and the snorting of the ponies, but the camp was already out of sight among the darkening trees. Twigs and boughs rustled over her head, and she ducked instinctively. But no swords or masks came screaming out of the trees—only a few flakes of moss trickled into her hair.

Quite apart from the mysterious rustling, Deanna sensed the presence of a being watching her. More vegetation shook to her right, and she realized with a start that whoever it was had just crossed from one side of the road to the other, over her head.

"Hello?" she said cheerfully, trying to follow the tiny noises in the brush.

An abrupt chattering sounded in response, making Deanna jump back. Languorously, a large simian unfolded itself from a tree limb and swung toward her, arm and leg over arm and leg, landing gracefully in the center of the road. Now she could see it wasn't an apelike creature at all, but something thinner and more exotic. This creature couldn't stand upright on its hind legs, because they were nearly as long and slender as its undulating tail. It smiled at her and shook its round shaggy face.

"You're probably one of those creatures we saw the first day," she remarked. "But you're not scared of humans, as those were."

The werjun leapt into the air and did a somersault before it landed on all fours. Deanna applauded in spite of her gloomy mood.

"I wish I were having as much fun as you are," she said, "but I'm frightened. Are the captain and Worf all right? Even if they are, what's going to happen to us?"

The lanky creature chattered words of advice, but Deanna couldn't understand them. It did another leap, only this time it ended up hanging by its tail from a tree branch. Then, with a few graceful movements, the werjun was gone.

"You could have stayed longer," Deanna called.

"Hey," came a distant call in response to her raised voice. "Who's there?"

Deanna peered north into the gloomy forest. She could hardly see the road at all anymore, but she could make out a couple of vague shapes flitting between the giant tree trunks. They were running toward her.

"Captain?" she called.

"Deanna!" came a relieved voice.

The Betazoid took off at a run toward the jogging figures, and somewhere in the middle of the vast forest they met. She hugged Captain Picard welcomingly, then grabbed Worf's grimy hand and shook it. There were smiles all around.

"I'm sorry," she apologized, stepping back and blushing with embarrassment. "I'm just so glad to see you!"

"No need to apologize," said Picard. "We're rather relieved ourselves."

Worf's shoulders heaved as he caught his breath. "What are you doing here alone? Has Piercing Blade made camp yet?"

"Just ahead," answered Deanna. "She'll be glad to see you, too, Captain."

"She may not be glad to hear what I have to tell her."

"Why?" asked the counselor. "Are the raiders close behind us?"

Picard shook his head. "The raiders are the least of our worries. We've just met a couple of Ferengi."

Piercing Blade didn't embrace Picard the moment she saw him, but she did look up from yanking a fish line from a spewing bog. She didn't look at him again until the line was out of the spring and Spider Wing and Medicine Maker were harvesting the squirming fish.

"Ah, Picard," spoke the Thunder Mask, "you've decided to come back to us. Did you see any raiders, or has Medicine Maker been dipping into his elixirs again?"

Both Lorcan men laughed, and so did Picard. They

were all relieved to have the new trainer and page back. They were also relieved to be laughing about the raiders.

"Medicine Maker was correct," answered Picard. "We waited for them in a tree and watched them pass beneath us."

"What a fine idea," exclaimed Medicine Maker.

Piercing Blade wiped some mud from the thin fabric stretched over her breasts. "How did you get past them?"

"We talked to them."

This brought Piercing Blade up short, and the two men jerked to their feet, dropping the fish. Blade strode angrily toward the captain. "You must be in league with them, or they would've killed you."

"*We're* not in league with them," countered Picard. "The Ferengi are. It was Ferengi with whom we talked."

"Ferengi traveling with raiders?" scoffed the warrior. "Now *you* are imagining things."

"No, I'm afraid not," replied Picard. Now he wished he hadn't asked Counselor Troi and Lieutenant Worf to stay behind stripping wood for the campfire. "The Ferengi are looking for the Wisdom Mask, the same as you. I'm certain the Ferengi are trying to take over or influence the leadership."

"Ha," she laughed. "How can they influence what doesn't exist? Besides, how do I know you're telling the truth? We know how *you* stole the Ambassador's Mask from *them*."

Jean-Luc's real snarl matched the one on his fearsome Trainer's Mask. "I've told you and I've told them that that was the action of one person, Fenton Lewis. I don't know where he is now, but I refuse to be held accountable for his actions. You can take what I've told you as the truth!"

"Come to my tent," the warrior suggested, her

sinewy legs lifting her out of the muddy bog. "And we'll talk further about this." She pointed back to Spider Wing. "See that we're not disturbed."

"Yes, my lady." The Ambassador's Mask bowed.

Jean-Luc followed Piercing Blade into the oilskin tent and was again reminded of a gaily painted circus tent. The Lorcan pages were arranging lamps, rugs, and pillows on the floor for dinner. Piercing Blade motioned to them, and they quickly finished and left. The noblewoman pulled some clean garments from her pack and knelt out of sight in a dark corner of the structure.

Picard stood waiting, still fuming over Piercing Blade's apparent loyalty to the Ferengi. Didn't the Lorcans know what kind of people the Ferengi were? But he had to curb his tongue and quit preaching against them so vociferously. If it was the Lorcans' wish to ally themselves with the Ferengi instead of the Federation, then they should be allowed to make that decision. The Lorcans had fared pretty well in this hostile environment, but maybe the Ferengi were in for more than they bargained for.

When the woman emerged back into the light, she was wearing the white feathered gown, which revealed a breathtaking amount of her sumptuous figure. But the most startling part of the apparition was her unmasked face, angelic and pure, so unlike her sleek battle-hardened body.

"I'm not really mad at you," she cooed. "Perhaps I shouldn't be surprised that the Ferengi are allied with the raiders, because their attacks have been bolder and better organized lately. If the Ferengi are responsible for killing any of our citizens, they will be punished."

But the Ferengi were far from Picard's mind as he tore off his mask. "You are so beautiful, Piercing Blade."

She ran to him and began running her fingers over

his cheeks, his forehead, and his scalp. He reached behind her and filled his hands with supple flesh, roughly pulling their bodies together.

"Picard," she moaned, tightening her powerful arms behind his shoulders. "Stay with me. I'll give you Lorca."

"I don't want Lorca," he rasped. "I want *you*."

His mouth found hers, and all talk was over.

Chapter Eleven

JUST BEFORE THEY BROKE CAMP the next morning, Day Timer assembled his colorfully masked entourage, which now consisted of a nobleman, an herbalist, a teacher, an archer, and a messenger. He had gone back to wearing the simple and comfortably broken-in Peddler's Mask, which was by far the least impressive mask on display.

As the peddler stood atop his quaint wagon, sun began filtering through the trees behind him, burning away the rose-colored mist. The clay was almost dry, and the topsoil was almost devoid of worms. It promised to be an unusually warm day.

"Starting today," Day Timer told them, "our journey becomes dangerous."

Katherine Pulaski glanced at Commander Riker. Though they could only see each other's eyes, they easily expressed to each other their amazement over the suggestion that anything could be more dangerous than what they had already faced.

"We are coming to a crossroad," Day Timer explained. "From this point on, we will meet many more travelers, and not all of them will be friendly."

"Will we meet more raiders?" asked Data, in his pale mask of strange scribblings.

The Lorcan shrugged. "We could. Certainly we will meet travelers like ourselves, headed for the fair. Your behavior must be appropriate to your new masks, or we'll have to defend ourselves every step of the way."

"How should we behave?" asked the doctor.

"Act as if you were born with that mask on," the peddler answered. "Act as if you will die with it on. A moment's weakness or hesitation, and you may face a challenge. Also, we are a troupe united. An affront to one of us is an affront to all of us.

"Were I still a simple peddler traveling by myself," he continued, "I would pose little threat to anyone. Even as a proprietor with all of you as my apprentices, we would attract little notice. And you, as proper apprentices, could remain silent and obedient, allowing me to speak for you. But now you are all important personages in your own right. Especially you, Riker. Everyone we meet will want to talk to the wearer of the Forest Mask. I will be ignored."

Will touched the polished wood covering his face and realized for the first time how ostentatious the Forest Mask was, with its gleaming jewels and exquisite workmanship. What right did he have to represent himself as a member of the Lorcan nobility? He was honored by the prize and, in an odd way, would have hated to go back to the crude clay mask, but he didn't want to let his own vanity endanger his crew.

"Day Timer," he suggested, "if you think we should go back to wearing the Apprentice's Masks—"

"No!" the Lorcan shouted, aghast at the idea. "You have earned these masks. The villagers selected well, and I want you to wear them. You don't know this, Riker, but they *purchased* the Forest Mask from me in order to present it to you. Of course, I gave them a very good price."

He bowed his head. "That's not entirely the whole of it," he admitted. "I've been looking for someone to wear that mask ever since its rightful owner, an old friend of mine, was killed in a skirmish by his own son."

Day Timer waved his hand, dismissing the tragedy. "But there are many stories like that on Lorca. The torch is never passed easily." He rose to his full height and looked at each one of them in turn. "You will wear the masks, but you will do so correctly. As we always say, 'If you honor the mask, the mask will honor you.'"

Day Timer jumped down from the wagon and picked up his pony's halter. "Of course, Riker, if you were to hide in the wagon whenever there is a threat of trouble, no one would see the Forest Mask. It would be appropriate for a nobleman to ride instead of walk."

"I'll bear that in mind," the commander answered with a faint smile no one saw.

A few minutes later, they were on the move again, marching in single file behind the funny little wagon, with its blue paint and gold lettering. Commander Riker walked directly behind Fenton Lewis, keeping an eye on the man in the feathered Messenger's Mask. Fenton Lewis had been spookily quiet ever since Day Timer's lecture, and Will scrutinized him with half-closed eyes from behind the knotholes of the Forest Mask.

"Lewis," said Will, "we've come far beyond the point to which the first away team could have traveled. Yet you haven't pointed out a single place and said, 'This is it—maybe it happened here.' You're just walking along, biding your time. What do you hope to get out of this?"

"Peace of mind," Lewis replied. "You don't want to be here on Lorca, but I do. I feel a certain kinship with this planet. So why don't *you* leave? I'll stay and find the captain's remains, and I'll also finish the mission. I'm sorry things worked out the way they did, but we knew this would be a dangerous mission. There's no point in more people getting hurt."

"What would you do if we left you here alone?"

"I'd probably stop traveling with this crazy coot," answered Lewis, pointing toward the rickety wagon. I'd go on to the fair to see who ends up with the Wisdom Mask. If it's Piercing Blade, then we're all out of luck."

"Perhaps you should leave," Riker suggested. "You're the one who's had all the hard luck."

"No," snapped Lewis, shaking his mask and his shoulder-length hair defiantly. "I'm alive, and I know more than I knew coming in. That's progress! You said I was biding my time, and you're right. I happen to be very patient."

"Well, I'm not," said Riker. "If you don't substantiate your story by the end of the day, I'll have you beamed back to the *Enterprise* and placed under arrest."

"For what?" scoffed the ambassador. "For having bad luck, as you put it?"

Now it was Riker's turn to shake his head. "No, Ambassador. There's a Ferengi vessel orbiting this planet. They might be very glad to welcome you aboard."

The Messenger's Mask whirled around. "You can't do that, Riker. That's a death sentence." Lewis took a deep breath and reassumed some of his cocky assurance. "There's no extradition treaty between the Federation and the Ferengi. You have no authority to do their bounty-hunting for them."

"It was just a thought," Riker said, slowing down

and letting Fenton Lewis walk far ahead of him. He unzipped his inside pocket and took out his communicator badge.

"Riker to bridge. Come in."

"Wesley here," came the reply. "Lieutenant La Forge is in the image laboratory studying infrared scans of the planet. We're concerned about the warming trend you're having down there."

"The last thing I'm worried about is the weather," grumbled Riker. "Don't interrupt Geordi. What are the Ferengi doing?"

"Just sitting here, like us," Wesley answered. "But their transporters are getting more use than ours."

The commander sighed, then spoke again, keeping his voice low. "Ours are going to get some work tonight. Let Geordi know that one or more of us will beam up at nightfall."

"Regardless of—"

"That's right, Ensign. The personnel we have down here are too valuable to risk . . . on top of the others." His voice clouded up like the salmon-colored sky.

"Yourself included, sir," the young man reminded him.

Riker didn't contradict that remark. "We need to put together a search party to look for them over a longer period of time."

"Yes, Commander," Wes answered softly.

"Out."

"Out, sir."

Will Riker soon found himself walking at the rear of the column, beside Lieutenant Commander Data. "You don't believe Fenton Lewis, do you?" he said to the android in a dry whisper.

"No, sir, I do not," Data rasped, trying to match Riker's lowered voice. "Everything we have seen on this planet indicates that his story is simply not plausible."

The Forest Mask nodded solemnly, but the fears

180

came surging back. "His story is still possible, isn't it?"

"Many things are possible," Data acknowledged.

"You know, Data," Riker said hoarsely, "we can't spend years on this planet. We have to leave eventually, whether we find them or not."

"Of course," Data said softly.

"If that happens, I'd like to leave somebody from the *Enterprise* behind here . . . to keep looking."

"May I volunteer?" asked Data.

Riker put his hand on the android's shoulder. "I was hoping you'd say that. You seem to get along with Day Timer, and maybe he'll look after you. You might develop an affinity for this place."

"I already have," Data replied. "With all of us wearing these masks, I feel less different than the rest of you. Nobody knows I am an android. They think I am human."

Will patted the android on the back, happy that somebody had found something to like about Lorca. "This would be a wonderful land to explore," he agreed, "if our purpose here wasn't so serious."

"Do not despair, Commander," said Data. "If we find them, they will be alive."

Will Riker nodded, unwilling to face Data's "if" and unwilling to consider the alternative to "alive." Never to see Deanna or the captain or Worf again? Never, perhaps, to know what really happened to them? They would just no longer be at his side. They would be gone from his life, as they were now. It wasn't a future he cared to contemplate. The thought of the combined loss was so monstrous that he could hardly conceive of it.

He forced himself to see the irony of the situation— that his shipmates should vanish on a primeval planet instead of in space, where they spent so much of their lives.

"Whoa!" came a loud cry from ahead of them. Day

Timer had stopped his wagon, but Riker could see only the latticework atop the cab because a thick stand of cane blocked his view. Ensign Greenblatt rushed past Data and Riker and ran toward the stalled wagon. Something was happening; Fenton Lewis was slowly edging his way into the forest, keeping out of sight.

Dr. Pulaski joined Data and the commander. "What happened? What's going on?"

"Unknown," said Data.

"Let's wait for Greenblatt to return," Riker ordered, keeping the other two from pressing forward.

The ensign returned a moment later. "The crossroad is at the bottom of this incline," she explained, "and we can see at least two riders down there. From this distance, even Day Timer can't tell who they are. He says the commander should get in the wagon."

"This is ridiculous," grumbled Riker. "I'm not going to hide."

"Part of Day Timer's plan is to have some hidden reserves, to keep our full strength unknown to them," Greenblatt said. "The element of surprise often works."

"Like the Trojan Horse," added Pulaski.

"All right," Riker muttered. "But let's do everything we can to help Day Timer deal peacefully with them. Doctor, you and I will hide in the wagon."

"Very good."

"Data, if they look reliable, ask them about the captain."

"Yes, sir."

"And, Greenblatt," said Riker ominously, "keep an eye on Ambassador Lewis. Tell me later how he behaved and what he did."

"Yes, sir."

The doctor and the commander cautiously approached Day Timer's wagon. Wordlessly, they lowered the tailgate and climbed inside. As far as Data could see, Day Timer never even looked back or acknowledged them, but he snapped the reins as soon as they had closed the wagon door. The pony plodded on, unmindful of her hidden cargo.

Data and Ensign Greenblatt hurried to catch up with the wagon. The android saw the young security officer reach for her phaser and realize with a start that it was still in the wagon.

"Have courage," Data told her. "Perhaps that is another reason our cagey guide wanted someone in the wagon."

The blond woman nodded, then looked around. "Where's Ambassador Lewis?"

Data pointed to his left and behind him. "He is doing a very good job of staying out of sight. I would not worry about him."

"We have enough to worry about without him," the ensign agreed, striding toward the crossroad.

The two riders sitting at the crossroad astride their ponies were very impressive. Their masks were of smooth unadorned silver metal, as if the riders had no identity except for their obvious wealth. Sweeping wings on their masks did much to hide the most impressive aspect of their appearance, their monstrous ears, but the appendages were still eye-catching.

The travelers were Ferengi, concluded Data. He did not find this surprising, because he knew that a Ferengi ship was orbiting the planet. He was, however, disappointed, because he had been looking forward to meeting more Lorcans.

Day Timer straightened up in his seat and scratched under his mask, as if surprised to meet another bunch of off-worlders. He must think his planet is being invaded, thought Data. In a way, it was.

"Good morning to you," Day Timer hailed the mounted Ferengi. "Will you please allow my humble wagon and my traveling companions to pass?"

"Absolutely." The nearest Ferengi nodded, pulling

savagely on his reins and forcing his pony back. "Where are you headed?"

"To the fair at Cottage Meadow," the peddler answered. "On, girl," he barked, encouraging his plodding pony to move along. Data and Greenblatt walked nonchalantly behind him.

"The new king will be crowned there, isn't that so?" asked the second Ferengi, not moving out of the way.

Day Timer bowed reverently. "If the dragon is willing."

The big-eared trader rode out in front of Day Timer's wagon, forcing the peddler to pull up sharply. The Ferengi drew a slender whip from his saddle and pointed it at the Lorcan. "You're a peddler, aren't you?"

"As poor as my mask." Day Timer nodded. Then he abruptly dropped the obsequious tone. "Why are you delaying me?"

"We want to see what you have to sell," he answered. "We are customers."

With his unassuming Peddler's Mask, the Lorcan found it easy to slip back into a submissive attitude. "I have nothing for the likes of fine noblemen like yourselves, only simple things for poor people—fire starters, clay masks, and bits of fabric."

Now the other alien rode to the side of the wagon and stared into the peddler's face. "You have masks for sale?"

Day Timer averted his eyes. "Only clay ones, fit for serfs, apprentices, and assorted vassals."

"We'd like to look," his inquisitor demanded.

Day Timer took a jocular tone. "Then come to the fair. I'll have my own place and will be easy to find. A couple of noblemen such as yourselves will have a grand time there."

"Oh, we'll be there," the Ferengi assured him. "But we'd like to look at your wares now. Frankly, I don't understand your reluctance to display your goods.

Why are you in business? We're collectors, and we pay very well, especially for fine masks."

Day Timer held out his hands in a helpless gesture. "No offense, but I'd rather save my wares for the fair. Why can't you honor my position and let me pass?"

A Ferengi pointed to Ensign Greenblatt in her darkly handsome Archer's Mask. "What about you? How much will you take for that mask you are wearing?"

"It's not for sale," said Greenblatt proudly. "I was born with this mask on, and I will die with it on."

"A noble sentiment," agreed the Ferengi. "And typical for the barbarians of this planet."

Data felt it was time to intervene. "You are Ferengi," he said loudly enough for those inside the wagon to hear. "We are Lorcans. We have more right than you to travel this road. So why do you molest us?"

Data's stern tone worked, at least temporarily. "Forgive our rudeness," said one interplanetary trader, "but we are short of time. We have to make our acquisitions as soon as possible. So, please, show us what you have for sale."

"I will be delighted to do so," Day Timer replied, "at the fair. Now *please* let us pass. We are late already."

"I think not," the other Ferengi snarled. He held up his hand and made a circling motion. At once, the trees rustled, the cane snapped, and red-masked Lorcans sprang out of the forest, brandishing swords and pikes. They growled and snarled like badly kept animals.

Data and Greenblatt hurried toward the wagon. "Surrounded by raiders," said Data loudly, "a large party."

"Whom are you talking to?" a Ferengi asked the teacher. "And how did you know I was a Ferengi? Have we met before?"

"Word travels," Data explained. "But we had not heard that the noble Ferengi were thieves."

"What have we stolen?" asked the other Ferengi, sounding injured by the accusation. "Our red-masked friends here have been known to steal, however, so it would be wiser to deal with us. We will *buy* your masks, but there's no telling what our companions might do. Also, we pay top price for information—if you know where the Wisdom Mask is."

Erupting like a volcano, Day Timer stood in his seat and harangued the arrogant traders. "If you travel in the company of thieves, you must be thieves. Why aren't *you* wearing red masks?"

"Careful, peddler," warned the nearest Ferengi, shaking his lithe whip at him. "Our friends here know how to kill, but we know how to inflict pain."

Inside the wagon, Riker held his communicator close to his lips and whispered urgently, "Riker to *Enterprise*. Riker to *Enterprise*. Keep your voice down when you respond."

"Understood, Commander," Wesley whispered. "This is Ensign Crusher."

"Wesley, I haven't got time to explain, but I need a diversion. Can you arrange a mild temblor down here?"

"Uh, sure." The teenager sounded puzzled. "A photon torpedo would work, but the effects could be disastrous. We could also beam a detonator into a seismic fault."

"That would take too long," muttered Riker. "I need something right now."

"What about a dummy torpedo, like the ones we use to test the launchers?" suggested Wesley.

"Try it," said Will, checking his chronometer. "In exactly sixty seconds."

"But the risks," Wesley protested. "If the cloud cover increases, we won't be able to beam you up tonight."

"Do it," said Riker. "Out."

The commander handed a pistol phaser to Kate Pulaski. "I know you hate these things, Doctor, so I don't have to tell you to use it only as a last resort."

"No, you don't," agreed the doctor, hefting the weapon. She removed her mask and smiled bravely at him.

"Who's inside there?" demanded an angry Ferengi voice, accompanied by pounding on the side of the wagon. "I hear voices in the wagon!"

Will adjusted his Forest Mask, kicked open the tailgate of the wagon, and leapt out. He was careful to quickly close the gate behind him to keep anyone from seeing Kate and her phaser.

"The Forest Mask," exclaimed one of the raiders in awe.

Riker strolled cockily to the center of the crossroad, staring down the red-masked Lorcans, many of whom lowered their weapons.

"He is a follower of Almighty Slayer," said another raider. "He may know where the Wisdom Mask is."

The Ferengi spurred their ponies and jockeyed for position in front of the stoic nobleman.

"I'll match your weight in aluminum for that mask," claimed one of them.

"Where can we find more like it?" squealed the other.

Riker pointedly ignored them and appealed to the raiders. "Fellow Lorcans," he intoned, "the dragon who lives at the center of the earth is displeased with your actions. He can't understand why you would strip your motherland of her most precious possessions in order to enrich these scavengers."

"Hold your barbaric tongue," growled the Ferengi with the whip, "or I'll silence it for you."

Where are you Wesley? thought Riker. *Come on, Wesley!*

* * *

Wesley Crusher stood at the weapons console on the bridge of the *Enterprise,* double-checking his co-ordinates. He couldn't be certain that the planet's dense atmosphere wouldn't alter the flight of a nonfissionable missile, so he targeted it directly at an active volcano. More than likely, no life-forms would be endangered inside a volcano, and a hit in such a place would have the best chance of causing the diversion that Commander Riker needed. He thought of a dozen other measures he wanted to take, but his time was up.

"Torpedo away," he announced, pressing a flashing red button.

The Lorcan atmosphere had minimal impact on the course of the missile as it sliced through strata of dust and ash. It struck a volcanic peak near the planet's equator, causing a small crater. But the impact compressed the seething lava inside the volcano, forcing air bubbles to the top, which took up more room and further weakened the crust. Seconds later, when the lava expanded again, the peak of the mountain exploded, spewing tons of molten debris into the air. One shuddering explosion touched off another, as a ring of interconnected volcanoes belched up their fiery contents.

While explosions echoed in the distance, the ground in the forest pitched wildly. The clay crust ripped apart, sending geysers of steaming water spouting thirty meters into the air. The gigantic trees swayed and groaned ominously while branches snapped off and plunged down to the forest floor. Somehow Riker stayed on his feet, but the Ferengi in front of him wasn't so lucky. His pony unceremoniously dumped him and bolted.

The Ferengi stood up, his mask askew, and started to come after Riker with his whip. But he was knocked off his feet by one of his own raiders, who rushed past him in screaming fear. Panic was the order of the day, with everyone rushing for cover, which didn't exist. Will Riker tried to account for his own people but could spot only Data, standing serenely in the center of the road, staring up. Then he saw Day Timer, crouching by the side of the road, covering his head with his arms. Where was the wagon? Where were Dr. Pulaski, Ensign Greenblatt, and Ambassador Lewis?

Suddenly Data ran to Day Timer, scooped up the peddler, and carried him out of the way—just as a tree trunk crashed down on the spot where he had been huddled.

Within seconds, the sky turned blood red and as dark as night. Riker stumbled around in the darkness, calling his shipmates' names, but the groaning of the earth drowned him out. Finally he felt someone grip his arm and he whirled around gratefully—only to find Fenton Lewis tugging on his sleeve.

"Beam us out of here," Lewis yelled, his Messenger's Mask perched on the back of his head.

"Are you kidding?" Riker barked. "They couldn't even *find* us in this."

With both hands, Lewis gripped Riker by his collar. "You've got to try."

Will shoved him away, then stumbled up the road, calling, "Doctor! Greenblatt! Data!"

Suddenly, in the darkness, something clubbed him on the back of his head, and Riker fell into the mushy clay, unconscious.

Until the darkness struck, Captain Picard had managed to keep track of his traveling companions throughout the devastation. They had stopped only moments before to rest the ponies, and they were fortunate that no one was mounted at the time. Counselor Troi maintained a steady grip on Picard's arm while Lieutenant Worf stood back-to-back with him in a typical Klingon battle position, batting away any branches that hurtled toward them.

Until the red darkness fell, the captain could see Cold Angel valiantly trying to restrain and comfort the ponies, with little regard for his own safety. He could also see Piercing Blade gathering up her charges, trying to protect Medicine Maker, Spider Wing, and the two pages while they in turn tried to protect her.

Then came the darkness, and Jean-Luc was extremely grateful for Worf's and Deanna's presence. He fought the urge to run to Piercing Blade's side and remained where he belonged, with his crew.

He could do nothing but ride out the eruptions and hope that the planet stayed in one piece.

Chapter Twelve

LIEUTENANT LA FORGE burst onto the bridge from the turbolift, waving his arms agitatedly. "Ensign Crusher," he barked, "what is going on? What in blazes are you doing?"

"Obeying orders," said Wesley glumly, leaning over the Vulcan officer who sat at the Mission Ops station. "Can you raise them at all? Do any frequencies work?"

"Negative," the woman replied. "But the eruptions are starting to subside."

They all stared at the main viewscreen and could see a patch of burgundy clouds swirling over the planet, like an ugly bruise on a peach. Geordi took several deep breaths and tried to calm himself. "Keep trying to raise Commander Riker," he ordered. "Ensign Crusher and I will be in the captain's ready room."

He waved curtly, and the young ensign lowered his head and started to follow him out, but the Vulcan officer spoke again: "The Ferengi vessel is hailing us."

Geordi flapped his arms, as if to ask what else could

happen. He turned quickly to Wesley. "Give me the short version. What did you shoot? And why?"

"I launched a neutralized torpedo," Wesley answered, "in response to the commander's request for a diversion."

Geordi glanced around the bridge and saw nods of affirmation from everyone except the Vulcan woman, who kept her eyes riveted on her instruments. "The Ferengi commander demands a response," she said matter-of-factly.

"On the screen," Geordi said. He waved Wesley to his post at the conn station and turned to the main viewscreen, forcing a friendly smile.

He was greeted by a half-dozen angry Ferengi faces. "This is the captain of the *Lazara,*" growled the shortest and ugliest of the big-eared humanoids. "Why are you attacking Lorca? We have personnel on that planet."

"There's been a mistake," Geordi replied. "We were testing a photon torpedo launcher with a dummy torpedo, and the torpedo was mistakenly fired toward the planet."

"Directly at an active volcano?" the Ferengi snarled. "Don't you know how volatile that planet is?"

Geordi feigned innocence. "We do now."

The Ferengi's eyes narrowed with suspicion. "*Why* are you testing your photon torpedoes? Do you expect to engage battle soon?"

"No," answered Geordi, pretending to take umbrage at the suggestion. "It's part of the routine maintenance schedule we perform while in orbit."

The Ferengi captain looked extremely skeptical. "Such actions are incredibly reckless."

Geordi shot a glance at Wesley Crusher. "I would agree."

"If any of our personnel or property have been harmed," warned the Ferengi commander, "we will hold the Federation responsible. And we will demand full restitution."

"I understand." Geordi nodded. "We have personnel on the planet as well. It wasn't intentional."

"You won't frighten us away from Lorca," concluded the Ferengi captain, slicing the air with a white-gloved hand. The viewscreen went blank.

Geordi sighed and slumped into the captain's chair. "Ensign Crusher, I want a full report, accompanied by the transcript of your conversation with Commander Riker."

"Yes, sir," the boy muttered.

"In particular," said Geordi, "I want to know why I wasn't notified. Now put the planet back on the screen."

"Yes, sir." Wesley brought the inflamed clouds and curved horizon back into view.

The Vulcan at the Mission Ops panel straightened her back. "Reception is faint," she said, "but we have a signal from Lieutenant Commander Data."

"Enhance it," Geordi instructed, leaning forward excitedly. "Data, this is Geordi. Is everybody all right?"

"Unknown, at present," answered Data, rising from his knees beside Will Riker's unconscious body. Day Timer, who remained with the fallen figure, was carefully removing Riker's Forest Mask. A few meters away, Fenton Lewis paced nervously.

The android peered into the artificial dusk. "I am fine. Commander Riker is with me, but he is unconscious. Ambassador Lewis is accounted for, but I cannot find either Dr. Pulaski or Ensign Greenblatt."

"How badly hurt is the commander?" asked Geordi worriedly.

"At the very least," said Data, "he has a concussion. But his reflexes remain good. When we find the doctor, we'll know more."

"Shall we beam him up?"

Data shook his head. "No. In these cases it is best not to move the patient until we're sure there's no spinal or neurological damage."

"Agreed," said Geordi. "I can't tell you how sorry we are about what happened. It showed a terrible lack of judgment on our part."

"Under the circumstances," answered the android, "Ensign Crusher couldn't have done anything else. I overheard only part of his conversation with Commander Riker, but we were about to be attacked by a combined force of Ferengi and Lorcans. Obviously the diversion was substantially larger than we would have wished, but it did disperse our attackers."

"I see," Geordi answered, turning to look at Ensign Crusher. He gave the teenager a weak smile.

Data continued to peer into the gloom. "I think I see the doctor," he said. "I will contact you again later."

"Please," answered Geordi. "Out."

The acting captain stood and walked behind Ensign Crusher at the conn console. He briefly clasped the boy's shoulder. "Ensign Crusher, you have the bridge again. I'm going back to the lab to see if we can determine what effect all those eruptions had on the planet."

"Yes, sir." Wesley nodded, appreciating the vote of confidence. "I'll have a report for you . . . on the incident."

"Belay that order," said Geordi softly. "We could spend the rest of our careers writing reports about this mission. Just inform me as soon as you hear more about Commander Riker."

"Yes, sir."

Data rushed down the road toward the two slow-moving figures. He was followed at a respectful distance by Fenton Lewis, who was pulling his mask back on. Katherine Pulaski had her arm around Ensign Greenblatt and was obviously favoring one leg. She carried her Herbalist's Mask, and Greenblatt was carrying her Archer's Mask as well as another mask that Data had never seen before. Masks were the least of his concerns at the moment.

"Doctor," he exclaimed, relieving the ensign and transferring Dr. Pulaski's weight to himself. "Are you injured?"

"Just my ankle," she muttered. "It could be far worse. When all the commotion started, Day Timer's pony took off like a shot. And what a ride he gave me in the back of that wagon." She pointed behind her. "We crashed into the trees somewhere down the road. Thank heavens Ensign Greenblatt ran after me and pulled me out. Is anyone else injured?"

Data nodded glumly. "Commander Riker is unconscious."

"Let me see him," demanded the doctor, brushing away Data's arm. "It's all right, Data. I have to try to walk on it, or it may stiffen up."

They watched wordlessly as Kate Pulaski hobbled to the spot where Commander Riker lay unconscious. Day Timer rose to his feet and let the healer take over. After a moment, the old peddler saw Greenblatt and rushed angrily to her side.

"That mask," he hissed, pointing to her hands. "Give it to me."

The blond woman held up her black Archer's Mask and another, much older, piece of facial armor. In the dim light seeping through the crimson clouds, Greenblatt couldn't make out the details of the unfamiliar mask, but Day Timer evidently had no trouble recognizing it. He grabbed it from her hands and wrapped his arms around it protectively.

"I'm sorry, Day Timer," said Greenblatt, "but I have bad news for you. The eruption scared your pony, and . . . she ran head first into a tree. She's dead, and there's not much left of your wagon. I was looking for our equipment when I found that mask in the wreckage—"

Fenton Lewis stepped forward. "May I see it?"

"No," growled the peddler, tightening his arms around the artifact. "It's nothing—just an old mask."

"I was in your wagon before," Greenblatt remarked, "and I didn't see it. You must have kept it in a secret compartment."

"Where I kept it is no concern of yours," growled the peddler with surprising testiness. After a moment, he spoke again, softly. "I'm sorry. With everything that's happened . . . Where is my wagon?"

"Past the crossroads," answered the ensign, pointing down the dark road.

Day Timer nodded and jogged off, still clutching the newly discovered mask to his chest.

"He's acting quite suspicious," observed Fenton Lewis. "Did anybody get a good look at that mask?"

A moan came from the ruddy gloom behind them. They turned to see Commander Riker struggling to sit up as Kate Pulaski guided and restrained him.

"Agh, my head," he groaned, gripping the back of his skull as if expecting it to pop off.

"Good old smelling salts did the trick," Pulaski remarked proudly. "He's all right, but he'll have a terrific headache until I find my hypo."

"I'll live," moaned Riker, craning his neck and grimacing with the pain. He stared at the treetops, now deceptively still. Lorca's sun was struggling to peek through the darkness, and Riker had to remind himself that it was only midmorning.

He blinked his eyes, which burned from all the pollutants in the air, and looked down. A small group of people had gathered around him, and he felt lucky to have such loyal comrades. Then he saw the owlish Messenger's Mask and he exploded angrily.

"You hit me," Riker accused Fenton Lewis. "You're the one who knocked me out."

"You're crazy," scoffed the ambassador. He pointed to a huge crooked branch, one of many littering the forest floor. "That's what hit you."

"Most likely," observed Data.

Riker took a deep breath and shrugged it off. With Data's help, he staggered to his feet. "At least," he groaned, "the eruptions are over. When you ask Ensign Crusher for a diversion, he doesn't hold anything back."

"But it was effective," said Data. "The raiders have fled."

"The Ferengi will round them up," muttered Dr. Pulaski.

Riker scowled, still massaging the back of his head. "If the Ferengi are helping the raiders, it means they're taking an active role in determining Lorca's future. If past performance is any indication, the Ferengi may try to enslave the entire population of this planet."

"The Lorcans need the Federation," said Kate Pulaski. "But how can we convince them?"

Riker shook his head. "I don't know. Where's Day Timer?"

Pulaski pointed down the road. "His pony's dead, and his wagon has been destroyed. He's gone to look at it."

"Was nothing salvageable?" asked the commander.

"A mask," said Fenton Lewis. "A mask that he had kept hidden from us."

Reminded of masks, Riker bent down and picked up his own Forest Mask. He was grateful to see that it had remained in one impressive piece. "Has anyone contacted the ship?"

"I have," answered Data. "They are concerned about us."

Commander Riker sighed loudly. "I don't blame

them. We can't just stumble around down here, accomplishing nothing. We're no closer to finding the captain, or anyone in charge of government affairs. Until we find someone to deal with, we're not going to get anywhere."

"That's what I've been trying to tell you," said Fenton Lewis. "All of you are wasting your time. I've offered to stay and look for the captain's remains. I'll also go to the fair and see who emerges as Lorca's leader. Why don't you let me do my job while you go back to doing yours?"

Although his head was still throbbing, Will Riker forced himself to make a decision. Lorca was volatile in more ways than one. Its problems couldn't be solved in a matter of days; months or years could be needed to sort out the ascendancy to the throne. Now, with the Ferengi exerting their influence on the Lorcans, diplomacy was called for. As much as he hated to admit it, Riker thought maybe Fenton Lewis, a professional, was the right one for the job.

Another incident like the one they had just survived, and the *Enterprise* wouldn't have a captain at all. It was foolish and stubborn of him to remain on the planet. He had argued against Captain Picard accompanying the away team, and look what had happened. Now *he* was the captain, and he had to use the same logic to persuade himself to return to the ship.

"All right," sighed Riker, "a small party will remain on the planet. Data has already agreed to stay behind, to keep looking for the captain, Worf, and Counselor Troi.

"Ambassador Lewis will also stay," he continued, "to fulfill his original mission, in however much time it takes him. Ensign Greenblatt, I would like you to stay as well, but I can't order you to. You're assigned to the *Enterprise,* and I can't transfer you permanently to a post on this planet unless you volunteer. At this point, you know as much about the planet as anyone, and I believe you will be useful to Lieutenant Commander Data and the ambassador. Of course, you know the dangers—"

The ensign jutted her chin forward. "I'll be honored to stay, sir."

"So the rest of us are going back?" asked Kate Pulaski, not hiding her disappointment.

Riker nodded. "We're too valuable to stay here. The *Enterprise* needs us."

"We need you, too," insisted an urgent voice.

They whirled around to see a familiar figure emerging from the shadows, wearing an unfamiliar mask. Gone was the simple clay affair. In its place was an old mask, older than any Lorcan artwork they had yet seen. On a bronze frame shaped like an elliptical shield lay a bed of beautiful mosaic in aquamarine, coral, and gold-flecked ivory. The tiny tiles formed a whirlpool, or maybe a spiral nebula in deep space. The effect was hypnotic, drawing the viewer's eyes into the knowing eyes of the wearer. With each movement of Day Timer's head, the fragments of the mosaic seemed to shift and re-form in new designs.

Contrasting with this ethereal whorl but somehow emanating from it was a border of ruby crystals. From a heavy wooden ring they fanned outward like feathers to form a crimson mane around the mask. While the mosaic suggested eternity and serenity, the crystals suggested explosion and force, like a sun's corona. It was a perfect mask for Lorca. Like the planet itself, the mask was full of beauty and promise but constantly changing and slightly sinister. Will found it hard to believe that the artist hadn't traveled extensively in space. Judging by the apparent age of the mask, maybe he had.

No one spoke as the ancient and somewhat frightening mask bore down on them. "The peddler's wagon is gone," rasped the old peddler. "So Day Timer is gone, too. Now you can meet the person you've been seeking—Almighty Slayer."

"The Wisdom Mask," Fenton Lewis gasped, reaching out toward the prize.

The Lorcan knocked his hand away. He put his hand on the hilt of his sword, but he didn't draw it. "I've killed many more than your number to guard this mask. Whether I choose to wear it or not, it's mine. I'll not give it to you, to the Ferengi, to Piercing Blade, or to anyone. So put that thought out of your minds."

"We don't want your mask," said Riker. "But why didn't you tell us who you were?"

"Because," their old guide said hesitantly, "I ceased being Almighty Slayer. I hid the Wisdom Mask and became a peddler. Was that cowardly of me? I don't know, but I didn't think I had any more to learn as a warrior. I had fought my share of battles and duels, and fighting was like a nagging wife I couldn't get rid of. I met an old peddler on the road one day and bought him out.

"Since then," he continued, "my life has been full of freedom. My responsibilities have been only to myself. For the first time, I could stop sharpening my sword long enough to enjoy a good meal, some idle conversation, or a sunny day. But now," he murmured, "Day Timer has died with his wagon and his pony. The clay masks are shattered, and so is that way of life."

"By letting someone else wear the Wisdom Mask, you could return to being Day Timer," suggested Data.

"No," said the man in the mosaic mask. "I knew this day would come. I was going to the fair to resume my rightful leadership, and I might as well go as who I really am. Lorca needs a ruler more than a peddler."

Ensign Greenblatt looked concerned. "You'll be challenged everywhere you go."

"Probably," the leader agreed. "Without your help, I may be killed before I get to Cottage Meadow."

Out of respect, Dr. Pulaski slipped her mask back on. "We can't help you, Day Timer—er, Almighty Slayer. We can't get involved in your internal affairs."

"Just come with me," the legendary warrior begged. "I must have an entrourage, if I am to survive."

"I'll go with him," Lewis offered. "We can discuss trade agreements and treaties on the way, and I can tell him about the Federation. It's better than leaving him to the mercy of the Ferengi."

Commander Riker rubbed his eyes before putting on his own mask. Why did he feel such a sense of responsibility to this place? Was it because the Lorcans were descended from Earth stock? Or was it simply because they were unique in the galaxy? More than likely, it was the wiry old man in front of him, now wearing the grandest mask of all, who compelled him to help the Lorcans.

"All right," said Riker, his voice sounding hollow within the mouth chamber of the Forest Mask, "we'll stay with you as far as the fair. Do you think Piercing Blade and her band will be there?"

"I'd be very surprised if they weren't," answered the man in the Wisdom Mask. "She'll be the hardest one to deal with."

"I want to verify the ambassador's claim that the first away team was killed," replied Commander Riker, staring at the Messenger's Mask, "since we have no bodies to verify it."

"You're a stubborn fool," Fenton Lewis snapped, shaking his head in disbelief. "You'll risk your life and the life of your ship's doctor just to prove me a liar. Well, that's fine. The *Enterprise* doesn't deserve a captain as reckless as you."

This pushed Riker over the edge, and he lunged for

Lewis. No sooner had he grabbed him by the collar than the ambassador pulled a stiletto from his shirt-sleeve and stuck it under Will's chin. Data pulled the long-haired woodsman back as Greenblatt and Dr. Pulaski restrained Riker.

"That's enough," barked Kate, forcing her way between the combatants. Commander Riker heaved his big shoulders and composed himself, while Fenton Lewis shook off Data's grip and slipped his knife out of sight.

"Why not let them fight?" suggested Almighty Slayer. He pointed to Fenton Lewis. "This one seems determined to get himself killed, and Riker may be warrior enough to do it."

"Federation personnel don't fight each other," Pulaski exclaimed.

"It won't happen again," muttered Riker. "We're all on the same team, and I wish we would start cooperating."

Lewis straightened the sleeves of his hide jacket. "I wish everyone would act rationally," he said. "We now know that the dangers on Lorca are far worse than we had expected, and I'm the only one who has to be here. Why can't the rest of you admit that beaming down here was a mistake and staying here is an even bigger mistake?"

"The captain would do the same for us," said Pulaski.

"You cling to your sentimentality," answered Lewis. "Just be careful it doesn't get you killed. I'm walking ahead to make sure the Ferengi have really gone."

The ambassador turned on his heel and walked into the dusky gloom. A few rays of sun trailed after him, and it looked as if the worst of the cloud cover had started to disperse.

"He has something to hide," said Riker. The commander turned to Ensign Greenblatt. "How did he behave when we were confronted by the raiders and the Ferengi?"

"I don't know," she answered. "He stayed in hiding the whole time."

"I rest my case," murmured Riker.

The peddler-turned-king waved them all forward. "We're wasting time. We have to get to the fair and enlist some supporters. Come."

He strode down the road, as the others glanced at one another. "Go ahead," said Riker, reaching for his communicator badge. "I'll contact the ship and let them know we're all right. Go ahead—don't keep the king waiting."

Data, Greenblatt, and the doctor adjusted their masks and dutifully followed the departing figure. Well, thought Riker, watching them go, at least part of their mission had been a success. They had found the mysterious Almighty Slayer.

The death of a friend was never easy to accept, even when the living were prepared to face it. But to lose a comrade unexpectedly to an accident of blind fate was doubly painful and frustrating. Piercing Blade had beaten the ground, cursed the dragon, and screamed with anger, but there was no resurrecting the immobile figure lying in the damp clay. There was no denying the dried blood around his neck and chest. There was no consoling his friends, who stood gathered around his body, staring helplessly.

Spider Wing was dead.

Long after the volcanic chaos had ended, while his comrades were busy comforting the ponies, Spider Wing had gone ahead to ensure safe passage for his would-be queen. No one had seen the blow that felled Spider Wing, but the attitude of his body suggested that he had been inspecting a small bog when it had erupted. A stone about half as large as a man's fist had struck him in the Adam's apple, missing the protection of the Ambassador's Mask by a centimeter. Had he not been so determined to protect his queen, thought Deanna Troi, he would still be alive.

She felt like a ghoul for thinking about it, but she wondered whether the resplendent mask would be buried with him? Or maybe they didn't have conventional interments on Lorca. Deanna had once done a study of the burial customs of various cultures, and she knew they could range from elaborate funerals to cremation to dismembering the body and distributing the parts to friends and family members as souvenirs.

She preferred Starfleet's custom of beaming a body into space. It was elegant and simple, but it didn't leave a lasting monument, as required by some societies. The Klingons, on the other hand, threw a body out with the trash, considering it totally worthless after the spirit had departed. Much could be learned about a culture from the way it buried its dead, Deanna thought, waiting to see what the Lorcans would do.

Everyone was apparently waiting for Piercing Blade to vent her grief. She had knelt over the body for a long time, her mask hiding her emotions. But her hands gave her away, as she wrung them in anguish. Finally, she laid her open palms on Spider Wing's chest and turned her eyes heavenward. Captain Picard, Worf, and the Lorcans stood perfectly still.

"Mighty Dragon," she intoned in a quavering voice, "you have chosen to reclaim one of your children, our noble companion, Spider Wing. He had only recently worn the Ambassador's Mask, but he was always *my* ambassador, my protector, my first-line defender. Some resented his closeness to me, his arrogance . . . But he was my shield when I needed a shield and my spear when I needed a spear.

"The tasks he performed for me were necessary, and he performed them without complaint, without concern for his own safety." Now the warrior's voice broke, and she lowered her head and gripped Spider Wing's chain mail. "No longer will he help me pull fish from the bog. No longer will he help me sow the barley or shoe the ponies. He was always delighted with a good catch or a good crop. He wanted his countrymen to eat well, to live a dignified life."

Her voice rose in volume, and the Thunder Mask gleamed like an amber flame under the red skies. "I swear, as surely as the dragon breathes fire, that Spider Wing's sacrifices will not go unrewarded. I will honor him in battle, if I must, to bring harmony to Lorca."

"Aye! Hear, hear!" shouted her companions.

She ripped the mask from Spider Wing's face. The calm peace of his pale unlined face made him appear much younger than Deanna had imagined him to be. He looked like a boy with a reddish beard.

Piercing Blade stood up and drew her sword. "To the bog that killed him!"

"To the bog that killed him!" echoed her followers.

Worf raised his sword with the others. "To the bog that killed him!"

They surrounded the spring that had hurled the projectile and began hacking at it with their swords. In a frenzy, they took out all their anger and frustration on the mushy wormy clay, carving out a hole and letting loose a torrent of grimy water that covered everyone. But it didn't matter, for their task was to widen the sinkhole until it could accept a body, and they weren't about to quit until they had done it.

When the diggers began to slip, and it appeared one or more of them might go down with Spider Wing, Piercing Blade dragged them out of the hole. She was still clutching the Ambassador's Mask, which she used like a baton to direct their actions. They lifted Spider Wing and propelled him head first into the frothing geyser, then watched solemnly as he was sucked out of sight by the water.

The diggers cheered lustily as the earth consumed the body.

Biologically sound, thought Counselor Troi, if a bit gruesome. Worf was at her side, a thick layer of fresh clay now covering several layers of old dirt. Every indication of his status as a Starfleet officer was long obscured.

"That was exhilarating," he panted.

Captain Picard joined them, the hair of his animal mask still dripping wet from the geyser eruptions. "We need to get back to the *Enterprise*. Do you have any ideas?"

Worf heaved his big shoulders. "We can't go back to the place where we beamed down. It's too close to those volcanoes."

"We could ask the Ferengi to help us," Deanna suggested.

"Their price is too steep," Picard reminded her. "But we must try to talk to them again."

Jean-Luc turned to see Piercing Blade striding toward them. She was tossing the Ambassador's Mask back and forth between her hands the way a kitten might toss a ball of yarn.

"Picard," she said, stopping in front of him and bowing her head. "I would like you to wear the Ambassador's Mask. Like any worthy mask, it is trying to find its rightful owner. Perhaps you are the one."

"I am honored," answered Jean-Luc. But he didn't immediately reach for the gleaming mask. Picard had never been superstitious, but the Ambassador's Mask did seem to be cursed. First its Ferengi owners had been murdered. Then Fenton Lewis was discredited. Now Spider Wing had been killed. Jean-Luc didn't aspire to become such a clear target.

Nevertheless, he took the mask, marveling at how light the silverish alloy was. "Thank you." He bowed. "I shall wear it proudly."

Piercing Blade's mind was elsewhere. "I'll miss him," she murmured. Then she turned and walked back to her crestfallen comrades.

Picard regarded the mask made by the legendary Fazool, as Worf and Deanna edged closer to see it.

Traveling without the peculiar blue wagon was not an altogether pleasant experience, thought Data. As members of a peddler's retinue, the second away team had been relaxed and at ease. Now that they were part of a king's entourage, they were serious and tense. They had trusted Day Timer to take them to the fair, but they were apprehensive about Almighty Slayer.

Nevertheless, the old Lorcan seemed little changed by his sudden rise in status. Data found himself walking beside Almighty Slayer, wondering what the famous warrior was thinking. Was he plotting military strategy? Was he composing a speech to woo the undecided? What did a king think about?

"That was a fairly exciting boggle, wasn't it?" Almighty Slayer asked the android.

"Are you talking about the eruptions?" asked Data.

"Sure, and the ground bucking like a farm girl." He laughed. "You don't have boggles where you come from?"

"Not usually," Data admitted.

The ruler's voice took on a serious tone. "Data, if I'm killed, I want you to take the Wisdom Mask."

Data held up his hand as if to protest, but Almighty Slayer gently lowered it. "I don't mean you have to wear the mask. I wouldn't play such a dirty trick on somebody I liked. But I sense that you are a wise man, Data. I think you will know what to do with the Wisdom Mask. Don't give up your life for it, but try to see that it gets into the right hands. It's a powerful symbol."

"I will," pledged Data. "But there must be some way for you to win followers without fighting them."

"It's not the followers I'm worried about fighting," said Slayer grimly. "It's the thieves."

"Maybe I can help you," offered Data.

Chapter Thirteen

GATHERING WOOD for that night's fire was as easy as opening one's eyes and looking down. As a result of the eruptions, the forest floor and the clay road were choked with fallen boughs. Almighty Slayer mentioned that he was almost glad his wagon had been destroyed; they would have broken their backs clearing a path for it. As it was, their legs were aching and their shins were scarred from climbing over branches all day, and Commander Riker had never been so glad to make camp.

The more Will Riker saw of the Wisdom Mask, the more the ancient mosaic design reminded him of a spiral nebula. Almighty Slayer himself seemed accustomed to the beauty of his unique mask as he searched for a fir tree still in good enough condition to harbor them for the night. Finding one, he immediately put everyone to work stripping the moss off the plentiful firewood, while he went to find a bog for fishing. He warned them that fish might be hard to catch so soon after a big boggle. But he would try.

Riker watched with some trepidation as the famous warrior ventured into the woods by himself. The man was casually wearing the most sought after possession on the whole planet, thought Will, the key to the leadership of Lorca. Without the Wisdom Mask, all the other pretenders to the throne were just that—pretenders.

Not that he blamed the old peddler for keeping the mask hidden. What had happened to the king's earlier entourages? he wondered. What had become of previous wearers of the Forest Mask? They had been killed, all of them, defending the Wisdom Mask.

The first officer wanted to tell the old warrior to hurl the mask into the woods. He wanted to tell him to live out his years in the peace and serenity of an old peddler's wagon. But something in the man's straightforwardness and determination told Will that Almighty Slayer knew what he was doing. Now *was* the time for Lorca to have a ruler who had seen enough of killing, a ruler who had found wisdom behind a simple clay mask.

What had the old peddler said, before turning himself into a king? "The Wisdom Mask chooses who will wear it." Maybe the Wisdom Mask had chosen a warrior out of necessity, then had waited years for him to become a wise man.

This realization, that he wanted his friend to succeed in regaining his throne and the people's respect, was disturbing to Commander Riker. Such a wish was in direct conflict with the Prime Directive. What would he and his shipmates do when they met a band of ambitious Lorcans? Would they defend Almighty Slayer or let him be killed for his mask? Could they stand by and watch the Ferengi steal the Wisdom Mask, only to auction it to greedy collectors thousands of light-years away? With the Wisdom Mask gone permanently from Lorca, the planet could be condemned to centuries of bloodshed. There would be nothing for individual factions to rally around— nothing but their own swords.

Like every other Starfleet officer, Will Riker had vowed not to interfere in the development of another planet. Starfleet personnel could defend their own lives—as they already had—but that was the extent of it. His personal concern for Almighty Slayer was immaterial. For two hundred years, the strong had wrested the Wisdom Mask from the weak, always by force, and that was the means of ascension to power the Lorcans had chosen. Who was he to put an end to it?

Nevertheless, when a scream came from the woods a few seconds later, in the direction Almighty Slayer had headed, Will Riker was the first to draw his phaser and go running. Data was right behind him and nearly ran him over when Riker pulled up sharply. As the others caught up, Riker and Data stood gawking at the sight of an old man in a fanciful mask dancing with a dirty, bedraggled werjun.

"It's Reba!" he cried joyfully, swinging the red-haired animal by its gangly arms. "She's come back."

The werjun apparently had no trouble recognizing her master in his new mask, for she chattered sweetly and nuzzled his neck. Then the animal leapt to the ground and began a gawky dance, accompanied by wild whoops, leaps, and gestures.

"Is she all right?" asked Data with concern.

"She is telling me of her adventures," said Almighty Slayer.

Reba's performance went on for several minutes, ending with a thrashing about and thumping on the ground that even Riker could tell was a werjun's impersonation of a giant boggle. Then the slothlike creature cackled proudly and jumped back into her master's arms.

"Piercing Blade's band is not far ahead of us," warned Almighty Slayer.

"How do you know that?" asked Dr. Pulaski.

The old warrior shrugged. "Reba told me. She said the camp ahead of us has women in it. She met one of them. That would probably be Piercing Blade's band, because she is one of the few to accept women as pages."

"I know I'm grasping at straws," said Commander Riker, shaking his head at his own ridiculousness, "but did she see any sign of our missing comrades?"

"Wait," said Fenton Lewis. "Now you're asking a *chimp* to discredit me. That's going too far, Riker!"

Will gnashed his teeth beneath his polished mask and ignored Fenton Lewis. "Did Reba see anyone like that?" he asked the Lorcan.

Almighty Slayer shook his head sadly. "To Reba, most humans look the same. She doesn't know one from another." He hugged the scrawny animal happily. "Except for me, of course."

With Reba's help, Almighty Slayer managed to catch enough fish to feed his troupe. The fire was blazing comfortably by the time he and his nobleman, teacher, herbalist, archer, and messenger began settling down under the tree to sleep.

Commander Riker couldn't settle down, however. He leapt up and began nervously pacing the golden perimeter of the firelight. He couldn't get the idea out of his mind that the Wisdom Mask was about to engulf them in trouble. He didn't much care for the oppressive darkness, either. The sky was still shrouded in opaque clouds, and being unable to see the stars made the *Enterprise* seem even farther away.

He drew his communicator from his pocket. "Commander Riker to the bridge," he said softly, not wanting to alarm his sleeping companions.

"Lieutenant La Forge here," came a voice that sounded weary.

"Hi, Geordi. Just checking in to see how long it will be before you can beam us up."

"We're working on it," answered Geordi. "We can try now, if there's a real emergency, but that cloud cover makes locking on extremely difficult. We need full enhancement just to pick up your voice. If the winds stay steady, conditions should be much better in a couple of days."

"Great," muttered Riker. "I suppose it's my own fault for asking for that diversion."

"About the diversion," said Geordi. "We think it did the planet some good."

"How's that?"

"Well," the engineering officer continued, "we defused a whole chain of volcanoes along the planet's equator. There probably won't be another major eruption for several months."

"If there's ever a demand for volcano sweepers," joked Riker, "we'll be all set."

"That's the way I look at it," answered Geordi. There was a moment's uneasy silence in which the joviality faded away. "No word about the captain's party?"

"No," sighed Riker. "Nothing around us but Lorcans and Ferengi."

"Take care of yourselves," Geordi offered.

"Thank you. Out."

Commander Riker tucked away the insignia badge borrowed from Ensign Greenblatt and looked back at the fire. Reba, exhausted, was hanging by her tail from an upper branch. A number of bodies lay motionless under the fir tree's gently swaying canopy. Almighty Slayer and Lieutenant Commander Data emerged from the shadows at the base of the tree and wordlessly found places on the cushions of humus. They were the last, except for Riker, to bed down.

The tiles of the Wisdom Mask glistened softly in the warm firelight, the design subtly shifting every time the Lorcan moved. Data didn't remove his pale Teacher's Mask, either, and Riker marveled at the way they were all getting so accustomed to their masks that they seldom removed them anymore, even to sleep.

The commander thought about keeping himself awake for guard duty, but he knew that Data didn't really sleep. With so many bodies curled up under the giant pine, the crackling fire was beginning to look more inviting. Riker yawned and forced his aching legs to carry him to the tree. Within seconds of stretching out on the tender needles, he was asleep.

When the scuffle started, the fire was still blazing, casting more than enough light on the horrible scene in front of Riker's drowsy eyes. He saw Fenton Lewis, in his feathered mask, shooting Almighty Slayer repeatedly with a pistol phaser while he tried to tear the Wisdom Mask off the Lorcan's face. Something was wrong, however, because the phaser blasts had no effect on the Lorcan, who was rising to his feet, valiantly protecting his mask.

Not believing what he was seeing, Riker blinked and tried to shake off his exhaustion. Fenton Lewis stumbled backwards, unable to believe it either, and bolted into the darkness.

"Lewis stole my phaser," shouted Ensign Greenblatt.

"Day Timer!" shouted the doctor, bounding to her feet.

There were more shouts and confusion, and Riker found himself running into the woods, finally awake. But the pervasive darkness afforded him no chance of seeing, let alone catching, the fleeing ambassador. He stopped before he took a nasty tumble over the fallen branches.

When he returned to the glow of the fire, Riker was startled to see Almighty Slayer calmly removing his mask, as the others looked on curiously. To their astonishment, the Wisdom Mask didn't conceal a gnarled old warrior at all—but a smooth-faced android.

The lieutenant commander quickly handed the Wisdom Mask to the man wearing the Teacher's Mask. The teacher deftly turned around and switched masks, becoming Almighty Slayer. The king handed Data's mask back to him, thumping the android on the shoulder.

"You were right," roared the Lorcan. "He was no good. I'm glad *you* decided to be *me*!"

"I assumed he would act quickly," Data admitted. "He is very determined."

Dr. Pulaski examined Data quickly. She was no mechanic, but he looked okay to her. "Data, you should be happy he left the phaser on stun. At a kill setting, you'd be a lump of iron by now."

"I am fortunate, Doctor," Data agreed. "I had no idea he would use a phaser—"

"Which he stole from me," said Ensign Greenblatt.

Data nodded. "I thought he would make a simple attempt to snatch the mask and run."

"You should've talked to me about this first," Riker insisted. "You endangered yourself, Data."

"I couldn't talk to you, Commander," explained the android, "because Ambassador Lewis had you under observation."

Almighty Slayer interrupted, throwing his arm around Data's shoulders. "Riker, we only decided to do this a short time ago. Be thankful that you have such a clever lieutenant commander and I have such a clever friend. Data saved my life, and I won't forget such heroism."

"His job isn't to save your life," snapped Riker, instantly regretting his words. "Day Timer, we can't become involved in a power struggle down here. We will capture Fenton Lewis, because he is our responsibility, and we'll protect you from the Ferengi, if you request it. But we won't defend you from other Lorcans."

The old warrior put his free arm around Will Riker's shoulders. "My noble friend, wearer of the Forest Mask, I know precisely what you will and won't do. I know how loyal you are. Believe me, if you keep your own people and the Ferengi off my tail, I will be forever grateful."

He let go of their shoulders and clapped his gnarled hands together. "At least we have gotten rid of the traitor in our midst."

Commander Riker looked down the pitch black road where Fenton Lewis had vanished after his thwarted attempt to steal the royal mask. Will's voice echoed within the Forest Mask as he vowed, "I'm going to get him. And when I do, I'm going to take him to the most distant starbase I can find. He will never disturb Lorca again."

The Thunder Mask and the Ambassador's Mask lay forgotten in the shadows in a corner of the tent, which was illuminated only by a flickering lamp. Their owners slowly uncurled from a naked embrace that had lasted long after the lovemaking. Jean-Luc started to sit up, and Piercing Blade reached out her sinewy arms to pull him back. He was happy to oblige her needs by again nestling within her soft breasts and strong limbs.

He could feel her arms tightening around his back as she buried her little girl's face in the crook of his shoulder. What drove this incredible woman? he wondered. She could best any man in a swordfight, and that would be enough for most Lorcans. She could love a man to death, he knew that much. She was a warrior in the noblest, most chivalrous sense. In the span of a single day, she could be an inspiring leader, an insatiable lover, and a vulnerable child. She commanded the loyalty and allegiance of some of Lorca's best citizens, and yet she expected the impossible from them.

No matter how brave they were, how could half a dozen Lorcans unite an entire planet? Jean-Luc knew their grief for Spider Wing was real, but the loss of one man had only served to demonstrate how short-handed they were for the task set before them.

Now Piercing Blade clung to Captain Picard as the moss clung to the fir trees above them. She wanted so desperately to rule Lorca, but Picard wondered if such a thing was possible. A land of vast wilderness areas, far-flung population, and seething volcanoes did not seem a good candidate for the rule of law. The planet's very atmosphere was anathema to electronic devices, and the people were committed to a bloody form of feudalism. With the Wisdom Mask, he supposed, Piercing Blade might stand a chance of achieving her goal. But having the Wisdom Mask hadn't made Almighty Slayer's job any easier; he had vanished without a trace.

Despite the odds against them, Jean-Luc would have given anything to share Piercing Blade's dream with her. He longed to be two people, one of whom could proudly wear the Ambassador's Mask and fight and love at her side. But he was already the other person, the one who wore the tight-lipped starship captain's mask.

"Picard?" she breathed, stroking the fine gray hairs on his chest. He normally thought of himself as fair, but next to her smooth body, he was the swarthiest of men.

"Yes," he murmured.

"When will you leave me?"

He sighed deeply and shifted onto his back, his body sticking to the slick oilskin. The bedding had felt like silk a moment before, and now it felt like what it was—clammy fish skins. "I don't know," he answered honestly. "At the moment, we have no way to go back."

"Back to your ship in the sky?" she asked, her innocent face glowing guilelessly. "To your wives? The captain of so fine a ship must have many wives?"

"Maybe he should," laughed Picard. "After these last few nights, I might consider it. But I am a prime example of a captain who is married to his ship."

"That is sad," Blade replied, nuzzling his neck.

"No sadder than a queen," he countered. "When does a queen take time off to be a woman?"

"Right now," she purred, running her hand down his chest and across his flat stomach. "Oh, Jean-Luc," she moaned, "why is our time so short?"

He drew her into his arms and hoarsely replied, "So that we will be forced to make the most of it."

As their lips met, an irate voice sounded outside: "Intruder! Halt! Who goes there?"

"Come out slowly," called another.

In the space of time it took Piercing Blade and Captain Picard to dress, several more cries and shouts echoed throughout the camp. Worf's bass voice could be heard above all of them, bellowing, "Captain!"

Picard pulled on his mask and followed Piercing Blade outside into the dim glow of the campfire. There, surrounded by pages with swords drawn, stood a man in a feathered mask and rawhide leggings.

"Lewis," exclaimed Picard in astonishment.

"None other," the man answered, nodding his owlish Messenger's Mask. "Please put the swords away. I'm unarmed and can't do you any harm. In fact, I bring important news to Lady Piercing Blade."

"Where have you been?" growled Worf.

"Mostly lost," the ambassador acknowledged. "But do you really need to know how I spent every instant I was gone? Can it suffice for you to know that I've been with Almighty Slayer?"

"Almighty Slayer," gasped Piercing Blade, rising to

her full height. She drew her sword and leveled it at Fenton Lewis. "If this is a trick, not even the dragon will be able to stop me from taking your head."

"No trick, my lady." He bowed, his sandy hair tumbling over his shoulders. "They are, in fact, right behind us on this same road. I have just come from their camp."

Picard pointed angrily at Lewis. "You mean you ran away from them, just as you ran away from us?"

"Never mind that," snapped Piercing Blade, waving the captain down with her sword. "Do you know for sure it's Almighty Slayer? Have you seen the Wisdom Mask?"

"Yes," said Medicine Maker suspiciously. "What does the Wisdom Mask look like?"

"Like nothing I've ever seen," admitted the messenger. "It's a swirl of mosaic in a beautiful whirlpool pattern. Surrounding the mosaic tiles is a ring of red crystals—"

"That's it," crowed Cold Angel, leaping into the air and doing a joyful little dance. "The fates are with us, my lady. We can have the mask tonight."

"Just a minute," said Medicine Maker, holding up his hands to quiet the murmurs. "He could have heard a description of the mask from any traveler in any village." The healer turned to Fenton Lewis, his eyes narrowing behind the twining serpents on his mask. "What kind of man is Almighty Slayer?"

"How do you mean?" Lewis shrugged. "He is not a young man anymore. He plays at being dumb, but he's a very smart man."

Cold Angel roared, "What difference does it make if it's Slayer or not? All we need to crown our queen is the Wisdom Mask. I say we take it."

This declaration was met with several shouts of approval. Captain Picard looked at Counselor Troi; he didn't need to see the Betazoid's face to know how alarmed she was at the growing shouts for violence.

Piercing Blade sheathed her sword. "How large is this force behind us?"

"About the same size as yours," replied Fenton Lewis. "But I believe your force will be superior in battle. The others lack training and discipline."

Medicine Maker still didn't sound convinced. "One more question, Messenger. What other masks did you see in this camp?"

"Mostly masks I didn't know, but there was one called the Forest Mask."

That turned Piercing Blade completely around, and she stood staring at the owlish Messenger's Mask. "Now I know you speak the truth," she breathed, her eyes glazing over as if she was remembering something from long ago. "It can be none other than Almighty Slayer, for his first lieutenant always wears the Forest Mask." She pointed to Lewis and declared, "When I am queen, you will be rewarded for this."

Piercing Blade whirled on her heel, waving her followers to action. "Come. Saddle the ponies. We march!"

Captain Picard dashed in front of her, grabbing the hand that had stroked his chest just moments before. "Are you going to attack them?" he demanded.

"No." She shook her head vehemently, pulling her hand away. "We are not raiders. I'm surprised that you would think like that, Picard. I will challenge Almighty Slayer's right to wear the Wisdom Mask. He will either hand it over or defeat me in battle."

"Why can't you wait until daylight?"

"Tomorrow he may be stronger," said Piercing Blade, leveling her intense green eyes at Picard. "Or he may go into hiding again. We have to seize the moment. Only one thing worries me, and that is you."

"Me?" the captain gulped.

"Yes, *you!* You are the only one to have defeated me in a duel, so now I know it can happen. That knowledge weakens me, I think, but I will have to overcome it. When you defeated me, there was not as much at stake—I must remember that. I don't believe Almighty Slayer can withstand my challenge. He will give me the Wisdom Mask."

"And if he doesn't?" the captain persisted.

"Then I'll take it."

"By force, with your warriors fighting his warriors?"

"Those who are brave enough to come with me," she snarled, pushing past him. Picard could do nothing but watch the remarkable woman stride toward her pony, which Cold Angel was saddling as they spoke.

Deanna Troi reached his side a moment later, followed by Lieutenant Worf. "Can we stop them?" asked Deanna.

"No, we cannot," declared the captain.

"Can we help them?" pleaded Worf.

"No, we can only stay neutral."

"And watch them die?" Worf murmured.

"Don't you think *I* want to help them? I do, but we don't know any of these other factions, and we can't influence the outcome. We have to sit back and let it occur naturally."

"In a way," said Deanna, "this society, with their use of masks, is a natural experiment in human interaction. We have to avoid disturbing it."

"Can we follow them?" asked Worf. "To see what happens?"

"Absolutely," answered the captain. "I want to make sure there are no Ferengi involved."

Worf cocked his mask slyly. "You know, Captain, now that Fenton Lewis has returned, we have the price of our fare back to the *Enterprise.*"

"Yes, I know." Picard nodded. "But dealing with the Ferengi must be our last resort."

"Fenton Lewis isn't upholding the Prime Directive," Deanna pointed out.

"You're right," the captain agreed, craning his neck in a futile attempt to spot the Messenger's Mask. But Fenton Lewis had apparently returned to the forest road with the first of Piercing Blade's band. The pages had gone ahead on foot, noisily clearing away branches for the benefit of the ponies and lighting the way with their lamps. Jean-Luc felt certain that this group would not sneak up on anybody. They were going to arrive as a proper entourage to a noblewoman. Fenton Lewis was probably making better time alone, skulking through the woods.

"Fenton Lewis will be arrested as soon as we get back to the *Enterprise*," vowed Captain Picard. "The charge will be violating the Prime Directive."

Moments later, riders and mounts pranced nervously into the darkness, following the vague glow of the pages' lamps. The Starfleet officers were left alone in camp, standing beside a dying fire, silently collecting their thoughts.

Lieutenant Worf took his hand phaser from his pocket and checked it thoroughly. He glanced around and, seeing no one, fired a brief blast into the sickly embers of the fire. At once, the fire blazed, and a puff of sparks shot into the air and danced away on the breeze.

"Set to stun," said the Klingon. "But all settings are functional."

Kate Pulaski tried to go back to sleep, but she ended up just watching the campfire sputter and collapse, shooting errant sparks into the darkness. She stood and tossed the last of the stripped branches on it. Not that she was cold—she was uncomfortably warm— but she had nothing better to do with herself. Keeping the fire burning was at least *something* to occupy these last lonely hours before dawn.

The doctor remembered the old saying that it was

always darkest before the dawn. This night certainly was.

"Are you troubled, Doctor?" asked a voice, startling her.

Kate whirled around to see Data sitting up in the darkest corner of the tree shelter. His yellowish eyes glowed disconcertingly in the darkness.

"You're the one who should be troubled," she remarked with bravado. "An attempt was made on *your* life tonight, not mine."

"Not my life," he corrected her. "On Almighty Slayer's life."

"That Wisdom Mask is like a red flag," Pulaski muttered, careful to keep her voice down. "I wouldn't give you a plug nickel for Slayer's chances of staying alive."

"That is too bad," said Data. Then he cocked his head quizzically. "Is a plug nickel very valuable?"

"No," she grumbled. "That means I don't think much of his chances."

"He would appear to need more followers," Data admitted. "We are limited in the help we can offer him."

Twigs snapped overhead, and both the doctor and the android looked up. Reba, the lanky werjun, uncurled from her branch and swung lazily to the ground. She arched her back like a cat, undulated her prehensile tail, and stretched her gangly limbs one by one.

Kate Pulaski would have petted the friendly werjun, if her coat hadn't been so filthy. Of course, she thought, looking down at her own grimy clothing, none of them were ready for the queen's ball.

"Do you really suppose Day Timer can converse with that creature?" she wondered aloud.

"I do not know," replied the android. "Shall we try an experiment?"

"What experiment?"

Data turned to the slothlike animal and, in a perfectly serious tone of voice, asked, "What is your favorite food?"

"Fish," answered Reba.

"You see," said Data matter-of-factly. Then he blinked and looked back at the werjun.

"He . . . he talked," sputtered Pulaski.

"She," Data corrected her.

Kate forced her excitement into a whisper. "That thing . . . that werjun talked. Ask her something else." The doctor leaned forward excitedly.

"Very well." Data turned to the sloth. "What kind of animal are you?"

"Fish."

Data shrugged, and Dr. Pulaski slumped back onto her haunches, disappointed. "I thought we had something there," she sighed.

The werjun brushed away some pine needles and picked up a scrap of fish from the ground. She plopped the treat into her mouth, gibbering contentedly. But before she could scrounge for more, something made her raise her furry face and rotate it like a tiny satellite disk.

"Now what is she doing?" Kate asked.

Data listened intently. "She is listening to something . . . Noises. And voices."

"Where?" Kate gasped, no longer drowsy.

"Out there." Data pointed, rising into a crouch and running out from under the tree. The doctor scurried after him and stood by the android's side, staring down the gloomy road. Incredibly, like a mirage, a faint glow appeared deep within the black woods. The light bobbed along, illuminating row upon row of ghostly trees as it crept closer. The night wind carried a very faint lilt of voices.

"Shall we wake everyone?" breathed Kate.

Data cocked his head, still listening. "That may be

unnecessary, Doctor. I do not know why these people are traveling by night, but they are obviously not trying to approach furtively. They probably have no idea we are here. Let us go forward to meet them and allow the others to rest."

Kate Pulaski pulled her Herbalist's Mask over her face and fixed the strap. "Lead on," she said.

Lieutenant Commander Data and Dr. Pulaski picked their way carefully along the road, avoiding the fallen branches and bottomless shadows. Thanks to his superior vision, Data made better time than the doctor and paused occasionally to let her catch up. The voices were very clear now, and they could see several shapes that weren't human in the wavering halos of light about thirty meters ahead of them.

"Ponies," Data whispered.

Kate gripped his arm. "It isn't the raiders again, is it?"

"Unknown," said Data. "Perhaps you should turn back."

She shook her head. "No, Data, I'm with you. I think we should find out who they are and what they want before we let them see the Wisdom Mask."

Data straightened his own Teacher's Mask. "There is nothing in the Prime Directive against making inquiries."

"Damn right," said Pulaski. She studied Data's mask; like hers, it was little more than a heavy sheet of metal with a fresh coat of paint. But there was something about its quaint ivory color, elegant markings, and faint smile that made the Teacher's Mask particularly amiable. "You know, Data, you look almost human in that thing."

The teacher and the herbalist boldly strode into the circle of light. Katherine Pulaski didn't know what to expect, but she was ill prepared for the magnificent display of masks among the equestrians. A regal woman at the head of the pack was wearing an

225

astounding mask, but Kate tore her eyes away from it to study something much more startling—a mask identical to her own, though much finer, with jeweled serpents instead of painted ones. She found it hard to stop staring at the mask even as Data was speaking.

"Hello," he greeted the Lorcans pleasantly. "This is a dark night for a walk."

"We aren't on a walk," answered Cold Angel. He appeared to be scowling, because Picard had given him back his gruesome Trainer's Mask.

The woman in the astounding star mask leaned forward. "Are you from Almighty's Slayer's band? And don't lie to me."

Data glanced at Dr. Pulaski, but unfortunately the android had not been programmed to lie. "Yes, we are. May I ask how you knew that?"

"That's not important. Tell your master to prepare to receive me."

"Who shall we say is calling?" asked Data.

She stiffened in her saddle, and her voice took on an imperious tone. "Tell him it's his daughter."

Chapter Fourteen

FROM THEIR HIDING PLACE about thirty meters away, Picard, Worf, and Deanna watched the confrontation between Piercing Blade and the two Lorcans. One of the strangers was tall and well built and wore an unfamiliar white mask; the female wore a less elaborate version of the Herbalist's Mask. On first impression, the two looked like formidable and intelligent foes, and Picard's opinion of Almighty Slayer went up a notch. They weren't close enough to hear all the conversation, but they clearly made out Piercing Blade's loud announcement that she was Almighty Slayer's daughter.

Picard blinked at Deanna from beneath the graceful curves of the Ambassador's Mask. "Well, what do you make of that?"

"We have to remember," said Deanna, "that masks are not inherited—they are fought for. Birthright doesn't grant any special consideration. Only the possessor of the mask has claim to the title."

"It might explain why she wants the Wisdom Mask so badly," remarked Worf.

Picard heaved a sigh. "I think she would want it anyway."

The two Lorcan strangers now turned and headed back up the road. The sky was minutely brighter than it had been an hour before, but the mammoth trees and dense clouds of ash made the sun's job impossible. Jean-Luc was thankful for the tall trees, however, because they were catching most of the ash as it drifted to the ground.

He brought his attention back to the two unfamiliar Lorcans, as they vanished into the woods. "Counselor, did you get any impressions from them?"

The Betazoid nodded. "They seem familiar to me somehow."

"It's very interesting," noted Picard, "how every party we've seen has a healer."

"If you're bashing each other with swords all the time," said Worf, "you need a healer. That white mask looked like heavy armor."

The Ambassador's Mask nodded. "They both did. Let's not underestimate any of these Lorcans. Be extremely careful and try to stay out of sight."

Giving the ambassadors from Almighty Slayer a brief head start, Piercing Blade waved her arm, and her entourage lumbered forward. With the pages clearing and lighting the road, the unearthly glow disappeared into black silhouettes of the tall trees.

"Let's stay with them," ordered the captain, rising into a crouch and slinking after the departing figures. Wordlessly, his subordinates crept after him.

Lieutenant Commander Data and Dr. Pulaski glanced back over their shoulders. They could tell they were being followed, but none too quickly. Data was experiencing mixed reactions—the satisfaction of having again been accepted as human and guilt over the dressing-down Commander Riker had given him earlier, after he protected Almighty Slayer from Ambassador Lewis. What had Commander Riker said? That it was not his job to save Almighty Slayer's life. The implications of that statement plagued him.

"Doctor," he said, as they cautiously picked their way along the road, "the continuing mission of the starship *Enterprise* is to seek out new worlds and new life-forms."

Dr. Pulaski looked askance at the android, even with her mask on. "That's hardly news, Data."

"To seek out new life-forms," Data repeated. "But not to save their lives or to offer assistance?"

"You're thinking about what happened earlier tonight," Kate sighed, "and what may be about to happen?"

The android nodded. "You *have* biological life, Doctor, so perhaps you do not appreciate the uniqueness of it. I am not sure I can stand by and watch Day Timer be killed."

"I'm not sure I can either," Kate admitted.

"Then you will violate the Prime Directive?"

The doctor shrugged. "I won't know what I'll do until it's time to do it."

Data cocked his head quizzically. "That seems irresponsible."

"I'm sorry," sighed the doctor, "but that's the way humans think. We don't always do what's right or what's best, because we don't always know."

"Then my confusion is not unusual?"

"No, Data, it's not," said Dr. Pulaski, peering into the darkness. "At some point, you learn to look at rules and regulations as guidelines, not gospel. In the end, you have to trust your own judgment. At least, that's what humans do."

"So the Prime Directive may not apply in every instance?"

"Oh, it always applies," said Kate forcefully, "but

it's sometimes subject to different interpretations. Now, where is the tree where we made camp?"

Data pointed behind them. "We passed it about ten meters back."

Dr. Pulaski shook her head in amazement at the way Data's mind worked. "I'll wake up Commander Riker and Ensign Greenblatt and tell them what happened. You tell Almighty Slayer to get ready."

"Yes, Doctor."

Data found the Lorcan leader dozing peacefully beneath his mask of swirling pastels. Pinpricks of light glinting off the fire gave the mask an otherworldly quality. On the other side of the tree, Dr. Pulaski knelt over Commander Riker and gently shook him. Data shook Almighty Slayer.

"Wake up, Your Highness."

The Lorcan rolled onto his back, and his aged eyes blinked warmly at Data. "What is it, my friend?"

"Your daughter is here."

"What?" he roared, bolting awake. His thunderous voice brought the others to their feet.

"What is it?" Riker demanded.

Dr. Pulaski pointed down the road to the light glimmering eerily among the stark tree trunks. "We're going to have visitors very soon, and they know that Almighty Slayer is here with the Wisdom Mask."

"Lewis must have told them," Riker said. "How else could they know?"

Almighty Slayer stomped angrily around the campfire, plunging his heavy sword into the dirt. *"I have no daughter.* She's made that claim once too often. I'll skewer her!" He sliced the air with his sword for emphasis.

Commander Riker stepped away from the giant fir and stared at the approaching party, which was little more than vague shapes trapped within a halo of light. "How many are there?"

"Three riding ponies," answered Data, "and two on foot."

"We can take them," vowed Almighty Slayer. He turned to Ensign Greenblatt. "Archer, get your fire arrows ready."

"Wait," shouted Riker. "I told you before, Day Timer, we're not going to interfere in your internal affairs."

"My internal affairs?" scoffed the old Lorcan. "My internal affairs are going to be spilled out all over this ground if you don't help me. I'm no match for Piercing Blade in a duel. Not anymore."

"Then you do know this woman?" asked Pulaski. "She claimed to be your daughter."

The king banged the Wisdom Mask with his fist, demonstrating, if nothing else, that the antique mask was still a solid piece of armor. "Daughter or not, she has only one thing on her mind—to take my mask." He appealed to them. "Will you stand with me?"

"We have time to make a run for it," suggested Greenblatt.

"Run," wailed Almighty Slayer. "What kind of friends are you? Why don't you kill me yourselves and take the mask?"

Commander Riker clenched his fists in frustration. "Day Timer, what would you do if you didn't have us?"

The king's wiry shoulders slumped noticeably. "I probably would have remained a peddler."

Several other pairs of shoulders slumped as the herbalist, the teacher, the archer, and the nobleman confronted their conflicting loyalties. The *Enterprise*, the Federation, even the stars seemed far away. The reality was the breath steaming out of their mouths, the ash clogging the air, the worms in the ground, and the mounted warriors approaching through the tree-shrouded gloom, surrounded by a weird halo.

"Phasers set to stun," Riker muttered. "And keep them hidden. We're going to try to talk our way out of this."

"I don't have a phaser, Commander," Greenblatt reminded him. "Fenton Lewis took mine."

"That's unfortunate," Riker replied. "Doctor, would you mind giving your phaser to the ensign?"

"Not at all," answered Pulaski, handing the weapon to Ensign Greenblatt. "But you won't mind if I stand close to you, will you, Commander?"

"I'm not sure that's wise," answered Will, straightening his Forest Mask. He was acutely aware that Almighty Slayer might not be the only one who would face a challenge for his mask.

"Hail, Almighty Slayer," called a voice from the forest, cutting off further conversation. "Prepare to receive Lady Piercing Blade."

With the pages holding their fish-oil lanterns as high as they could, the small but stately procession wound its way out of the woods and into the stretch of rutted road claimed by Almighty Slayer. The king strode in front of them and put his hands defiantly on his hips as Kate Pulaski edged closer to Commander Riker.

Riker was astounded by the three mounted Lorcans. They were the most imposing figures he had yet seen on Lorca. The woman was one of the most perfect physical specimens he had ever seen. Flanking her were two men—a brute in a brutish mask and a dignified healer with a sword that had to be two meters long. Even the pages were clear-eyed and wary as they planted their lanterns in the moist clay and took their places in front of their leader.

The woman shook her gleaming mask, as if suppressing a private laugh. "So, Father, you have decided to come back to the land of the living?"

The old king spoke through the ancient nebula mask. "You may call me a wormhole maggot if you wish, but you can't call me your father."

"Right." She nodded. "Women are playthings to you, like my wretched mother. You can't lower yourself to acknowledge the weeds that have sprung from your windblown seeds."

"Your mother was a farmgirl," the king countered. "In my day I had many such women."

"Yes, you did," snarled the noblewoman, leaning forward in her saddle. "But you had my mother for seven cycles, until she died for you, driving your wagon into an ambush. You should respect her enough to recognize me as your daughter."

Almighty Slayer lowered his head and said nothing.

Piercing Blade sat back in her saddle and squared her shoulders. "For years you dragged us from camp to camp, from campaign to campaign, and I watched scores of brave warriors die for you. I watched as you used up scores of women. And through it all, there was that Wisdom Mask, making the whole mess seem right somehow. Well, you have misused the Wisdom Mask for over thirty cycles, and now it's time to give it up."

"I am not that man anymore," Slayer protested, his voice barely audible.

But Piercing Blade wasn't listening as she drew her deadly short-sword and pointed it at the old warrior. "Almighty Slayer, by the fire of the dragon, I challenge your right to wear the ancient and hallowed mask of royalty, the Wisdom Mask."

Her green eyes narrowed within the stunning Thunder Mask. "Hand it over now or die at your daughter's hand."

During the tense moments before Almighty Slayer's response, Data sidled up to Commander Riker and pointed to the left of the mounted Lorcans. "That is not their entire force," he whispered. "I count four more hiding in the forest, three over there and one behind the ponies."

"I hate this," muttered Riker. "I don't want to let

him fight that woman, but I must. We can't involve ourselves in a full-scale battle. The Wisdom Mask is his, and he's the one who must defend it."

But Almighty Slayer had other ideas. He pointed confidently to Ensign Greenblatt in her black Archer's Mask. "I have an archer who will set your breast aflame. She will fight in my stead."

"Are you going to let more brave warriors die for you?" moaned Piercing Blade. "Will you never learn? This land is crawling with off-worlders, like the Ferengi, who have no respect for our traditions. Innocent villagers are massacred by marauding bands of raiders. When will you realize that your reign has been a failure and that Lorca needs new leadership?"

"When I am dead," seethed Almighty Slayer. He motioned to Greenblatt. "Archer, show her your flaming arrow."

Ensign Greenblatt hesitated for a moment, then dropped her hands to her side, away from her pistol phaser. "I cannot."

Almighty Slayer whirled around to face Data. "My good friend, you will fight for me, won't you? As you did last night."

Lieutenant Commander Data stepped forward. "I respect you a great deal, Almighty Slayer, but you have not ruled as king for a long time. I believe this lady's concerns are the same as your own. You should consider passing the leadership to someone who is younger and more willing to serve."

Almighty Slayer shook his head sadly and turned to the nobleman in the stolid Forest Mask. "Will you help me, or is that mask just a decoration?"

"Give her the Wisdom Mask," Riker urged. "You've lost your taste for it."

"This is very strange," said Worf, crouching behind a stand of cane with Captain Picard and Counselor Troi. "Apparently, his own entourage is not going to defend him."

"It *is* strange," agreed Deanna Troi. "This is not consistent behavior for the Lorcans as we know them."

Picard pointed to Almighty Slayer's followers. "There is something odd about them."

"As you humans say," added Worf, "they are selling him down the river."

The dawn sunlight struggled to penetrate the massed clouds, infusing the surface of Lorca with a few rays of hazy scarlet. One of them struck the Wisdom Mask, turning it into a field of swirling red lava, within which two dark eyes glowed determinedly.

Almighty Slayer drew his sword. "I vowed long ago to protect the Wisdom Mask with my life, and I shall never break that vow. Piercing Blade, child of mine you may be—but after today, I will be childless."

"Or I will be fatherless," she said, stepping down from her pony and leveling her sword at the old man. "I will make your death quick."

They lunged at each other, and their swords clashed over their heads, locking at the hilt. Piercing Blade, with her superior height and strength, bore down on her father, pushing him to his knees. But the wily old warrior reached a hand behind her boot to trip her. Blade stumbled backwards, barely regaining her balance before the king slashed upward with his sword, catching her on the collarbone and ripping open an ugly gash.

Jean-Luc bolted forward, but he felt a hand—not restraining but comforting—on his shoulder. He turned to see Deanna Troi, shaking her head.

"Captain," she said with deep sympathy, "it is not our fight."

Jean-Luc lowered himself back into the cane and buried his mask in the moist clay. He couldn't stand to watch.

Despite the crimson blood streaming from her

shoulder and flowing down her breastplate, Piercing Blade fought valiantly on. She had abandoned her initial recklessness and was now parrying Almighty Slayer's attacks. Having smelled blood, the older warrior was trying to finish his younger opponent off, while she was plotting to tire the old man and outlast him.

Slayer adopted a bashing technique, swinging his sword up and around in a spectacular arc, trying to split Piercing Blade's skull open. But the woman parried each blow, steering her father's sword harmlessly out of range. And each time, Data could see her measuring and counting the old man's reaction time before he regained his balance. One of these times, thought Data, she was going to slip her short blade between his ribs.

Slayer stepped back, trying to catch his breath. The tiny tiles on the Wisdom Mask continued to swirl within the mane of red crystals, giving the king an aura of the supernatural. But Piercing Blade wasn't deterred; she lunged low and slit open his thigh.

Now blood was flowing from both of them, and Almighty Slayer leaned back, laughing. "You shrew! You're just like your mother. She could always draw blood—but only in bed."

"Give me the mask, you old werjun."

"I'll give you the point of my boot," vowed Slayer, trying to kick his daughter's shin. She swung her sword with such force that it knocked several tiles off the Wisdom Mask. The king tumbled backwards, dazed, clutching his mask. A moment later, he shook his head and tried to sit up, but he found Piercing Blade's sword at his throat.

Before she could force it deeper, Data dashed across the road and grabbed her arm.

"Data!" shouted Riker. "Don't hurt her!"

"I have no intention of hurting her," said Data.

Cold Angel and Medicine Maker drew their swords

and spurred their ponies forward, but they were arrested by a thunderous shout from Deanna Troi.

"Stop!" she cried. "These are our friends! Will Riker, is that you?"

"Yes!" cried Riker, who tore his mask off and threw it to the ground. Deanna Troi broke from the cane and ran toward him, shedding her own mask.

Dr. Pulaski tore off her mask, as did Data and Ensign Greenblatt. From the cane, Worf and Picard lumbered into the light, ripping off their own masks.

The deluge of naked faces so horrified the Lorcans that they wailed and covered their faces until the laughter and shrieks of happiness tempted them to uncover their eyes and witness one of the happiest reunions ever to occur in the galaxy.

"Captain!" shouted Riker, grabbing his commanding officer by the shoulders. "You're alive!"

"Obviously," the captain replied. "How long have you been looking for us?"

"Since the day you vanished."

"Excuse me if I'm impertinent," the Klingon said, "but your naked face looks very good to me, too."

"Impertinence accepted." Kate smiled.

Lieutenant Commander Data let go of Piercing Blade's sword arm. "I am sorry. You may have the Wisdom Mask, but you may not slay Almighty Slayer."

"I never wanted to kill him," she breathed, massaging her wrist. "All of you are from the same place . . . this ship in the sky?"

"Yes." The android nodded, not noticing the man in the feathered mask sneaking up on Almighty Slayer, who was still lying dazed on the clay road.

The messenger snatched the Wisdom Mask off the old man, laying bare a pale creased face with a gray beard. Ensign Greenblatt, who was closest to the perpetrator, grabbed for the mask with both hands. But Fenton Lewis had set his stolen phaser to kill, and he drilled her with a red beam. Greenblatt twitched for an instant before slumping to the ground dead, most of her torso eaten away.

Shock gave way to confusion in the early Lorcan dawn as Fenton Lewis darted into the shadows of the great trees. With their own phasers drawn, Worf, Riker, and Picard cautiously gave chase. But the cagey woodsman was not about to give away his position by shooting at them. He had the mask, a head start, and darkness.

"Spread out," whispered Picard, motioning Riker and Worf to either side. "But keep in eye contact, so we can use hand signals. I'd like to take him alive."

"Understood, Captain," said Worf with grim determination.

"Try not to damage the Wisdom Mask," Riker reminded them.

The three officers fanned out into the forest, stalking the most dangerous game of all. Away from the road and the lamps, darkness ruled supreme, and Will Riker found himself stumbling over a tangle of rotting branches and vines, wishing the sun would break through. He concentrated on keeping his footing. He glanced at the vague shadow that was the captain, and he saw an encouraging wave.

At least they were all together again, even if their ordeal was not over yet.

Kneeling beside the lifeless body of the young ensign, Dr. Pulaski looked up at Data and Counselor Troi and shook her head glumly. She pressed Greenblatt's eyes shut and reached into her inner pocket for her communicator badge. "Dr. Pulaski to the *Enterprise,*" she murmured.

"Enterprise here," answered Geordi. "This is Lieutenant La Forge. Please speak up, Doctor. The reception is not terrific."

"I have good news for you," Kate began, letting her

happiness override her grief. "We have found Captain Picard, Counselor Troi, and Lieutenant Worf. They're all fine."

Kate could hear the exuberant cheer on the bridge of the *Enterprise,* and she hated to interject a note of sorrow. "But we have a body to beam up."

"Ambassador Lewis?" asked Geordi.

"I wish," she muttered. "No, it's Ensign Greenblatt."

After a moment, the lieutenant replied, "We're not sure how well the transporters will work in that atmosphere."

"She's dead, Geordi," said the doctor, brushing a strand of blond hair from the peaceful freckled face. "You can't hurt her. Lock on to my signal." She set her badge on the dead woman's lapel.

"All right," said Geordi slowly. "Locking on."

"Good-bye, Ensign." The doctor smiled at the brave young woman before retrieving her medical insignia and stepping back.

The Lorcans stared in astonishment as Greenblatt's body dissolved in a shower of crystalline sparkles, leaving a slight indentation in the clay.

"Witchcraft," muttered Cold Angel.

"No," said Deanna Troi, "it's something your ancestors were able to do, but you've forgotten."

Piercing Blade bent down and picked up the discarded Ambassador's Mask, which she handed to her cowering father. "Clothe yourself, Father. You deserve this mask more than these naked-faced offworlders. Now *they* have our Wisdom Mask."

"Fenton Lewis is as much our enemy as yours," said Kate Pulaski. "Do you think we wanted to see one of our own people killed?"

Medicine Maker jumped off his pony and strode toward them, drawing his immense sword. "One life is a cheap price to pay for the Wisdom Mask."

Deanna Troi leapt in front of him, grabbing the

hilt of his sword. "Please," she begged, "trust us. We don't think as you do. We consider one person's life more valuable than all your masks put together."

As the healer peered into the Betazoid's beautiful olive-skinned face, his anger abated and he shoved his sword back into its scabbard. "Then don't wear our masks. Show us who you really are."

"From now on, we won't wear your masks," vowed Deanna.

Almighty Slayer stood up, adjusting the gleaming Ambassador's Mask. Its smooth curves and bold colors suited his wiry, energetic physique, and the others turned their attention to him, waiting to hear his words. "I have spent many days with these people," he testified, "and I am willing to believe that they don't want the Wisdom Mask for themselves. I can also vouch for the fact that they didn't trust the messenger, this Fenton Lewis. In fact, he made an earlier attempt to steal the mask, and Data protected me."

Piercing Blade lowered the Thunder Mask and pressed her fist to her shoulder to stanch the bleeding. "I am to blame. I let the messenger manipulate us into coming here. Picard warned me about him, but I was too eager to face you, Father."

Almighty Slayer limped to his daughter's side, blood still oozing from his thigh, and put his arm around her. "I always knew I'd have to face you, and that you would best me."

"For what purpose?" she asked bitterly. "Now we have lost the Wisdom Mask."

Kate Pulaski glanced at the tall healer in the jeweled Herbalist's Mask. He nodded, and together they walked to the reconciled father and daughter, seated them on the ground, and began to administer to their wounds.

"We brought Fenton Lewis here," the doctor admitted, ripping a gap in Almighty Slayer's pant leg. "And we take full responsibility for his actions. I'm sure Captain Picard, Commander Riker, and Lieutenant Worf are doing all they can to bring back the Wisdom Mask."

"They had better be," snarled Cold Angel, drawing his sword, "because you are our prisoners until they return it to us."

Chapter Fifteen

FENTON LEWIS thrashed through the woods like a hunted animal. He didn't care if his pursuers heard him; he knew they couldn't see him. He wanted to put as much distance as he could between himself and his pursuers before daylight flooded the woods. Thus far he hadn't fired a single phaser blast at them, but he was prepared to do so if they got too close.

He regretted having had to kill that young ensign. But the brutal murder had worked to his advantage, paralyzing everyone for those few precious seconds he needed to seize the mask and escape. The Lorcans were probably still in shock from the sight of all those naked laughing faces. Fenton Lewis grinned under his Messenger's Mask at the easy success of his heist, then clutched his prize all the tighter.

He was now the sole owner of Lorca's Wisdom Mask. He was the king.

Unfortunately, even if his escape went as planned, he still had his work cut out for him before he could claim the throne. Just wearing the Wisdom Mask wouldn't do. He had to assemble a force of mercenaries, recruited from around the galaxy, to help him keep the Wisdom Mask. The ignorant and fearful villagers of Lorca wouldn't challenge him, but the well-heeled nobility might. He would put them in their place quickly, by coming after *them* before they had a chance to come after him.

He hefted the pistol phaser. Until he assembled his royal bodyguard, the hand weapon would have to do. He knew the Lorcans would not stand up to a phaser, but the greedy Ferengi and the Federation busybodies were a different matter. He knew, however, that if the Lorcans accepted him as king, the Ferengi, the Federation, and everyone else would have to do the same. And as far as the Lorcans were concerned, his credentials were impeccable. He stroked one of the ruby crystals jutting from the rim of the Wisdom Mask.

A phaser blast sheared off some branches a good twenty meters away and far over his head. It was probably that hot-headed Klingon trying to flush him out, thought Lewis. But he wasn't going to play that game. If they wanted to catch him, they would have to track him down the hard way. He wasn't about to stand toe-to-toe with them and shoot it out.

Nevertheless, Fenton Lewis did try to deaden the sound of his movements, stepping over tangles of branches instead of leaping over them. He had no idea where he was going and was only trying to head in a straight line, to keep from accidentally doubling back and running into Piercing Blade. What a woman, he marveled. He would try to save her life, once he took over. In fact, he would save her for himself; having Almighty Slayer's daughter as his queen could only enhance his power.

Lorca was the perfect retirement home: a non-aligned, sparsely populated wilderness where he would rule as an absolute despot. Of course he would be a benevolent despot, keeping his people happy but ignorant. Now that Lorcan masks were hot items on the black market art circuit, he could count on a steady income as king. The masks would also increase awareness of Lorca, making intergalactic tourism a strong possibility.

These were wonderful plans, but he would have to survive the next few hours if he was to carry them out. Behind him, he could hear the clumsy lumbering of his pursuers. They were no match for him in a short-term contest of survival skills, but they had the *Enterprise* to back them up. They could commit fresh troops to the manhunt and keep running him down until he was exhausted. He would have to find someplace to hide until the *Enterprise* gave up and moved on.

But where could he bide his time while assembling a force formidable enough to cower the locals? Not the upcoming fair, where there would be too much scrutiny and too much unbridled ambition. One of those backward villages might do, like the one where Riker and his party had been so warmly welcomed. He had spied on them during the mask presentation ceremony, and he was certain he could use the Lorcans' slavery to tradition for his own benefit. After all, didn't he possess their greatest icon? If he couldn't win over a bunch of superstitious villagers, then he didn't deserve to wear the Wisdom Mask.

As if fate had been listening to his fevered plans, Fenton Lewis saw a light glimmering far ahead of him in the forest. It could be Piercing Blade, he knew, and he ran the risk of losing all as he cautiously made his way toward it. But he couldn't outrun a starship full of security officers forever. He needed to slow down his pursuers, somehow, and throw them permanently off his trail. If the light came from a party of Lorcans or from a village, maybe the Wisdom Mask would persuade them to help him. If not, maybe the pistol phaser would convince them.

A few moments later, Jean-Luc Picard saw the light as well. He had no idea how long or how far they'd been running or even in what direction. They could have doubled back on the others, but somehow he didn't think they had. This light was small, steady, and unwavering, like a streetlamp. He wondered whether Fenton Lewis would avoid it or keep running in that direction.

The only sounds came from Worf and Riker on either side of him, two big men who couldn't take a step without noisily crushing the forest debris underfoot. The captain stopped and waved to his subordinates to join him.

Reluctantly, they suspended the chase. "Captain," complained Riker, panting heavily, "I'm sure we were gaining on him."

"I'm not," answered Jean-Luc, taking a few deep breaths. He pointed to the light. "There's a village or something ahead of us. I don't want to risk shooting an innocent villager, and I think it's dangerous to sneak up on it."

"Commander Riker," said Worf, hardly winded, "is your communicator working?"

Will nodded. "I've kept it in my inside pocket."

"I wish we had done that," groused Picard.

The Klingon continued his thought. "May I suggest, Captain, that we ask the *Enterprise* to send reinforcements? With enough personnel, we can surround this area and close in on Lewis."

"Negative," said the captain, "until we have full daylight to work with. Lewis has a phaser, and we know he'll use it. I don't want any Lorcans or any of our own people to be caught in a cross fire."

"I think he'll head for that light," said Riker.

Captain Picard looked warmly at his first officer,

immensely relieved to have him back at his side, beard and all. "Why do you think that, Number One?"

"Because he has the Wisdom Mask," answered Will. "With his ego, he'll want to try it out."

"I agree," seconded Worf. "And with the pistol phaser, he won't be worried about facing challenges."

The captain nodded. "Very well. Let's proceed toward the light . . . with caution."

He motioned them forward, and the three bridge officers continued to stalk the renegade ambassador through the murky forest.

Armed with medical supplies beamed down from the *Enterprise,* Dr. Pulaski made quick work of Almighty Slayer's and Piercing Blade's sword wounds. They were deep but clean, and no arteries had been severed. Medicine Maker could do little more than stand back and shake his jeweled-serpents mask in amazement.

"How did you stop the flow of blood so quickly?" he asked. "What is that instrument you used? Does its glowing tip cauterize the wound?"

"You'll learn all about that . . . in time." She smiled enigmatically as she clamped a bandage around Piercing Blade's shoulder. In her own sickbay she wouldn't have bothered with a conventional bandage, but Lorca was not exactly a sterile place.

Almighty Slayer sat nearby, prodding his bandaged thigh with a grimy finger. "Pulaski," he said, "I've been sewed up by the best of them, and you do good work. You can still wear your Herbalist's Mask. In fact, you *deserve* to wear it."

"No, thanks," replied the doctor, tying a sling around Piercing Blade's arm. "Your masks are beautiful, but they make us into something we aren't."

Kate slid the warrior's forearm into the sling and tugged on it to make sure it would hold. She wiped her hands and stood up. "Piercing Blade, you'll have to wear that sling for at least a week. No duels."

The Thunder Mask shook ominously. "I can't promise that. I can't rest until the Wisdom Mask is safe."

Kate shrugged. "Then you'd better keep your healer close by, because any fighting is bound to reopen that wound."

Like a recalcitrant child, Piercing Blade stood up and tore off the sling. "This isn't a time to sit like old werjuns. We need to find that mask."

"Aye," snapped Cold Angel, who had been prowling through the camp like the wild animal his mask depicted. "I say we can't believe these people from the sky. The thief who stole the mask is one of *them.*"

Kate Pulaski looked helplessly at Lieutenant Commander Data and Counselor Troi. No one, including Deanna, knew what to say to the distraught Lorcans. They could not deny that they had brought Fenton Lewis with them to the planet. They had turned loose a plague of ruthless ambition, and, as in all plagues, the carrier was blamed as much as the virus.

More subtly, Deanna realized, the crew members' relationship with the Lorcans had changed since they had cast off their masks. Their naked faces made them alien again. Whereas moments before, they had been part of two Lorcan factions, now the "sky people" had reverted to type. That had to be, Deanna decided. They shouldn't try to shield the Lorcans from encounters with off-worlders. Their masks were already acclaimed throughout the galaxy. Not even the blackest clouds of soot and ash could keep Lorca and its remarkable culture isolated.

Also, the Lorcans needed the Federation to help them tame their wild planet. This was not, however, the time to try to explain that to them. Something had to be done to win back the Lorcans' trust, and it had to be done quickly.

"I, for one," declared Deanna Troi, "will give myself up as hostage—in guarantee of the safe return of the Wisdom Mask."

"No!" shouted Kate Pulaski. She appealed to Almighty Slayer, who remained seated on the ground, running his gnarled hands over the sleek contours of his new Ambassador's Mask. "Vouch for us, Day Timer. Tell them we wouldn't steal the mask."

"I've already told them that," he said. "But I surrendered the Wisdom Mask, so I am not important anymore." He leveled his aged eyes at his daughter, who stared back at him with a mixture of emotions that confounded even Deanna Troi. "My daughter won and lost the Wisdom Mask in the blinking of an eye. She must live with that."

The old peddler struggled to stand, and Data rushed to help him to his feet and give him support. He nodded gratefully to the smiling android. "Perhaps Piercing Blade should remember that the Wisdom Mask chooses the ruler of Lorca—not the other way around," Data said. "If she is destined to wear it, it will be returned to her."

"Superstitious nonsense," growled Cold Angel. "The Wisdom Mask goes to the strongest. The one with the quickest blade. That's how you held on to it for so many cycles, old man."

"True." The old man nodded. "That's how I held on to it. But do you know how I came by the Wisdom Mask?"

"I've heard this story before," sighed Piercing Blade.

"You can never hear it often enough," Almighty Slayer replied, leaning on Data for support. "I was a page, as green as any of these in your band. Oh, I had some skill with the sword, and I had strength and youth on my side—but I had no aspirations to the Wisdom Mask. I was part of Whistling Arrow's band, and we were chasing the old king, just as you have

248

been chasing me. But Burning Cloud was a wily old man, and by the time we caught up with him, he was naked-faced. He had buried the mask, he said, instead of giving it up.

"I'm not proud to say," the deposed king continued, "that Burning Cloud died under our torture, never telling us where the mask was hidden. So our leader instructed us to retrace the king's trail, digging wherever we thought the mask might be. We toiled for weeks, digging up every stone and every mound of clay. Many gave up and went home to their villages, but I had no intention of returning to the farm, becoming a serf, chained to the land. I kept looking."

With Data's help, he rose to his full height and pointed to the shadowy clouds hovering over the tremendous trees. "It was on a morning darker than this. The others were asleep. The first ray of dawn broke through, and I saw a werjun sitting in an old tree. He seemed not the slightest bit afraid of me, as he sat there, eating a seed pod. After a bit, he swung to another tree, then another, and I followed. He moved so slowly, it was as if he *wanted* me to follow him.

"I found him perched upon an old stump, chattering comically and leaping about. Then, to my utter amazement, he reached into a hole in the stump and tried to pull something out. I could see that, whatever it was, it was too heavy for him, so I went to help. Imagine my amazement when I saw the red crystals glinting within that deep hole. I carefully drew the ancient mask from its hiding place, as the werjun watched calmly from a branch overhead. I had the Wisdom Mask, and it had been given to me by a werjun! I knew then that *I* was destined to rule Lorca.

"Without a second's thought, I threw the Page's Mask aside and put on the Wisdom Mask. I had to kill many warriors, including Whistling Arrow, to keep it, but I held on to that mask for thirty winters and thirty summers . . . until today. And I have maintained my friendship with the werjuns. So, Piercing Blade, you don't need to take hostages. You don't need to molest these visitors from the land of our ancestors. You only need to know that the Wisdom Mask is yours—if you are worthy of it."

The old warrior slumped against Data's shoulder and lowered his mask. "Now, my good friend, set me back on the ground. I have earned my rest."

The android carefully lowered Almighty Slayer to the ground, then turned to face his daughter. "I do not believe that the Wisdom Mask has supernatural properties," Data said, "but I do believe that a certain amount of patience is called for in the acquisition of it. You have waited this long. One would think you could wait until our comrades return."

"All right," declared Piercing Blade, looking pointedly at Cold Angel, "we shall wait. But only until the sun has risen above the treetops."

Picard, Riker, and Worf crept cautiously forward on their hands and knees, brushing aside the twigs before they had a chance to snap and alert the guards. A few hardy rays of sun infused the forest now, and they could see the guards confronting Fenton Lewis as he strolled brazenly into the periphery of the camp. They could also see the glint of red on the guards' masks.

Jean-Luc led them a few meters closer, close enough to make out the murmur of voices and see details of the camp. The light they had been heading toward was a disembodied globe that hovered steadily over three pre-fab geodesic huts, none of which appeared to be native to Lorca. As the red-masked guards escorted Fenton Lewis into the center of the camp, the globe strobed for a moment, then turned bright orange. Seconds later, the two silver-masked Ferengi emerged from their huts.

The *Enterprise* officers inched forward until Picard

held out his hands to stop Riker and Worf. He wanted to hear the conversation that was just beginning.

"What have we here?" asked a Ferengi, circling Fenton Lewis warily. "A Lorcan with a Federation phaser pistol?"

"Everybody stay in front of me," Lewis ordered, waving the weapon assuredly. "I know how to use this phaser."

The Ferengi motioned the raiders to step back, but one of them dropped to his knees and prostrated himself before the intruder. "The Wisdom Mask," he intoned.

"This is indeed an honor," said a Ferengi with a low bow. "If you are Captain Picard, rest assured we will uphold our end of the bargain and get you back to your ship."

"No, I'm not Picard," Lewis announced. "But he's probably not far behind me."

"Who are you, then?" asked the other Ferengi suspiciously.

"What you call me doesn't matter," answered Lewis. Haughtily, he threw back his head and gave them a good look at the swirling mosaic. "What matters is that I am the ruler of Lorca. I have the mask."

"But you are only one person," a Ferengi pointed out, "a person who looks as if he has been scrambling for his life."

The long-haired human cocked his mask at the elephant-eared humanoid. "One person and one *phaser*. I will be happy to do business with you, but I will be just as content to do business *without* you. You don't want to rule this planet—you just want to conduct commerce at advantageous rates. Well, I'm a man who thinks as you do. Wouldn't it be wise to have someone you can deal with as ruler of Lorca? I'll make it worth your while."

A Ferengi nodded his silver mask thoughtfully.

"That is for the future. I assume you will want something in exchange today."

"Well"—Lewis glanced behind him—"my immediate requirements are to slow down the party that is right behind me. I don't know how many there are, but they also have phasers."

"They would be the ones you stole the Wisdom Mask from?"

"Look," said Fenton Lewis, leveling his phaser at the closest Ferengi. "I'm not asking for much. If you let me pass through your camp, that should be enough to slow them down. Then, later, we can do all sorts of business—masks in exchange for weapons and equipment."

"All very agreeable," replied a Ferengi, stroking the slender whip stuck in the garish sash around his plump middle. "We can start the trade with the Wisdom Mask."

"How much?" asked the other.

Lewis shook his head, refusing the deal. "You don't listen, do you? This mask is not for sale, but if you'll help me now, I'll repay you later . . . in masks or aluminum or anything you want."

"But the Wisdom Mask is here now," a Ferengi calmly pointed out. "And all those other masks aren't."

"Yes," agreed his partner, "why don't you give us the mask now? We'll be happy to delay whoever is behind you."

"We'll even give you safe passage on our ship," pledged the other. "To anywhere in the galaxy you want to go. First class."

Lewis waved the phaser at them. "I'm done dickering. The Wisdom Mask is *mine,* and it's going to stay that way. Now stand over there, so I can get through your camp. We'll talk another time."

But neither of the Ferengi moved. One of them spread his arms and motioned to the raiders to close

252

in on Lewis. "I'm afraid we can't let you leave. We have to give you time to reconsider."

His companion drew his whip from his sash. "It would be wise to cooperate with us."

"Don't you get near me with that thing," Lewis threatened, dropping into a crouch and trying to cover them all with his phaser gun.

The Ferengi ignored him and stepped closer, emboldening their red-masked minions. One of them brandished a long pike, which he jabbed playfully at Lewis. Driven back against the wall of a hut, Lewis spun out of the way and fired his phaser at the pike-wielding Lorcan. The beam went a scant few centimeters before being deflected into the trees.

Aghast, Lewis fired blast after blast at his approaching foe. Each time, the phaser beam bounced harmlessly off an invisible force field.

"Antiphaser field," explained a Ferengi, pointing to the glowing orange ball, which strobed gently over their heads. "Very effective against Federation weaponry."

Fenton whirled in the other direction and tried to escape into the forest, but three massive raiders were upon him in an instant. They grabbed the would-be king by his long hair and dragged him back, kicking and struggling, to face the Ferengi. Only the Wisdom Mask gave him any dignity at all.

The short humanoids had to stand on their tiptoes to reach the mask, as the Lorcans forced Lewis to lower his head. "Let's see who you really are," cackled a Ferengi, removing the Wisdom Mask.

The Lorcans gasped as they looked at the ambassador's face, and some of them reached worriedly for the Wisdom Mask. But they needn't have worried, because the Ferengi were handling it like the precious commodity it was.

"Let me hold it," squealed one Ferengi.

"No, let me." The fatter one wrenched the mask

away. "*You* check the human's identity. If he is the one we are looking for, there will be an even *bigger* bonus."

With that, Fenton Lewis bolted from the arms of his captors, but he only got a few meters before the brawny Lorcans tackled him again. A few upended him and suspended him in the air by his heels while the others kicked and punched him ruthlessly. When Lewis stopped struggling, they dropped him to the clay and stomped on his long hair with their boots to hold him down. Blood pouring from his mouth, he sputtered up at the Ferengi who leaned over him: "I am a Federation ambassador. I demand diplomatic treatment. I demand to speak to your purser!"

The Ferengi turned back to his partner and clapped his hands. "I think we're in luck."

"Be positive."

The Ferengi nodded and turned to the globe hovering overhead. "Correlate this human's identity with known felons."

A violet beam shot out of the globe and engulfed Lewis. He screamed in agony, as the raiders dropped him and backed fearfully away. The scanner probed his every molecule, dissected his DNA, and sped up his heartbeat to a high rev before it illuminated his nostrils and entered his brain. Fenton Lewis wasn't dead when the procedure had ended, but he wasn't moving, either, except to cough up tiny bits of phlegm.

"Federation Ambassador Fenton Lewis," squealed a shrill voice. "Convicted of murdering two Ferengi. Sentence: death. Bonus alive: 900 primes. Bonus dead: 900 primes."

"No difference," one Ferengi said to the other.

"I don't relish having a human on board," said the other. "Not a *live* human."

"If he escapes, we'll lose our bonus."

"It's too risky to keep him alive," the other Ferengi

agreed. He motioned to the raider with the long pike, and his pantomime left no doubt as to what he wanted the raider to do.

From their hiding place, Riker raised himself up to a crouch, but Jean-Luc put a restraining hand on the commander's shoulder. "Our phasers are useless in there," he whispered.

"Primitive weapons apparently still work," said Worf, gritting his teeth as he watched the red-masked Lorcan plunge his spear through the ambassador's chest. With a loud wheeze, Fenton Lewis stopped moving entirely.

The Ferengi again addressed the glowing ball. "Relay to our transporter bay that we have a body to beam up: one human felon named Fenton Lewis. Please be sure we get the performance bonus."

"Yes, your lordship," the artificial voice squeaked.

The other trader sidled up to his partner. "Do you think we should beam up the mask?"

His partner studied the mesmerizing swirls of the nebula mask. "No. Let's keep it and wear it to their fair. We can use it to collect more masks, if nothing else."

"I think we should recruit more raiders. We've lost so many."

"Then let's stay another night," his partner agreed, staring into the vacant eyes of the Wisdom Mask. "I believe this is going to be our most successful trip ever."

"Can I hold the mask for a while? Please."

"Oh, all right." Reluctantly, he handed the mask to his partner.

The Ferengi never took their eyes off the priceless artwork as the whole camp became infused with a violet glow. The raiders bowed their red masks and watched reverently as Fenton Lewis's body disintegrated into a million dancing shapes before disappearing entirely.

"Double the guard," ordered the Ferengi, disappearing into one of the domed huts. "There are probably more of them out there."

The red masks turned suspiciously toward the forest, and Picard reached out and touched Riker's and Worf's shoulders. They turned and slowly crept back the way they had come. Worf took up the rear, training his phaser often on the raiders behind him, but the Lorcans didn't look anxious to leave the protective glow of the hovering ball.

After having crawled to a point where they could no longer see the guardian light of the Ferengi camp, Jean-Luc stood and wiped off his clothing. He knew he couldn't get off even half the dirt, but it was worth a try.

Riker and Worf rose to their feet. "That solves the Fenton Lewis problem—permanently," Riker said.

"But not the missing-mask problem," said Jean-Luc. "There has to be some way to get it back."

"For Piercing Blade or Almighty Slayer?" asked Will Riker.

Picard shrugged. "We'll let them sort that out." He turned to Worf. "What is your evaluation, Lieutenant?"

The Klingon made a low growl. "Their defense against our weapons is complete. To attack them, we would have to either disable that antiphaser field or use Lorcan weapons. We could, of course, ambush them on the trail."

Picard shook his head almost imperceptibly. "I don't want to turn this planet into a battleground between us and the Ferengi. On the other hand, negotiation would be a waste of time. They would probably demand the *Enterprise* in exchange for the Wisdom Mask."

Commander Riker was stroking his beard when his whole face brightened into a grin. "I know how we can get in there. With the exception of mine and Day

Timer's, all of the masks we wore were old Raider's Masks that had been captured in battle and repainted. All we have to do is paint them red again, and we can stroll into their camp and be taken right in."

"An excellent idea," Worf agreed. "Then we bide our time until we can steal back the mask. If we're clever, they may not even know who took it. I volunteer."

"As do I," said Riker.

Jean-Luc smiled and patted their brawny shoulders. "I appreciate both the idea and your enthusiasm. But it's a very dangerous plan. You wouldn't stand a chance unless you had someone like Cold Angel or one of the other Lorcans to cover for you, to say and do the right thing."

Chapter Sixteen

I KNOW THAT PLACE," said Cold Angel, nodding the shaggy Trainer's Mask thoughtfully. "It's an old gathering spot for raiders. Don't ask me how I know that, but I do."

The once warring Lorcans and the reunited sky people stood in an irregular circle, now one large band numbering twelve. They were six and six, the naked faces mingling with the masks. Riker had gathered up the three metal masks awarded for bravery in the tiny village north of them and had tossed the armor into the center of the gathering.

"That's our way in," he declared, pointing to the ivory Teacher's Mask, the vivid Archer's Mask, and the twining serpents of the Herbalist's Mask. "Those masks belonged to raiders until a few days ago. We heard the Ferengi say that they would stay at their camp another night to recruit more raiders. So we can paint the masks red, join their band, and just wait for the right opportunity to steal the Wisdom Mask."

"Aye, we can," responded Cold Angel, turning eagerly to the impassive Thunder Mask. "It would work, my lady. We can steal it right from under their noses."

Piercing Blade glanced at Picard, who stood next to her, frowning and massaging the cleft in his chin. He addressed himself to Riker. "Your plan has a chance to succeed, Number One, but it's still very dangerous. Are you forgetting those energized whips they have? Are you forgetting that our phasers will have no effect as long as that force field is protecting the Ferengi camp? You would have to use swords to battle your way out."

"I agree," proclaimed Piercing Blade in her most regal tone. "That is why Cold Angel, Medicine Maker, and I will be the three to infiltrate the raiders' band."

"Wait," Worf said, clearly disappointed. "This was *our* idea."

"Yes," added Commander Riker, "and we are responsible for what Fenton Lewis did."

"He's paid for his treachery," she responded, turning to Captain Picard. "I absolve you and your comrades of any wrongdoing. You have served me well by telling me where the Wisdom Mask is and how I can get it back. Now you must leave the rest to us."

Before Picard could respond, Medicine Maker stepped forward, bowing apologetically. "Pardon me, my lady, but you can't pass yourself off as a raider. You would be recognized instantly. You have attributes no mask could hide."

Whether the noblewoman blushed under her formidable mask, no one could tell, but she didn't immediately counter his argument.

"Besides," said Medicine Maker, "Lorca needs a living ruler, not another dead hero."

"I'll decide who should go," said Almighty Slayer. All eyes and all masks swiveled in the old man's direction as he hobbled forward. "Riker, Cold Angel, and I are the ones to do it. Cold Angel and I have the best chance of fooling the other raiders, and Riker claims to know something about these Ferengi." He touched his bandaged thigh. "This blasted wound will make us look all the more authentic."

"That is a very practical combination," proclaimed Data, stepping crisply to Almighty Slayer's side. "Because they are Lorcans, Slayer and Cold Angel will know how to speak and act, and there will be one great advantage in having Commander Riker with them. As soon as they seize the mask, he can signal to the *Enterprise* to beam them up. Escape will be instantaneous."

Picard turned to Piercing Blade, and they exchanged a look filled with longing and melancholy. "Very well," replied the captain, "if Lady Piercing Blade agrees, so do I. The least we can do is help the Lorcans get back the Wisdom Mask. Number One, you will go with them—with the proviso that you do exactly as Data suggested. I'm sure he can alter a communicator to send us a signal instead of a voice."

Riker nodded and glanced at Cold Angel. "We'll have to equip Almighty Slayer and Cold Angel with communicators, too, so that Data can lock on to all our coordinates."

Almighty Slayer clapped his hands excitedly. "I've got to make some red paint."

Dr. Pulaski glanced up at the brightening sky. "Can you make paint, paint the masks, and have them dry by tonight?"

"Certainly," answered the former peddler. "That's why the raiders chose red. It's a clay-based paint that's simple to make, so it's easy to chuck it all and become a raider anytime you want. Piercing Blade, can your pages help me?"

"Certainly, Father." She motioned to the man and woman in the bronze oval masks to follow the famous warrior. As they strode off, Data, Riker, and Cold Angel began to confer, and everyone in the camp was suddenly busy. Piercing Blade turned slowly to the captain. "What will you be doing, Jean-Luc Picard?"

"I have to return to my ship," he told her. "My crew has been like Lorca, a people without a leader. They deserve to see their captain again."

"Oh," she moaned, "to think that all those women can see your naked face while I will be deprived of the sight of you."

"And I of you," he murmured.

Before they could edge closer to each other, Data interrupted them. "I need to contact the ship, sir. Shall I tell Geordi you're beaming up?"

"Yes. Three to beam up—Dr. Pulaski, Counselor Troi, and I. You and Lieutenant Worf can beam up when preparations have been completed here."

"Yes, sir." Data nodded, taking his communicator badge from his inside pocket.

But Jean-Luc wasn't paying any attention to the android and his conversation with the *Enterprise*. His eyes were again on Piercing Blade, and he was trying to commit every centimeter of her statuesque frame to memory.

"If you keep looking at me like that," she cooed, "I may not let you leave."

"I can't apologize." He smiled. "It may be a long time before I come back to Lorca. I have a lot to remember."

"Come back, Picard," she insisted, taking his hand in hers. "I'll give you more memories."

He squeezed her hand. "Rule wisely."

"Captain," said Data, "they are ready. Geordi is at the transporter controls."

"Good-bye," rasped Picard, reluctantly pulling away from Piercing Blade. He was joined by Dr. Pulaski and Counselor Troi.

"I'll miss this place," said Deanna, peering up at the cloud-enshrouded treetops. "It has such majesty."

"Yes." Kate Pulaski grimaced, twisting her torso to demonstrate the soreness of her muscles. "But it'll be nice to sleep in a bed again."

Picard nodded to Data, who spoke into his communicator. Jean-Luc gazed at the stunning woman in the Thunder Mask until every molecule of his being had been dissolved and reassembled in the transporter room.

"Captain!" Geordi La Forge beamed as the three crew members stepped down from the platform. "It's good to have you back. You, too, Counselor Troi and Dr. Pulaski."

All three of them managed weary smiles. "Thank you, Lieutenant," said the captain. "How's the ship?"

"None the worse for wear," Geordi said, grinning. "Let me show you the data we've collected on the planet."

Jean-Luc held up his hand. "I'd love to see it, but first—and I think I speak for all of us—I need a shower. You help Data and Commander Riker assemble what they need, and we'll rendezvous on the bridge in half an hour."

"Yes, sir," Geordi replied, still grinning.

Data placed the communicator badge inside Almighty Slayer's tunic, buttoned it shut, and pulled the chain mail down over the old king's chest. The red mask angled quizzically downward. "What am I supposed to do with that thing?"

"Nothing," answered the android. "It merely tells us where you are, so when the time comes, we can beam you aboard the *Enterprise.*"

"Will it hurt?" asked the warrior worriedly.

The android shrugged. "I do not know for certain. I have heard some people say that it tickles."

"You really aren't human, are you?" asked Almighty Slayer. "I find that hard to believe."

"Thank you," answered Data. "You do not see many faces, or you would know how different mine is."

"I'm not king anymore," sighed the old warrior, "and I can't promise much. But I will always keep a mask for you, Data, if you ever tire of living in the sky."

"Thank you," Data replied, his pale eyes glowing brightly. "I shall always treasure the memory of Lorca, where I am no less human than anyone else."

"Ouch!" exclaimed Cold Angel as Worf clumsily placed a communicator inside his shirt.

"May this assist you in your victory," said the Klingon.

The animal trainer shook his red mask, as if in puzzlement. "With a face like yours, Worf, wouldn't you rather stay here, where you can wear a mask?"

"No," answered Worf. "I prefer to return to the *Enterprise,* where I only have unmasked humans to compete against in beauty."

Commander Riker slipped on his Raider's Mask and adjusted the straps. "How do I look?"

"Like a scoundrel," replied Almighty Slayer. "I've been meaning to ask you, Riker, what are you going to do with the Forest Mask?"

"Well, I . . . I hadn't thought about it."

"Take it back with you," the old peddler insisted. "It's an emblem of your courage and nobility. It belongs to you."

Lieutenant Worf picked up Riker's finely polished wooden mask from the ground and looked into its jeweled eye sockets. Piercing Blade had gone ahead to a meeting place farther down the road, taking the ponies and all the valuable masks, except this one. "I'll take it back for you, Commander," Worf offered. "A souvenir of battle."

Will nodded. "Thank you." His voice was barely

audible within the metallic Raider's Mask. "It's hard to imagine I'll be leaving Lorca soon."

"Commander?" asked Data. "Is there anything you want us to tell the captain? Remember, your communicator will not relay voice. As soon as you press it, the three of you will be beamed aboard the *Enterprise.*"

Data touched his own insignia badge, which responded with a soft beep. "Data to transporter room. Two to beam up—myself and Lieutenant Worf."

"Aye, sir," came the reply.

"Good-bye," said Data, as he and Worf stepped away from the others. Moments later they dematerialized in twin clouds of phosphorescence.

Almighty Slayer tentatively reached out to the place where they had been. "Are you sure that doesn't hurt?"

"Positive," Riker assured the old man, patting his shoulder. The three of them were alone now in the immense forest, all the others having beamed up to the ship or gone ahead to the meeting place. The commander looked up at the darkening clouds. "We'd better get going if we are to reach the Ferengi camp by nightfall."

Now it was the old Lorcan's turn to put his hand on Riker's shoulder. "Thank you for helping us, my friend."

"Come," said Cold Angel, stepping off the road into the dark forest and motioning to Almighty Slayer and Will Riker to follow him. Gripping the hilts of their swords to keep them from becoming entangled in the underbrush, Riker and Slayer plunged after him.

With the shadows lengthening and Almighty Slayer's limp getting more pronounced, the small band of ersatz raiders slowed to an amble. Cold Angel was occupied with following a trail he hadn't seen in many years, and Will Riker kept an eye on the old warrior hobbling along behind them, his red mask concealing his pain.

"How are you doing?" he asked with concern.

"Don't you worry about me," snapped Slayer. "I'm just saving my strength."

"Don't expect us to carry you," joked Cold Angel.

"You couldn't even carry my sword," scoffed the old warrior.

Riker shook his head. "We could have had the *Enterprise* beam us closer to the Ferengi camp. There was no need for all this walking."

"Beaming," repeated Almighty Slayer. "That's what you call all that disappearing and reappearing?"

"Yes," answered Will, "it's really a very safe procedure."

"Not for me." The deposed king reached inside his shirt and plucked out the communicator badge. With a shrug, he tossed it into the black woods.

"What are you doing?" exclaimed Riker, diving after the badge. But he could barely see three meters in front of him, let alone find a small insignia in thick underbrush.

"I know you meant well," Slayer explained, "but I would rather die fighting my way out than have my body turned into a cloud of burning ashes."

"Me, too," said Cold Angel, tossing his badge into the woods. "You go right ahead and beam out. We Lorcans must do things in our own way."

"Right," said Almighty Slayer.

But Will Riker was still shaking his head. "The Lorcan way is never the easy way, is it?"

They walked on in silence through the darkening forest. Riker hoped they would find the Ferengi camp soon, because they would need all their strength and wiles. What would be their best course of action? he wondered. Would they attack the Ferengi in their huts? Wait until they were on the trail? Create a diversion? He smiled at the recollection of the last diversion he had created and thought better of that idea. Probably the safest course would be not to do or plan anything until they had observed the situation for a while. The most important thing was to be accepted as raiders and invited to join the band.

They finally spotted a faint glow in the forest ahead of them. By now, total darkness had engulfed the woods, and they were all relieved to see their destination. Even though it was cold, Will found his palms sweating and his breath quickening as they picked up their pace and approached the eerie halo amid the trees.

"Let Cold Angel do most of the talking," Almighty Slayer cautioned him. "I'll just grumble about my wound and make up some wild story about how I got it. You can even play mute, if you like."

"I'll play it by ear," answered Will, swallowing nervously. Phasers would be ineffective, and the sword at his side was too foreign to give him much comfort.

As they drew closer, Riker squinted at the light in the woods, thinking that it wasn't the same light he had seen early that morning. The protective globe had hovered several meters off the ground, whereas this light throbbed feebly from the ground, like a campfire.

"Wait," he whispered, stopping Cold Angel and Almighty Slayer in their tracks. "I don't think this is it."

"Yes, it is," insisted Cold Angel, waving his hand impatiently. "Come on."

Then the wind shifted, and the putrid stench of death wafted into their noseholes. They looked warily at each other, and Slayer and Cold Angel drew their swords. Cold Angel was still in the lead, and he reluctantly waved them forward. Riker's hand drew near to his communicator badge.

The stench became sickening, but it was hardly worse than the sight that greeted their eyes when they reached the Ferengi camp. The two Ferengi were hanging naked by their heels from the tallest pine.

He averted his eyes, but the sight on the ground wasn't much better. Half a dozen raiders lay slain in bizarre poses. The scene was eerily lit by the Ferengi globe, now throbbing pathetically on the ground, a Lorcan pike stuck in the middle of its broken shards.

Most startling of all, in the center of the carnage, lying spreadeagle, was a dead raider wearing the Wisdom Mask.

Cold Angel was in a wary crouch, stabbing at the corpses with his sword. "I think they're all dead. Looks as if they jumped the Ferengi and then fought among themselves."

Almighty Slayer nodded his head numbly, as he kicked over one of the raiders and picked up his sword. "I've seen this happen before over an especially valuable mask. They kept challenging each other until there were none left. The winner had just enough strength left to put on the mask before he died."

"He was king for a day," remarked Cold Angel, bending down and carefully removing the Wisdom Mask from the victor's blood-encrusted body. Riker looked quickly away; worms were crawling all over the man's face.

Cold Angel wiped the worms out of the inside of the mask. "Y'know, Slayer, maybe I was wrong. Maybe the Wisdom Mask *does* choose its wearer. I'll never speak against it again."

Almighty Slayer nodded sagely and turned to Riker. "Tell Data about this. He didn't believe in the power of the mask, either."

Riker looked around at the carnage and was thankful he was wearing a mask. He didn't want anyone to see his face at that moment.

Cold Angel had wrapped the Wisdom Mask in oilskin and was trying to strap it to his back. "Slayer, could you help me?"

"Sure," said the old Lorcan, rushing to his aid.

Riker forced himself to think about something other than the scene around him. "What will you do now?" he asked the former king. "How will you promote Piercing Blade as the queen?"

Almighty Slayer held out his hands. "She'll be wearing the mask, and they'll know that *we* believe she should wear it. Perhaps they'll listen to her, perhaps they won't, but I believe they will. She might have to bash one or two heads, but that will be the easy part. If she can rule wisely, then all of Lorca will benefit. And I . . . I shall wear the Ambassador's Mask and try to deal with you off-worlders."

Cold Angel snorted into the cold wind, as if trying to clear his nostrils of the stench. "Let's get out of here." He hefted his precious cargo upon his brawny shoulders and trundled off into the woods.

"Good luck to you," Will said, clasping Almighty Slayer's arm. "We'll try to return soon."

"Come to the fair," crowed the old warrior proudly. "See my daughter crowned queen."

"I'll try," Will promised.

He watched as the men disappeared into the black woods, the crunching sound of their footsteps gradually dying away. With a peculiar sense of melancholy, Commander Riker reached inside his pocket and clicked his communicator badge.

He beamed aboard the *Enterprise* still in full raider regalia, startling several transporter technicians. The commander quickly removed his Raider's Mask and grabbed the hilt of his sword to keep it from swinging. He realized with a start that he had finished the mission with several noteworthy souvenirs, including the Forest Mask, brought aboard earlier by Worf.

"Sorry," he said to the transporter operators, stepping down from the platform. "Good work." He raised his voice. "Riker to the bridge."

"Back so soon, Number One?" Captain Picard

answered cheerily. "The Ferengi must not have put up much of a fight."

"They couldn't," Will answered. "They were all dead when we got there. The Ferengi were killed by the raiders, who, in turn, killed one another. We took the mask off a dead man."

"I see," the captain replied thoughtfully. "No wonder the purser of the Ferengi ship has been so testy. They've done everything but come out and accuse us of hiding their away team. Take some time to clean up, Number One, then report to the bridge. I'll try to figure out a way to break this to them."

"Yes, sir," Glancing self-consciously at the transporter operators, who were now smiling at one another, the filthy raider strode out of the room, his sword clanging in its scabbard.

When Commander Riker reached the bridge, he was greeted with brief smiles from Deanna Troi, Wesley Crusher, and Data, but Worf and Captain Picard remained stone-faced as they faced the angry Ferengi who was haranguing them from the view screen.

"And I want you to know," the feral humanoid ranted, "we hold the Federation fully responsible for what happened to our trading mission. We demand reparations, especially for a very valuable mask that should have been in the possession of our associates."

Picard held up his hand. "One moment, please. Commander Riker is now on the bridge. He has just returned from Lorca."

Riker stepped forward and nodded. "I didn't actually see what happened, but the evidence indicates that your people were killed by the Lorcan raiders with whom they were traveling. Perhaps you should choose more trustworthy allies next time."

The short humanoid sat up in his chair, his huge ears bristling. "And the mask?"

The commander glanced innocently at the Ferengi purser. "What mask?" he asked. "Lorca is full of masks."

The Ferengi made a growl that sounded more like a squeak. "We're returning to our base now, but you haven't heard the end of this."

"One last thing," said Picard, "if Lorca joins the Federation as a protectorate, as we fully expect it will, you will be allowed to trade here only if you observe Federation guidelines. If you can't do that, don't come back."

Angrily, the Ferengi punched off his viewscreen, and Will Riker grinned broadly at his commanding officer. "He didn't like that last part. But who's going to negotiate with the Lorcans? We're fresh out of ambassadors."

"That's up to you, Number One. Starfleet has given us permission to stay in orbit for a few more days. I thought, if you didn't mind, you and Data could attend the fair and talk to Piercing Blade about joining the Federation."

Will lowered his voice. "Sir? Wouldn't you rather do that yourself?"

Jean-Luc shook his head and smiled wistfully. "No. I would prefer not to have to say good-bye to her again."

Will nodded. "Understood, Captain."

"Besides," Picard added with mock seriousness, "I seem to remember someone saying that leading the away team should be the privilege of the first officer."

Now it was Riker's turn to smile. "Lorca would be a perfect place for shore leave, if it were a little less dangerous."

"But it's not," the captain reminded him. He cast his eyes downward. "That reminds me, Number One, now that you're back, I've scheduled Ensign Greenblatt's funeral for twenty-hundred tonight. Afterward, I'd like to drink a toast to her in the Ten-Forward lounge."

As Riker and Data stepped onto the transporter platform, they checked their equipment. Will had two communicator badges, one on his chest and another inside his parka. The second badge was the one altered by Data to signal the transporter room to beam them directly aboard the *Enterprise* and out of danger. After all, they still didn't know what to expect on Lorca. Data carried only a briefcase containing the articles and bylaws of the Federation, to be left with the Lorcans if they expressed an interest in joining.

They carried no phasers and no masks on this trip. They were coming in peace, and they were coming as themselves.

"Are you sure of our coordinates?" Riker asked.

"A small city is gradually forming on the planet," the android replied. "The cloud cover has been exceedingly mild, allowing us to monitor its development. I believe something extraordinary is happening on Lorca."

"Let's find out." Riker nodded to the transporter operator. "Energize."

Their sudden materialization on the planet attracted little attention, because it occurred directly behind a stage where a magician was mesmerizing a crowd of several hundred Lorcans. Hearing the awed reactions of the crowd, they peeked through the colorfully striped awnings and saw a figure shrouded in a sheet floating several meters above the wooden stage. Only his head and feet were visible.

"How is that possible?" asked an amazed Data.

"I hate to spoil it for you," whispered Will, "but he is probably holding a pair of false legs up in front of him. And he's standing under that sheet, not floating."

"Oh," said Data, clearly disappointed.

"Gentlemen," snapped a disapproving voice. They turned around to see a bent old man wearing the distinctive mask of a bearded human face.

"Trim Hands!" exclaimed Riker. "Don't you recognize us? We were in your village."

"Of course." The old maskmaker nodded. "But where are your masks? Where is the Forest Mask?"

"The masks are safe," Will assured him. "We decided not to wear them this trip. We didn't want to be mistaken for Lorcans."

"That is no problem," the maskmaker said, taking their arms. "That's why the queen sent for me—to design a special mask for sky people. Now you can wear masks and also be yourselves."

Will Riker glanced at Data and smiled.

"Come," said Trim Hands, leading them away. "My booth isn't far. If you walk around without masks, you'll be a bigger attraction than that faker out front."

They walked behind the colorful booths and awnings, so as not to attract the attention of the fair-goers. They could hear good-natured haggling, hammers beating aluminum, and potters' wheels spinning. They could smell meat and fish cooking on spits over open fires and the scent of perfume oils and burning incense. They also heard children squeal as they watched the tumblers and the acrobats.

"You mentioned the queen," said Data. "Has Piercing Blade been accepted as ruler?"

"For the most part, yes," said Trim Hands. "People are still pouring in from all over—there has never been such a gathering—but they are met at the gate immediately and informed of the new wearer of the Wisdom Mask. In due course, she holds audience with them, and she has proved to be a very persuasive young woman. All day and all night long, she has been meeting with people of all masks."

"Has anyone challenged her?" asked Riker.

The maskmaker shrugged his stooped shoulders. "A handful of stubborn noblemen, yes, but that was inevitable. She has postponed all duels until her wound heals, and we are hoping her challengers will have reconsidered by then."

He gestured to a tent. "Ah, here we are, my little booth." He untied the fishgut rope and let them in the back flap. His booth was far from little, and Riker knew that the queen must have sent a wagon to fetch him. Extraordinary masks, adorned with gems and feathers and other exotic materials in dazzling hues, covered the walls. Hanging from a fishhook was the startling Thunder Mask.

The kindly face painted on Trim Hands's mask almost winked. "You undoubtedly see many masks here that I did not make. I, er, supplemented my normal inventory with the help of my new partner."

From the dusty path outside, the Ambassador's Mask poked through the front tent flap. "It's about time you returned," a voice said. Then the massive mask reared back in surprise. "Riker, Data, what a welcome sight!"

Almighty Slayer limped into the tent and clasped their arms, and there were hearty greetings all around.

"We must show them their new masks," crowed the old warrior, but Trim Hands had anticipated that command and was already standing behind them with two identical aluminum masks painted the fairest salmon color imaginable and shot with jagged ruby streaks over the eyes. The masks clearly suggested the Lorcan sky in all its frightful unpredictability. Black jewels bordered the neutral eye, nose, and mouth holes. In many respects, thought Will, the design was a variation on the Ambassador's Mask.

"We call it the Federation Mask," said the maskmaker proudly.

Respectfully, Riker and Data accepted the matching works of art. "What an honor," said Will. "We will keep these aboard our ship forever in the hope of returning to Lorca."

"This mask will be registered with our computer," added Data, "so that all Federation visitors will have masks of the correct design."

The ex-king clapped his hands. "Let's go see the queen. She must have the pleasure of viewing you in your new masks." Then he stopped to reconsider. "Of course, we have to get some food first. I've been waiting a long time for this lazy roustabout to get back." He pointed to Trim Hands, who did not look the least bit chagrined.

"Excuse me, sir," said Data with concern.

"Yes, my brave friend?"

"Where is Reba? Is she well?"

The old peddler's eyes looked slightly older inside the shimmering mask. "She has returned to her own kind. I guess she knew I was king no longer. But I feel I have fulfilled my pact with the werjuns. I treated them fairly while I ruled, and I think the new queen will do the same."

Data added, "Perhaps someday we'll find out how intelligent they really are."

"Yes, but first let's see how much food we can eat."

After feasting on yamlike tubulars with green pulp and on blind fish that looked better skinned, they headed to Piercing Blade's tent. The fair threatened to divert them every step of the way, with tumblers, magicians, and performers of every stripe. One stage held a troupe of actors who performed mask quickchanges and lampooned the behavior of certain professions. Another featured dancers clad in nothing but masks and capes of translucent gauze. Artisans worked in every booth. Several of them were selling tent oilskin in bright colors to draw the eye. Others made masks and pottery, leggings and boots, swords and daggers. The smell of food came from everywhere at once.

The city was expanding haphazardly across the treeless meadow, which appeared to be a dry lake bed. Even with all the chaos, Piercing Blade's tent was easy to find, since a long line of well-wishers and curiosity-seekers waited outside. Their conversation indicated that most had come merely to see the Wisdom Mask and had no quarrel with Lorca's new queen. Several bowed reverently to Almighty Slayer as he passed. They were greeted at the front flap by Piercing Blade's pages, now augmented to four, who went about the job of screening and admitting callers with efficiency and diligence. Almighty Slayer and his two celestial guests were admitted right away.

It was dark and cool inside the tent, and an obvious effort had been made to keep the atmosphere regal yet soothing. There was no display of weaponry. In fact, there was nothing to distract a visitor's attention from the tall queen. Piercing Blade was dressed in a simple purple tunic, brown leggings, and a brown sling. The hallowed Wisdom Mask seemed subordinate to the majesty of the person, and yet its swirling mosaic and ruby mane cast a glow of authority on the lamplit proceedings.

Blade nodded to the visitors as they entered but continued conversing with two scruffy boys who looked to be in their early teens. They could have been brothers. Crude clay masks hid their expressions, but their excited gestures showed how enraptured they were with their new queen.

"Let us serve you, please," insisted the smallest boy. "We're old enough to fight for you!"

"We've grown strong from working on the farm," claimed his brother, whose voice crackled nervously. "We like the look of those Page's Masks."

"I'm sure you do," said the queen. "But you have to serve an apprenticeship in a trade before I can take you. What good are you to me now with no skill or craft?"

The two boys looked at each other. "We are good farmers," squeaked the elder.

"Then return home and farm. Grow food for all these people you see here. If that doesn't suit you, then apprentice yourselves to one of the merchants or artisans. When you've learned a useful trade, come back and see me. But I don't need fighters, for I am not building an army."

One of the pages motioned to the boys, and they awkwardly bowed their way out. "Thank you, Your Highness. We'll be back soon!"

The excited boys backed into Riker and Data, who gently steered them toward the tent flap. Very informally, Piercing Blade walked over to her visitors and offered her hand. Weakly, Riker returned the greeting; he was still in awe at the changes that had come over Piercing Blade and all of Lorca in the past few days. It was as if both the woman and the society had matured at once as a result of a single event: the passage of the Wisdom Mask to a new ruler.

"My father said you would come back," she said, gripping Riker's hand. "He has proved to be a very wise adviser."

Riker motioned around him. "We're impressed with your fair, and the way you have peacefully established your leadership. You must be very pleased."

"Yes, I'm the official ruler now," she agreed, self-consciously touching the mysterious nebula of the Wisdom Mask. "How do you like the Federation Masks?"

"They are exquisite," answered Riker. "These masks greatly honor us and the Federation."

The queen looked past him and out the door. "There are just the two of you? Jean-Luc Picard didn't come?"

"I'm afraid not," the commander replied. "Like you, he is a person of great responsibilities."

"He will come soon," Blade predicted emphatically. "We are going to make Lorca safe enough for all your people to visit. We have offered amnesty to all raiders who lay down their weapons, and we will trade no more with the Ferengi. I have talked to my father and Medicine Maker, and we see no reason not to accept the sky people as our brethren. The dragon once took you away from us, but now you've returned —and we have much to be thankful for."

The father hugged his daughter tightly. "*I* have much to be thankful for," Almighty Slayer said, "a wise daughter and a little wisdom in my old age. But it pains me to think that our land is not a fit place for our ancestors to visit."

Riker touched his communicator badge. "Riker to the bridge."

"Picard here," answered the captain. "How is it going down there?"

Piercing Blade leaned forward with great interest, studying the small badge from which Jean-Luc spoke. "Captain," Riker continued, "you would not believe how wonderful—and peaceful—the Lorcan fair is. I am with the queen and her father, the noble ambassador, and they assure us that the planet is safe for visitors. They have even created a mask especially for Federation personnel. I suggest we stay a few more days and give everyone shore leave. Yourself included."

"I am gratified to hear this," answered the captain. "Give the queen and her father my highest regards and tell them we have many people who are eager to visit Lorca."

Maybe Will Riker imagined it, but he thought he saw the Wisdom Mask smile.

STAR TREK®: THE LOST YEARS
by J.M. Dillard

What exactly became of Captain Kirk, Mr. Spock, and the rest of the *Enterprise* crew after their historic five-year mission? How did that mission end? What did they do before they were reunited for the STAR TREK movies? Even the most casual STAR TREK fan finds him/herself asking these questions from time to time...

Here, at last, is the book that provides the answers to those questions—a book as anticipated, in its own way, as SPOCK'S WORLD, the first STAR TREK hardcover and a major *New York Times* bestseller. In THE LOST YEARS, J.M. Dillard has written her best STAR TREK book to date—and the way she's answered the above questions will excite and delight STAR TREK fans.

Coming in October in Hardcover from Pocket Books

POCKET BOOKS

99-01

STAR TREK®

THE NEXT GENERATION

☐ STAR TREK: THE NEXT GENERATION: ENCOUN-
TER FARPOINT 65241/$3.95

☐ STAR TREK: THE NEXT GENERATION: #1 GHOST
SHIP 66579/$3.95

☐ STAR TREK: THE NEXT GENERATION: #2
THE PEACEKEEPERS 66929/$3.95

☐ STAR TREK: THE NEXT GENERATION: #3
THE CHILDREN OF HAMLIN 67319/$3.95

☐ STAR TREK: THE NEXT GENERATION: #4
SURVIVORS 67438/$3.95

☐ STAR TREK: THE NEXT GENERATION: #5 STRIKE
ZONE 67940/$3.95

☐ STAR TREK: THE NEXT GENERATION: #6 POWER
HUNGRY 67714/$3.95

☐ STAR TREK: THE NEXT GENERATION: #7 MASKS
70878/$4.50

☐ STAR TREK: THE NEXT GENERATION: #8 THE
CAPTAIN'S HONOR
68487/$3.95

☐ STAR TREK: THE NEXT GENERATION: #9
A CALL TO DARKNESS 68708/$3.95

☐ STAR TREK: THE NEXT GENERATION: #10
A ROCK AND A HARD PLACE 69364/$3.95

**POCKET
BOOKS**

**Simon & Schuster Mail Order Dept. NGS
200 Old Tappan Rd., Old Tappan, N.J. 07675**

Please send me the books I have checked above. I am enclosing $_____ (please add 75¢ to cover
postage and handling for each order. N.Y.S. and N.Y.C. residents please add appropriate sales tax). Send
check or money order—no cash or C.O.D.'s please. Allow up to six weeks for delivery. For purchases over
$10.00 you may use VISA: card number, expiration date and customer signature must be included.

Name _____

Address _____

City _____ State/Zip _____

VISA Card No. _____ Exp. Date _____

Signature _____ 100-05